MW01242130

BECOMING
SNAF-U

G. H. JONES

COVER ILLUSTRATION BY ANGEL DELA PEÑA

Copyright © 2013 by G. H. Jones.

Library of Congress Control Number:		2013906135
ISBN:	Hardcover	978-1-4836-1955-2
	Softcover	978-1-4836-1954-5
	Ebook	978-1-4836-1956-9

All rights reserved. No part of this book may be reproduced or transmitted in any form or by any means, electronic or mechanical, including photocopying, recording, or by any information storage and retrieval system, without permission in writing from the copyright owner.

This book was printed in the United States of America.

Rev. date: 4/10/2013

To order additional copies of this book, contact:
Xlibris Corporation
1-888-795-4274
www.Xlibris.com
Orders@Xlibris.com

Anyone who has passed through the regular gradations of a classical education, and is not made a fool by it, may consider himself as having had a very narrow escape.

—William Hazlitt (1778–1830), English essayist. "On the Ignorance of the Learned," printed in *Edinburgh Magazine*, July 1818; reprinted in *Table-Talk*, 1821.

CHAPTER I

DID YOU KNOW THAT there are only five truly great universities in the world? That's right, only five—ten at the very most. The rest are pretenders, every one of them. They try to make us think that they're great, but they really aren't.

My name is Tyrone McTavish, call me Ty, and let me cut right to the chase. How do most universities make us think they're great when they aren't? *They cheat.* I learned that early on in my time as dean of Arts and Sciences at Small but National, Aspiring to be Famous University (SNAF-U, pronounced as *snaff-you*). The SNAF-U tale is as bizarre as it is convoluted, and it is perhaps best to begin by telling you how I got there in the first place and exactly what kind of place SNAF-U actually is.

I was born and raised in a little town in southwestern Illinois. Growing up as a Negro (that's what we were called back then, you know; it was only later that we became "black" and even later that we were "African American") in that community was in many ways a unique experience. For one thing, the effects of segregation were much less pernicious in my hometown than in many other parts of the country. Even though I was born a few years after *Brown v. Board of Education*, I still attended all-Negro elementary, middle, and high schools. But I was not at all disadvantaged by this situation. On the contrary, I'm convinced that I got a much better education in my all-black schools than I would have gotten at the nominally "integrated" white schools in town. I was taught the value of education at an early age, not only by my parents but also by my whole community. It was always assumed in my household that I would finish high school and go off to college. The question was never if but only where. Where turned out to be PNEU, Prestigious NorthEastern University. I always had an interest in and an aptitude for math and science, so I pursued those subjects as an undergraduate at PNEU and was about to graduate with a bachelor of science degree in biophysics. So as I neared the end of my college education, it was time to have a conversation with my parents about the next step. I had come home between terms to spend some time with my folks and talked to my mom about my plans the day I arrived. It took a while for me to work up the courage, or whatever it took, to talk to my dad.

"Dad, I've decided to go to graduate school."

"Uh, I must be missing something here. Aren't you just about to graduate from school?"

My father, even though he only finished twelfth grade, didn't miss much.

"Yeah, Dad, but there isn't much I can do with just a bachelor's degree. I want to be a practicing scientist. At least I think I do. I want to have my own lab, do research, publish papers, and push back the frontiers of science. And to do that, I have to have a PhD. And to get a PhD, I need to go to graduate school."

"And what exactly is a PhD?"

"It's the abbreviation for doctor of philosophy."

"I thought you were a biophysi-something-or-other," my dad said in that cynical tone that fathers use when they think their sons are about to do something stupid. "Why are you changing to philosophy?"

"I'm not changing anything, Dad," I answered, trying my best to be patient with my old man. "That's just the name of the degree. It's sort of like an MD, only different. Instead of going to medical school, I plan to go to graduate school, and after four or five years, if everything works out okay, I'll graduate again, this time with a PhD. Then after I get my PhD, I'll do a couple of years of postdoctoral training, get a job, and start doing research, you know, pushing back the frontiers of science."

I repeated the "pushing the frontiers" phrase in the hope that my father would think that what I had in mind was important. He ignored that completely but picked up quickly on the "four or five years" part. I wasn't surprised.

"Who's going to pay for it?" My dad was a practical guy.

"Relax. I'm not going to hit you and Mom up for it. I hope to get a fellowship from the university that accepts me. That's usually the way it works. The fellowship will pay for my tuition and stuff and will give me enough to live on while I'm in school. So you and Mom shouldn't have to foot the bill for this part of my education. Plus, if I'm successful, I'll also be able to get a fellowship for my postdoctoral studies."

"I'll believe that when I see it. So what happens next?"

"Well, I've sent in applications to a bunch of schools, and I'm waiting now to see if any of them invite me for an interview. Then if I'm admitted, I can decide which one I want to go to."

"Well, good luck, Ty, if it's what you want to do. I guess there's no chance that you might go to law school or medical school instead. You know your Uncle Norman is the only Negro veterinarian in town, and he's getting pretty old. You could make a good living here by taking over for him."

"Not exactly what I have in mind, Dad. I've thought about law and medicine, but that's not what I have in mind either. I think a PhD is the route for me."

"Uh-huh."

My father was a good man and tried in his own way to support me.

He knew that there was little left of the "old" world in which he had grown up and that even though he hadn't gone to college, it was essential that I do so to be a success in the "new" world. Still and all, in his heart of hearts, I know he never really understood why his son wanted to be a biophysi-something-or-other.

I did graduate from the Prestigious NorthEastern University that spring, with a pretty good undergraduate record. It would have been better except for the fact that my undergraduate advisor, one William McWilliam McCloud, recommended that I take a graduate course in physics in my senior year. I knew pretty much from the start that I was at least somewhat out of my depth, and this judgment was driven home rather effectively by an incident that occurred about halfway through the fall semester. One of the instructors in the course came in one morning and began the session with an apology to the class for some mistake that he had made in the previous lecture. He then proceeded to pull a revolver from his pocket, pointed it at his head, and pulled the trigger. The gun was loaded with blanks, of course, but even after three years plus in college, this Negro kid (I know, I've already used the word "Negro" three times, but most of us still weren't black yet) from southwestern Illinois wasn't quite yet sufficiently sophisticated to deal with an episode like that. The rest of the class, almost all graduate students, thought that the stunt was hilarious. I was just happy that the instructor launched his actual lecture by reviewing the material from the previous period. That gave me time to go to the lavatory and clean out my undershorts.

The upshot is that even though I didn't do especially well in the graduate course (no, I'm not going to tell you what grade I got), I still had a more-than-respectable undergraduate record and graduated with honors (I will tell you that my grade in the physics course was the difference between honors and high honors, but I was thrilled to graduate with any kind of honors at all). So I was not at all apprehensive about applying to strong biophysi-something-or-other programs for graduate study. I made the interview list at several of my top choices and visited three of the schools that invited me. My first visit was to PERU (not the country, PERU—Private Eastern Research University). It was a school very much like my undergraduate institution, PNEU, but in a different part of the eastern US. The way these things work, in case you don't know, is that students show up, talk with faculty, meet with students already enrolled in the program, eat, drink, and generally feel pretty uncomfortable. At least that's the way it worked for me. Fortunately, because I had a good undergraduate record and had done well on the Graduate Record Exam (the SAT for grad school), I had no reason to believe that I was being considered by any of these schools just because I was Negro/black/African American—although there's a good chance that I was.

My first interview was with Professor Van Liplicur, one of the stalwarts of the biochemistry and biophysics program at PERU. From what I'd been told, Van Liplicur, although he was an outstanding scientist in his youth, hadn't done much at all in recent years. Rumor had it that he was pissed at having been passed over for the Nobel Prize ten or fifteen years earlier. I had no way of knowing exactly how old he was, but as I was barely twenty-one, he looked really old to me. Other than his age, which in hindsight, I guess, was somewhere between sixty-five and seventy, Van Liplicur's most distinguishing physical characteristic was the ring of reddened skin that surrounded his mouth, which explains the roughly half a dozen tubes of Chapstick that were lying around on his desk.

"So, Mr. Tyrone McTavish, is it? Hhmm, McTavish. That's an unusual name for a Negro, isn't it?"

"I guess it is unusual, Professor, but my mother is from South Dakota." As you might imagine, I'd been asked that question before, more than once; and in case you're interested, no, my mother was not from South Dakota.

"Oh. Well, Mr. McTavish, tell me a little bit about yourself."

At this point, I break out my "small-town boy from southwestern Illinois" routine. I try to keep it short and reasonably concise, but I'm only about halfway through when I notice that Van Liplicur is starting to nod. So I decide on a ploy to get his attention.

"So tell me a little about your research, Professor."

Van Liplicur moved his glasses down his nose, leaned forward across the desk between us, and fixed his eyes on mine. I knew immediately that I had asked the wrong question.

"*My research*. Well, let me tell you about my research, young man."

He glanced quickly at a calendar tacked to the wall next to his desk.

"In case you don't know, I was a nominee for the Nobel Prize in physics, that's the *Nobel* Prize that was awarded ten years, one month, and four days ago today. I suspect you didn't know that, did you? I was nominated for that Nobel Prize. I bet you didn't know that either, but I was nominated for that Nobel Prize. Anyway, I didn't get it. The bastards had no appreciation for the significance of my research. They gave the prize to some assholes from Japan. Since they were unwilling to give me what I deserved, I decided from that point on not to give them, or the rest of the world for that matter, the benefit of my scientific knowledge and capabilities. My lab has been closed ever since the day the announcement was made. But even if I was still active, I have no reason to believe that you would be capable of understanding my research any more than anyone else in the world could, even if I was inclined to tell you about it, which I'm not. Well, I see it's time for your next interview. Good-bye, Mr. McTavish."

Of course, it wasn't time for the next interview, not by a long shot.

But I knew that I had outstayed my welcome with Van Liplicur, so I left.

My next interview was with the young hotshot of the department, Professor Titus (pronounced *tightass*, or at least it should have been). He had just been promoted to full professor at the age of thirty-two. Though Van Liplicur hadn't won a Nobel Prize, I learned from the graduate students I talked to at PERU that in the minds of most in the department, Titus was a sure bet to do so someday. Rumor had it that he was going to be nominated for the National Academy of Sciences that very year. Titus certainly looked the part. He was dressed in corduroy slacks and a Harris Tweed sport coat with suede elbow patches, Oxford shirt with a "real" bow tie, not the clip-on variety. Problem was that the colors of the various components of his apparel didn't match very well. He clearly didn't care.

"Good morning, Mr. McTavish, is it? McTavish, that's an unusual name for a Negro, isn't it?"

"Yes, I suppose it is, but my father is from Nova Scotia."

"Well, Mr. McTavish, let's get down to business. Tell me a little bit about your hobbies."

Uh-oh. I wasn't really prepared for that one. I didn't expect to be asked about anything but my scientific and other scholarly interests. Why the hell did he want to know about my hobbies? Was this a trick question?

"Well, Professor Titus, I enjoy reading, especially science fiction, and I enjoy music, especially jazz. I like sports and still play a few, especially volleyball and basketball, and I enjoy bicycling."

"Oh. Okay. What's the normal pressure in the front tire of a ten-speed bicycle?"

"Uh, I don't think I know the answer to that one, Dr. Titus."

"Okay, let's try this one. Do you bump your head when you die?"

"Sorry... uh, I'm afraid I don't know that one either."

"Well, you must know something. Who's your favorite jazz musician?"

"That would be—" But before I could finish my sentence, Titus had opened a folder on his desk and was starting to speak again.

"Well, let's take a look at your undergraduate record. You know, I went to PNEU[1] myself. I took harder courses than you did, though, and I did better in them too. Yeah, I remember Physics 333. I did much better in that course than you did. Why did you even take it? If a hog and a half costs a dollar and a half, how much do two hogs cost, Mr. McTavish?"

"Professor, I really don't see what these questions—"

"Never mind. Tell me what you see yourself doing in fifteen or twenty years."

Finally, I thought, *a question I can sink my teeth into.* I had expected that someone would ask me this question, and I'd thought about my answer. I was ready, or so I thought. I leaned forward and smiled what I hoped would be a winning smile, one that would get me into grad school at PERU.

"Well, I certainly hope to have my own lab and to establish a productive research program. But beyond that, there are several members of my family who have been teachers at various levels of the educational hierarchy and some that have been academic administrators. I will certainly want to try my hand at teaching. I know that even at research universities, teaching is important. And I have thought from time to time about going into academic administration."

Now I wasn't really stupid, just naive. I thought that a faculty member at a prestigious university, at any university, would think that teaching was important; and I didn't know then that administrators were ranked just below cockroaches and just above lawyers in the eyes of university faculty. I caught on quickly though. My interview with Titus concluded

---

1   Prestigious NorthEastern University, remember?

just as abruptly as the one with Van Liplicur had, and for some reason, all my remaining appointments at PERU were mysteriously canceled. Not that it mattered. My two interviews had pretty much convinced me that I didn't want to go to school there.

By the way, in case you're interested, Titus was elected to the National Academy, but he never did win a Nobel Prize. In fact, he was kicked out of the university a few years after I visited there. Moral turpitude. More on that subject later.

My next interview was at Humongous University and Tech, number one (or HUT I for short since all HUTs have football teams). I won't bore you with all the details since this story is really about what happened to me after graduate school, but it is important to note that HUT I was located in the upper Midwest, and I went to interview there in March. Even at my PNEU, the weather had started to soften somewhat by then, and I knew that spring was on its way. But there were two feet of snow on the ground at HUT I. It was snowing when I got there, and it was snowing when I left. I knew immediately that HUT I was not the school for me.

So I finally settled in at another HUT, HUT II, which was located on the West Coast, and I had a great time in grad school there. And there's an interesting connection here to the question that got me whiteballed at PERU. After five years at HUT II, I'd learn how to be a smart ass when I needed to be and not to take any crap from tight-assed faculty. So if I'd been able to do it over again, my answer to Titus's question about what I saw myself doing in fifteen years would probably have been, "I see myself in a house on the Monterey peninsula with all the marijuana I can smoke." Actually, I don't do drugs, never have, but I would have gotten his attention. And that was certainly the kind of answer his question deserved.

CHAPTER II

I SPENT FOUR-AND-A-HALF YEARS at HUT II[2], which was shorter than the average time to degree in the biophysics department there, I produced a reasonable doctoral thesis, which resulted in three publications in a very respectable journal, and I got my PhD. And in contrast to the experience I had at PERU[3], I learned that most HUT II faculty really did think that teaching was important. I even got to teach a couple of classes myself. It was fun. After I left HUT II, I did three years of postdoctoral work, including two in Europe. Those were fun years too, although they would have been more fun if I'd had a bit more money. Even in those days, it was expensive to live in Europe. Still, it's an experience that I'm glad I had, and I'd do it again in a heartbeat. It was by sheer luck that I asked some of my faculty mentors at HUT II about the prospects of my landing a good job in the US while I was actually studying in Europe. They advised me that the prospects weren't good. So I began my job search before I left for Europe and was fortunate enough to land my first real job.

---

2   Humongous University and Tech, remember?

3   Prestigious Eastern Research University

That job was at HUT III, another West Coast university with a really good football team. I began there immediately upon my return from the European postdoctoral position; I rose through the professorial ranks at a reasonable speed and was made full professor after about eleven years. My research productivity was more than satisfactory although not spectacular. I produced a few graduate students, some of whom went on to do excellent science themselves, and some who did not (one or two of them got their PhDs with me and then went on to, ugh, medical school). I got a few research grants and published about seventy papers during my years as a research-active faculty member at HUT III, which was an acceptable if not an exceptional number, and I found that I really enjoyed teaching and that I was good at it. Shortly after I was promoted to full professor, I received a totally unexpected phone call from the president of the University. He asked me to take on a special administrative project that he had in mind. I was reluctant to do so at first but felt that I might benefit from a taste of academic administration; after all, it did run in my family, so I agreed to become the special assistant to the president. I managed to complete the project successfully, decided to stay on as the SAP, and so remained in that position for two years. In part because of the visibility I achieved as a result of my connection to the president, I came to the attention of a number of national headhunters. I threw my hat into the ring for several administrative positions at various institutions, and finally, I accepted the position of dean of Arts and Sciences at SNAF-U and moved back East once again. In addition to my position as dean, I was also awarded a full professorship, with tenure of course, in the Department of Biochemistry and Biophysics at SNAF-U[4].

I arrived at SNAF-U in the fall following the end of my nineteenth academic year at HUT III. Like lots of American universities, SNAF-U

---

4   As I've said, SNAFU is the abbreviation for Small but National, Aspiring to be Famous University. But note the other meaning of this acronym, Situation Normal, All Fouled Up, as you continue in these pages.

had been founded in the mid-nineteenth century. It was established originally by some religious order or another, and its initial charge was to train fencing coaches for mission schools in Borneo or something like that. The religious order was ultimately absorbed by a larger group (the Rastafarians, or some similar organization), and SNAF-U gradually evolved into a liberal arts university, with graduate and undergraduate programs and about ten thousand students. Many of its original buildings were still in use, and the more recent additions had been designed to blend with the original architecture. The resulting mix of the old and new produced a very attractive physical environment with lots of red brick, marble, and ivy.

The central campus was constructed around a traditional quadrangle enclosed by the usual categories of college edifices, classroom spaces, libraries, administrative offices, laboratories, the student union, the gym, and the like. The only blemish on the landscape was a truly revolting piece of modern sculpture situated at one corner of the quad. The title conferred on it by its creator was *Truth and Beauty*, but most of the people I met referred to it as *You Can't Get There from Here*.

It took me about a week to find a place to live and to get to know the staff in the dean's office. One of the most important members of that group was my administrative assistant, Jarvis Hall. Jarvis had graduated from SNAF-U with a degree in criminal justice. He had worked in the dean's office for about ten years, so he knew the university pretty well. Jarvis was about my height, that is, slightly over six feet, but was in better shape, that is to say he was thinner than I was. He was graying slightly, and I guessed, from the graduation picture on his desk, that he was a bit older than one would suppose from the date of his graduation. For personal as well as professional reasons, I decided that it would be a good idea for me to get to know him as well as I could. So to get that ball rolling, I invited him to lunch. We went to the University Club, the SNAF-U equivalent of a faculty club at other universities. The difference here was that the U Club was open to staff as well as faculty. We arrived around one o'clock, and the lunch crowd was already starting to thin out.

"Table for two?" The waitron was almost certainly a student. She showed us to a table overlooking the quadrangle. We got menus and ordered, soup and sandwich for Jarvis and a salad for me.

"So, Jarvis," I began, "tell me a little bit about yourself. How did someone with a degree in criminal justice end up as an AA in the dean's office?"

"Well, that's an interesting story, Dean McTavish, one that involves a particularly curious coincidence. I was all set to use my CJ degree. I thought about being a prison guard or maybe joining the FBI or the Secret Service. One day, shortly after I graduated, I was in my truck, actually on my way to the SNAF-U Career Office, when I passed this woman standing on the corner of Tucker and South U. She was surrounded by boxes and luggage, and she was crying her eyes out. Well, I couldn't just pass her by, so I parked my truck, got out, went over, and asked her what was wrong. She answered me in perfect English but with a thick Scandinavian accent. Turned out she was Swedish. She had come to SNAF-U for grad school, had just arrived from Sweden, had been dropped at the corner of Tucker and South U by the cab driver who drove her from the airport, and she didn't have a clue what she should do next. So she just stood there and cried. Well, what was I to do? Here's a damsel in distress, a damn good looking one at that, so I had to help. I learned that she had accommodations in grad student housing, but she didn't know where that was and neither did the cab driver. Fortunately, I did know. So I loaded her and her stuff into my truck, drove her to student housing, and helped her move in. I took her to dinner that night, and the rest, as they say, is history. We continued to see each other, and six months later, we got married. After that, I figured I needed to be close by, so I took the job in the dean's office. When she finished her degree, she got a job with the counseling service, and we've lived happily ever after. At least up to now."

"That's a terrific story, Jarvis. I guess romance isn't dead. And although I don't know you very well yet, I have to say that I don't quite see you as a prison guard."

He smiled, a smile that suggested that he didn't see himself as one either.

"So tell me. You've been here for ten years, actually longer than that if you count your years as a student. What do you think I need to know about SNAF-U?"

He rested his chin on his fist.

"That's not an easy question to answer, Dean McTavish, at least not in words of one syllable. You'll find that SNAF-U is a curious place. Don't get me wrong. It's a great university. There are some really smart people here, both faculty and students. But there are some really strange people here too, both faculty and students—and administrators. I'm not sure how much more I should say, especially about specific people. I may need to work for one of them at some point in the future. I think you'll just have to meet them, get to know them, and judge them for yourself. But rest assured that I'll always do whatever I can to help you deal with them. And I have to say, you will have to *deal* with them. In some cases, that will be easy, in other cases, it will be more difficult. And… in some cases, you'll find that it will be, well… just really odd."

Jarvis was honest, perceptive, and as it turned out, right on. We finished our lunches in casual conversation. As we were leaving the U Club, Jarvis returned to our earlier discussion.

"As I recall, Dean McTavish, you'll be meeting with President Sligh this afternoon. I hope that meeting goes well, but keep what I told you in mind."

"Thanks, Jarvis, I will."

As he had suggested, it was time for me to begin to make the rounds of the relevant administrative offices on campus. As dean of Arts and Sciences, I had responsibility for the undergraduate and graduate programs in the Arts and Sciences at SNAF-U, a somewhat different set of responsibilities than is associated with this position at other universities. My first stop on my administrative rounds was, indeed, the president's office.

President Robert Sligh had been in office for about three years when I arrived at SNAF-U. His academic training and experience were in some humanities discipline, and there was a very curious tale in circulation regarding his ascension to the presidency, a tale which if true, spoke volumes about the inner workings of SNAF-U. It went something like this. Sligh had been dean of the SNAF-U Honors College when the previous president resigned. The tradition at SNAF-U was for the board of trustees to select a new candidate from a slate of nominees, listing their first, second, and third choices via secret ballot. According to the rumor, when the vote was taken to select the new president, the ten trustees each listed a different candidate as their first choice. The majority vote getter as second choice was Elvis, but he was unavailable for the job (I was to learn later that it was highly unusual to find anyone with a sense of humor on any university's board of trustees. The SNAF-U Board was apparently an exception to this rule). Sligh was the near unanimous third choice since none of the trustees thought that anyone else would vote for him. So to everyone's surprise and perhaps to their chagrin as well, Sligh became the eventual president of SNAF-U. Now I know that this story is apocryphal, especially the bit about Elvis. But everyone I talked to had been surprised by Sligh's selection, no one thought that any trustee would have voted for him if they'd thought he had a snowball's chance of winning, and no one I talked to had any better explanation for how he became president of SNAF-U.

I guessed that Sligh was in his late-fifties, maybe early sixties, which made him a few years older than me. SNAF-U had sent me some stuff to read before I arrived on campus, and I'd seen some photographs of Sligh that were taken before he became president. Those pictures showed what appeared to be a trim, athletic man approaching his middle years. Three years as president had changed that. Sligh now had a considerable gut. As far as his administrative skills were concerned, he was apparently a master at currying favor with influential alumni, businessmen and women, and others. He was, in fact, admired by many for this ability, as it had produced substantial dividends for SNAF-U. On the flip side, though, Sligh had a reputation for making and implementing significant decisions without telling anyone, even after the deeds had been done. Sligh was sitting at his desk when I entered his office.

"Good morning, Tyrone. It's good to see you again. Welcome back to SNAF-U." Sligh rose to shake my hand, and we moved to leather easy chairs around a table in the middle of the office.

"Good morning to you, President Sligh. It's good to finally be here permanently. The traveling back and forth between here and HUT III was beginning to wear on me a bit, but I did rack up a bundle of frequent flyer miles." Sligh chuckled.

"Well, we're all delighted to have you here. Are you settling in okay? Did you find a place to live?"

"Yes, things are going very smoothly as a matter of fact. I've bought a house, or I should say I've closed on one, and I should be able to move in by the end of the month. I decided to buy right away rather than rent because I think, or perhaps I should say I hope, that I'll be here for a while. I'm getting to know the staff in my office, I just had a nice lunch with my administrative assistant, and we've already begun to make some plans for this academic year. So all things considered, I think I've made a pretty smooth transition."

"Good, I'm glad to hear it," Sligh said. "I suspect you have some questions for me, but there are a couple of things I'd like to discuss with you, if you don't mind." He paused and adjusted his glasses before continuing. "Ty, I'm a bit embarrassed by this, but it's been on my mind since the very first time we met. Now that you're a member of the SNAF-U family, I'd like to know a little more about you, so I, uh, I'd like to begin with a personal question… I do hope you won't mind. I'm sure it's one you've been asked before, so I trust you won't think it too personal. It's just a matter of my own curiosity. I've wanted to ask you this since we first met, but I was reluctant to do so. I hope you won't be offended by it." He paused. "It has to do with your last name. Isn't McTavish a rather unusual surname for an African American?"

"Well… yes, I guess it is, President Sligh, but my grandfather decided to change the family name when he immigrated to this country from Bulgaria."

"Hhmm, I see. What was your grandfather's surname, if I may ask?"

"Wang," I replied with a completely straight face. That was a lie of course. My grandfather's surname was McTavish, same as mine. And he was born and raised in Connecticut.

"Oh. Curious."

Maybe I should have been more forthcoming with my official boss, but I wasn't about to let him off that easily.

"I suspect you get some questions about your name too, President Sligh."

Sligh raised an eyebrow. "What exactly do you mean by that?"

"Nothing really, just that Sligh isn't an especially common name either." And I thought but didn't add, *Some might not consider it a name that would inspire confidence among the constituents of a university president.* "You mentioned other matters that you want to discuss with me?"

I'm usually pretty effective at directing the conversation away from uncomfortable or difficult subjects and decided quickly that I didn't want to continue with this one. Sligh frowned but didn't pursue the matter.

"Yes, there is one in particular. And it is another rather delicate one, although it's not particularly personal, I don't think. But it does involve some considerations that I feel the need to handle delicately. How shall I put it?"

Another pause.

"Tyrone, I want you to be assured that the fact that you are Negro, uh, black, uh, African American, uh, black, uh, the fact that you are black had nothing to do with your selection as dean of Arts and Sciences here. You were the best man for the job, and that's why we hired you."

"I'm glad to hear that, President Sligh," I offered, even though I was absolutely sure that although I was the best man for the job, my being black *did* have something to do with my getting it. And I was also pretty sure I knew what was coming next.

"Nevertheless, there are some ways in which your ethnic persuasion—you don't mind if I use that term do you?—in which your ethnic persuasion can benefit the university."

Here it comes, I thought.

"In particular, we think you can play a significant role in our efforts to recruit more minority faculty to the Arts and Sciences. As I suspect you know, there are only ten black faculty among the roughly four hundred in the Literary College, and five of them are in the African American Studies Department. We hope that your presence here will help us to increase those numbers and that you might even develop specific programs to attract more minorities."

Now don't get me wrong. I had already thought about ways to increase the number of minority faculty at SNAF-U. But I was a little put off by the fact that (a) the president had introduced this subject by claiming that my race wasn't important but had then (b) moved immediately to a discussion of a situation in which my race could be exploited to the benefit of SNAF-U. Still, I wasn't completely unprepared for this because I'd seen it before. Sligh was not as "sligh" as he thought.

"Let me assure you, President Sligh, that as I look at the overall issue of faculty recruitment, enhancing our efforts to recruit minority faculty will be a major component of the analysis. In particular, one of my goals will certainly be to increase the number of minority faculty generally and the number of minority faculty with tenure. May I ask exactly how many of the current black faculty in the Literary College are tenured?"

"You mean not counting you?"

"Uh, yeah, I guess so."

"Uh… One."

"And over the last, say, ten years, how many of the minority faculty that have been recruited here have received tenure?"

"Well, I'm not sure." Sligh was starting to squirm. He hadn't anticipated this line of interrogation. "You mean not counting you?"

"Yes, President Sligh. Not counting me." I would have thought that was obvious.

"I think the answer is one."

"Let me get this straight. In the last ten years, there have been at least eleven black faculty in the college at SNAF-U, maybe more than that. Only one has gotten tenure, and since I'm currently the only one with tenure, that means that the one other person who was tenured has left the university. Is that correct?"

Sligh's face reddened.

"Well, yes… it is. We can only do one thing at a time, Dr. McTavish (It was back to Dr. McTavish now). Right now, we need to have more minorities in our faculty ranks. We certainly want to see our minority faculty, indeed all our junior faculty, receive tenure. But we have to get them here first, don't we? Oh." Sligh glanced at his watch. "I see that it's time for my next appointment. Let's continue this conversation at a later time, shall we? I know you have other questions for me, and there are other matters I want to discuss with you too. Till then?"

I suspected that this conversation hadn't worked out exactly as he'd planned. Polite good-byes, then off to my next appointment—the provost's office.

The provost at SNAF-U was one Dr. Olan Azkizur. He pronounced his last name *oz-KY-zur*. His detractors on campus (and presumably elsewhere) preferred a different pronunciation. Provost Azkizur was doing a pretty good job according to the scuttlebutt, and he was held in especially high regard by President Sligh, but it was perhaps significant that almost everyone I spoke to mentioned that he owned a vacation home in Florida that was used with some frequency by the president and his family. Could it be that Azkizur owed his apparent success to something other than his administrative abilities? I checked in at the desk of his administrative assistant and was ushered into his office.

"Hi, Ty, great to see you again. You're looking fit. I guess the rigors of academic administration haven't begun to get to you yet." He chuckled. "Please, make yourself comfortable."

He sat down behind his desk, and I took a seat across from him. "Good to see you too, Olan." We had been on a first-name basis since the interview process some months earlier. Now with the president, on the other hand, I had made up my mind that at least for the foreseeable future, he was to be President Sligh no matter what he called me. Olan was of medium height and was starting to develop a slight bulge around his midsection. I suspected that he and the president attended a lot of the same functions and so showed the effects of all that good SNAF-U cuisine. The old meet-and-eat syndrome. The more I studied him, the more Azkizur reminded me of a somewhat pudgy Bela Lugosi. As a matter of fact—come to think of it—if I squinted and sort of turned my head to one side when I looked at him, Sligh might be mistaken for Lon Chaney Jr. Dracula meets the Wolfman or maybe vice versa. Interesting.

"Thanks for stopping by," he continued. "I know you've got a lot to do to get up to speed here, and I want you to know that I'm here to help in any ways I can. We'll have a chance to talk in greater detail about the job as the semester wears on, but I thought we could chat now about a few issues, if that's okay with you. Are you settling in okay?"

"Yes, thanks, Olan. Everyone has been very generous and helpful and the transition has been pretty smooth and almost painless so far. I do have a couple of questions for you, but they can wait until a bit later. Why don't you take the lead?" This was, after all, the president's man. Could I anticipate what was coming? You bet your ass I could.

"Ty, I want to say something to you that is difficult to say but that I think needs to be said." The obligatory pause. He leaned forward, rested an arm on the desk, and looked at me with an expression that I'm sure he intended to be his most earnest one. "I want you to know that your being Negro, uh, black, uh, African American, uh, black, uh, had nothing to do with your getting this position. You were far and away the best qualified candidate, and SNAF-U is damn lucky to have you."

"That's very generous of you, Olan," I said, responding in a rather generous fashion myself. Next shoe please.

"All the same, there are some ways in which we think that your ethnic persuasion—you don't mind if I use that term do you?—in which your ethnic persuasion can benefit the university. In particular, we hope that your presence here will help us to recruit more minority students to the Literary College and the graduate school."

Blah. Blah. Blah. Of course, recruiting minority students and faculty was important, but if my race was not a factor in my hiring, why was it that the only tasks that the president and provost seemed to have in mind for me were specifically related to my ethnic persuasion? I needed to move this conversation on to other matters. As I've said, I'm pretty good at that.

"Look, Olan, I do intend to address that concern and others related to minorities on this campus. In fact, I've already spoken with the president about it. But let me suggest that that's a conversation for another time. Right now, there are some other things I think we need to talk about. There are some matters that I'll have to deal with almost immediately. So if you don't mind, let's postpone that part of the conversation for a while, and, if you're agreeable, move on to some of those other matters."

"As you wish," he responded reluctantly. He leaned back in his chair and rested his hands in his lap.

"There is one question I have in particular, and I think you're exactly the person to answer it. I've been reading the materials that you sent to me, and I'm trying to familiarize myself with the various departments and programs in the Literary College. Most of the disciplines are familiar ones, and the departmental designations make perfect sense. Some of them seem a little curious though, and I'd like to talk to you in greater detail about several of them when we have time. Right now, my main concern is one specific program in the Literary College, or I guess it's really a department. Matter of fact, I'm not really at all sure exactly what the hell it is. Maybe you can clarify that for me. I don't know how I missed noticing it in my reading of the College Bulletin and the other stuff I had to read when I was interviewing for this job, but I did. I did notice it when I was reviewing some of that material the other night. Tell me about the Department of Nuclear, Uranial, and Theocratic Studies."

"I suspected you'd get around to asking about that," Olan responded. "People usually do. I'm surprised you didn't do so before now. You probably missed it earlier because we try our best not to make its existence very obvious. We *want* people to miss it. The reason you didn't see it in the College Bulletin is that it's not listed there. Anyway, as I'm sure you've observed, the department has only four members, and it's housed in a building that's situated off campus, as a matter of fact, it's on the other side of town."

"Well, I knew that there were only four faculty in the department, but I didn't know that it wasn't even housed on campus. But one other curious thing I did notice. As far as I can tell, the department doesn't offer any courses."

"That's right, Ty. No courses, graduate or undergraduate. We don't want any of those people in the classroom. The department has no chair, no undergraduate or graduate curricula, and therefore, no students. The faculty members don't serve on any college committees and don't do any advising."

"Then what in the hell good is the department?"

Olan rose, went to the window, and paused there for a moment. He turned to face me and continued.

"Ty, every university has some faculty that just don't fit in anywhere—the eccentrics, folks who got tenure then turned into pumpkins or worse. That's the case here. The department was created as a holding tank for the four most eccentric faculty in the college. We can't fire them, but we can put them in a place where the harm they can do is minimized. We're not any different in this regard than any other university in this country. I'll bet you had faculty like that at HUT III."

Maybe we did, but I sure didn't remember any phantom departments that housed them.

"Well, Olan, you may be interested in knowing that each of those four faculty has already made an appointment to see me. That's how I found out initially that the department existed. So you better tell me what I need to know about them now."

He sat again and leaned back in his chair.

"Okay, here's the scoop. The players are Michael Baccaliprati, Stoy Urgek, Ola Ebola-Shalaka, and Leonard Da Vinci, at least that's what the last two call themselves now. Ebola-Shalaka was Ola Mae Ballard when she got here, and Da Vinci was Nicholas Baldwin. But I'll come back to them. Let me begin with Urgek since he's the easiest to explain. Quite simply, Urgek is an Eastern European who never adapted to the American system of higher education even after more than fifteen years in this country. His teaching always bordered on the disastrous, and so he got tenure primarily because of his research, which to be fair was pretty spectacular. And in his heyday, he brought a ton of money to SNAF-U, supported a lot of grad students in English and philosophy, if you know what I mean. But the teaching situation came to a head a few years ago. He was assigned to teach an introductory physics class that met from twelve to one. It was apparently the first time in his career that he had taught a class that met at noon. He was outraged at having to teach during his normal lunch hour, so in protest, he brought his lunch to class every day and would spend the first fifteen minutes or so of each class period eating it, right there in the classroom. He also used to chain smoke Turkish cigarettes *during* his classes, and he developed the habit of spitting on students who answered questions incorrectly in class. We had to get him out of the classroom. Nucular, Uranial ,and Theocratic Studies seemed the best strategy."

(It's picky I know, but I just hate it when people mispronounce "nuclear.")

"Ola Ebola-Shalaka was the director of the African American Studies Program until a few years ago. She was removed after many complaints, primarily from students, about her behavior. She apparently used to stalk her students, at least some of them. Not in any life—or physically—threatening way, but to make sure that they were working. She would sit in the library and watch her students while they were studying, sometimes for hours on end. She would show up at the study lounges in the dorms and watch her students while they were studying. She would schedule additional time after classes in association with the courses she offered and would require her students to go either to a conference room in the Arts Building, or, if you can believe it, to her home, to study while she sat there and watched them. Sometimes her students would have to come to her home in the evening, occasionally before they had eaten their evening meal. When they got hungry, Ebola-Shalaka would give them peanut butter sandwiches and lime Kool-Aid. According to her students, it was always lime. Now her motives here might have been honorable, or maybe they weren't. Who's to say? Goodness knows a lot of our students need to spend more time in their books, and she never did anything really wrong, although these days I suspect her behavior would be described as harassment. In any event, she did take things just a bit too far. So we moved her to the NUThouse.

Olan paused and took a sip of coffee from a mug sitting on his desk.

"Michael Baccaliprati. You may have noticed as you walked around the quad that we have a new Physical Sciences Building. Baccaliprati blew up the old one. It was an accident, of course, or at least we think it was. We certainly can't prove that it wasn't. And there was no convincing evidence that the explosion was caused by any gross negligence on his part. It was just an accident, plain and simple. Nevertheless, for that and several other reasons that I'm sure you'll learn about, he had to go. And Nucular, Uranial, and Theocratic Studies was the logical destination for him. He has an office but no lab.

And that brings me to Leonard. There are a lot of things I could say about him, but let me sum them up by saying that as far as I can tell—and I'm neither psychologist nor psychiatrist—he's just plain crazy. Case in point. A few years ago Leonard was caught exposing himself to students in the library. Not really exposing himself... because he wasn't really... well, let me just tell you about the episode, and you'll see what I mean. What he would do was put on a raincoat and wander around the library opening the raincoat in front of students and staff, female *and* male, in the typical flasher's pose. The thing was that underneath the raincoat, he was fully clothed. So he wasn't really breaking any laws, he was just an annoyance. And he kept doing things like that. I have to admit that some of the things he did were truly funny, and they were all original, and he never did anything illegal. But we had to do something, so we sent him to the NUThouse."

I closed my mouth. "I can see, Olan, that I'm going to have an interesting time in my meetings with those four. I think they're all scheduled for the same afternoon. Maybe I should have my secretary try to do something about that. Anyway, thanks for the background."

"You're more than welcome, Ty. As I said, I'm here to help…"

We both stood, and Olan walked around to me and put his arm around my shoulder. "Uh, Ty? Before you go, and if you don't mind one more question from me, there is something else I'd like to ask you."

"Shoot."

"I'm curious about your name."

Uh-oh. Here we go again.

"I hope you're not offended by my curiosity. But it is somewhat unusual. I wonder… Are you by any chance related to Tyrone Power?"

Jarvis was right. Downright strange indeed.

CHAPTER III

J ARVIS," I SAID, TO call him into my office. His desk was close enough that I didn't have to raise my voice much above the conversational level to summon him. "I've been thinking about my meeting with the NUTS faculty. I believe you have them all scheduled for the same day."

"That's right, Dean McTavish. They each claimed that they needed to see you as soon as possible, and that was the first available date."

"Well, the provost gave me a quick rundown on each of them, and they sound like a pretty weird bunch to me. Did you think about asking whether I could meet with them all together?"

"You don't know me very well yet, Dean McTavish, but you will. So yes, I suggested a departmental meeting to each of them, and they each thought it was a pretty ugly idea. One of them called me a dirty name. I'll let you guess which one after you've met them all. Looks like you'll have to see them individually."

Damn! This wasn't exactly the way I'd envisioned the start to my career here, but there seemed to be no easy alternative. In fact, based on what I knew about them at that point, seeing them all together might be a whole lot worse than seeing them one at a time.

So the faculty from NUTS were scheduled, one at a time, for an afternoon a few days following my meetings with Sligh and Azkizur. My first visitor was Stoy Urgek. I wasn't exactly sure about his country of origin, but I knew that it was somewhere in the Balkans. He had been in the US for many years, but as the provost had said, he never quite caught on to how things are done in American higher education. Of course, that's true of a lot of people, including many who were born here. As far as his physical appearance was concerned, Urgek was pretty much a mess. His hair was disheveled, and although he wore a coat and tie, both the coat and the shirt underneath it were badly wrinkled, and the tie was pulled over to one side of his collar. One of the buttons was in the wrong hole. In addition to his ignorance of the niceties of the American educational system, Urgek had also obviously never acquired the habit of using deodorant. His teeth and fingernails were also heavily stained, probably from years of smoking those Turkish cigarettes. I ushered him into my office and sat as far away from him as I could.

"Good morning, Professor Urgek," I offered as my opening gambit. "I appreciate your stopping by. I am trying to make the acquaintance of as many SNAF-U faculty as I can."

"You don't have to pretend to be nice to me, Dean McTavish," Urgek spat. "I know that you know that I am one of the outcasts in the house of NUTS. I did not come here to be patronized by you."

Patronizing Urgek was the farthest thought from my mind. I was simply trying to be courteous and civil. It was clear that he did not intend to reciprocate.

"Well, then, perhaps you should tell me exactly why you did come here, Dr. Urgek."

"I know that all my fellow NUTS have made appointments to see you. I come here to make sure that they do not fill you with filthy lies about me."

"You are the first of the faculty from the department (I must admit that it was difficult for me to refer to NUTS as a department, but I did) to visit me, so I've heard nothing about you, good or bad, at this point." Of course, that last statement wasn't completely true.

"Very well. You should know then that Hyphen-Shalaka, Da Vinci, and the other physicist will try to get you to believe bad things about me. They will tell you I am an anarchist. They will tell you I threaten them with physical harm. They will tell you I break into their computer files. They will tell you I open their mail. They will tell you I do not use deodorant. Only last of those statements is truth."

"Let me assure you, Dr. Urgek," I began while Urgek caught his breath, "that I do not intend to ask the other departmental faculty about your habits or behavior nor do I plan to do anything to encourage them to volunteer that information. As dean, I am primarily concerned with how effectively you discharge your responsibilities to the institution. Since you have few such responsibilities, I have few concerns, at least for now."

"Good. And as you say, my responsibilities are few. I am theoretical physicist. I do not need lab. I have computer. I have grant. I pay overhead to the university. I do not have to listen to whining graduate students or teach snot-nosed premedical students. I leave others alone, they leave me alone. That is how I like it."

"That's fine with me, Professor Urgek, again, at least for now. I'm glad to know that you are reasonably happy with your situation."

"I am not happy, Dean McTavish, but I am content."

End of meeting. Urgek stood. I offered my hand, but he ignored the gesture. He waved his hand dismissively, wheeled, and walked out of the office.

Dr. Ola Ebola-Shalaka, or as Urgek referred to her, Hyphen-Shalaka (I confess that I tend to find hyphenated names a bit pretentious myself) was waiting when Urgek left. Neither acknowledged the other's presence as they passed. Ebola-Shalaka was the resident theocratician in the

NUThouse. Don't ask me to define theocratic studies, much less African American theocratic studies, because I can't. One thing I *had* learned about her was that she was one of the two African American faculty, *not* counting me, who had received tenure at SNAF-U in the last ten years. Sligh's count had been wrong, but it was true that only one of them was still here, and that was Ola. Ebola-Shalaka was perhaps ten years my junior, but she was painfully thin. That and the way she carried herself made her look much older. She bent slightly at the waist as she walked and moved slowly as if she were bearing some invisible weight on her stooped shoulders. We sat opposite each other across a table at one side of my office. I used my standard opening gambit.

"Good morning, Professor Ebola-Shalaka. I appreciate your stopping by. I'm trying to make the acquaintance of as many SNAF-U faculty as I can." I extended my hand. She accepted it and gave it a weak squeeze.

"Please call me Ola, Dean McTavish." Her voice was pleasant and made her seem younger than her appearance did.

"And please call me Tyrone, or Ty if you prefer."

"Thank you for seeing me. I know that you have appointments with all the inmates of the NUThouse today." There was no humor in her voice as she referred to the department and its denizens. "I also know that you have just arrived on campus, and I hesitate to bother you with my concerns so soon after that arrival, but I would have to raise them with you sooner or later."

"Exactly what are those concerns, Ola?"

"I want my old job back. I was stripped of it unfairly. I was the victim of lies, vicious rumors, innuendo, and sexism on the part of the senior administration of this university. I am hopeful that with a new dean in place, my case will be reviewed, and the decision to remove me from my former position and to put me in a so-called department with a bunch of misfits will be reversed."

Pregnant pause. I wasn't expecting this to be the major item on

Hyphen-Shalaka's agenda, although I'm not sure what I did expect. But in any case, I didn't have a good response ready. Fortunately, Azkizur had given me some of the background to her situation.

"Ola, let me say first of all that I don't know all the details of your situation, so some of what I will say next will be said from ignorance. I can say that I am sorry that you find yourself in this position. It's not one that anyone would envy. But if I may speak frankly, based on what I do know, it appears that your behavior was at least in part responsible for the decision to remove you as director of AAS."

"Exactly what are you referring to?" she asked through pursing lips.

"Well, as I understand it, there were some incidents that had to do with your monitoring your students study habits and—"

"And what's wrong with that?" she exclaimed, her voice rising. "You know as well as I do that these brats don't work nearly hard enough in most of their classes, and that's because the faculty have abrogated their responsibilities to see that they do! And not only college faculty. The same is true for high schools, middle schools, even grade schools. We wouldn't have to worry about grade inflation if we actually expected our students to work for the grades they get."

"There may be some truth to that, Ola, but that doesn't mean that you should follow your students around, intrude on their lives in the dorm, or schedule time to require them to study. Please do correct me if I'm wrong, but as I understand it, you did all of those things."

And I thought but didn't add, *You made them drink lime Kool-Aid. Orange might have been okay, cherry for sure, grape maybe, but certainly not lime.*

"Maybe I did, but if you look at the record, you'll see that my students always performed well in my classes."

"That may be true too, Ola, but there is no concrete evidence to the effect that it was your enforced study habits that were responsible, and in any case, there was clearly a cost associated with that outcome. As I'm sure you know, the initial complaints about you came from the students themselves."

She glared at me. What had begun as a reasonably pleasant conversation was clearly going south.

"I'm not going to argue with you, Dean McTavish. I want my job back. You're the person who can give it back to me, and if you don't do so, I'm planning to take legal action. The only reason I haven't done so up to now is because I thought it prudent to give the new dean—you—a chance to do the right thing. So if you don't intend to do the right thing, I have nothing more to say on the matter.

She paused to wait for a response from me. I had none.

"Good day, Dean McTavish."

I let out another "Damn" as she walked out the door. I didn't even have the chance to attempt a departure handshake. I could hardly wait to see what Baccaliprati had in store for me. But I needed a break, so I decided to go to the john. Too bad I couldn't lock myself in.

Michael Baccaliprati was waiting for me when I returned.

"Come in, Professor Baccaliprati." I escorted him from the outer waiting area into my own office. There was nothing especially distinctive about Baccaliprati's physical appearance. Neither his height nor his build were particularly remarkable. I guessed that he was about forty-five. He was casually dressed in the uniform common to university practitioners of the sciences: khakis, a blue oxford shirt with the collar open, and loafers. Although he was a physicist, he didn't have a beard, and he didn't wear a pocket protector either. Not all of the academic stereotypes are accurate.

"Good morning, Professor Baccaliprati. Please sit down." I began my opening gambit as I had done with the other two NUTS. "I appreciate your stopping by. I'm trying to make the acquaintance—"

I didn't finish the second sentence. Before I could, and as soon as he sat down, Baccaliprati burst into tears.

"Dean McTavish," he sobbed, "I have to have my lab back! It was an accident, Dean McTavish, I didn't mean to blow up the Physics Building. No one ever claimed I did! It was an accident! I'm a scientist, Dean McTavish, a research scientist. I have to have my lab back, you have to give me my lab back! Please!" More sobbing.

I handed him a tissue. Not Kleenex but a box of laboratory wipes of the sort I use in my own laboratory. Bad choice.

"Oh, lab wipes," he moaned. "I used lab wipes in my lab, at least I used to." I haven't seen that many grown men cry, at least not in real life, and although Baccaliprati's tears were obviously genuine, he was still beginning to annoy me.

"Please try to get hold of yourself, Professor. I know something of your situation although I admit that many of the details are lacking especially related to the explosion, but—"

"It was an accident!" he screamed.

"But," I continued, ignoring his outburst, "according to the information I have, there were other reasons for removing you from Physics and putting you in the Nuclear, Uranial, and Theocratic Studies Department."

"Department" continued to stick in my throat, but I forced myself to say the word, and you may also have noticed that in the previous interviews and in this one, I referred to the department by its full name until one of them used the term "NUTS" or "NUThouse" themselves. And with Baccaliprati, I was afraid that even my slightest gaffe might send him over the edge.

"There was, for example, the incident with the squirrel."

"That was an accident too," he said meekly. "I just forgot, that's all. I forgot."

I had learned about the squirrel incident from a subsequent

conversation with Jarvis. The incident in question took place a few months before the explosion in the Physics Building. Baccaliprati's specialty was low temperature physics, and he decided to demonstrate the effects of ultralow temperatures to one of his classes. Now Baccaliprati hated squirrels, and not without some justification, as there were almost literally jillions of them around campus, underfoot, inside buildings as well as outside—everywhere. So Baccaliprati trapped a squirrel for use in his demonstration. He brought the poor thing to class, put on a protective glove, pulled it out of its cage by its tail, and dropped it into a vat of liquid nitrogen. The temperature of liquid nitrogen is well below -100 degrees Centigrade, so the squirrel didn't last long and almost certainly felt very little, if any, pain. And maybe Baccaliprati would have gotten away with all of this if he'd let it go at that point. But no, he picked up a pair of tongs, pulled the dead squirrel, which was now stiff as a board, from the vat, and smashed it against the top of the counter in front of him. Remember, the poor squirrel was frozen stiff, so it shattered into a thousand pieces when he slammed it against the counter. The pieces scattered everywhere.

"Rocky the Flying Squirrel," Baccaliprati is reported to have said as the poor creature's remains were propelled around the classroom.

One must admit—it was a dramatic demonstration. But there were two problems. The first was that in a class of eighty students, there were bound to be some animal rights activists—and there were. They marched straight to the president's office immediately after the class. But Baccaliprati might still have survived if it hadn't been for the second problem. The second problem was that he didn't bother to clean up the squirrel fragments once the demonstration was finished. And although Rocky was frozen stiff when he encountered the bench top, he didn't remain frozen for long. The custodial staff was not at all thrilled at having to clean up the now room temperature squirrel guts they found later that evening. They too reported the squirrel incident to the president, and it was off to the NUThouse for Michael Baccaliprati.

"Nevertheless, Michael," I replied, "both of those incidents left doubts, in the minds of some at least, about your judgment. Those doubts made it necessary, again in the minds of some, to remove you from your position in Physics."

"But I'm an experimentalist, Dean McTavish. I'm not like Urgek. You're a scientist yourself, at least you were. You know what it means to want to do research and not to be able to do it. I'm still able to get grants. My proposals get good reviews. Except I don't have any place to do the experiments even if I do have the money to do them. I was even a pretty good teacher, and you know as well as I do that in the sciences, you have to be a strong researcher if you're going to be a strong teacher."

"Yes, I do know what you mean, Michael. I must admit that I still enjoy getting over to my lab myself after the administrative day's work is done, and although there won't be much time for teaching while I'm dean, I was a pretty good teacher too."

Baccaliprati looked at me in amazement. "You have a lab?" he asked, rising from his chair.

"Yes, I do. I still had about a year left on my research grant when I left HUT, and SNAF-U agreed to provide a small amount of space for me to continue my research. I have a technician and a student that I brought with me. It's a small operation but a workable one."

"You're a dean! A dean! And you have a lab." He began pacing back and forth in front of my desk. "You've got to help me, Dean McTavish." There was real desperation in his voice. "I have to get back to my research, and if you don't get me out of that NUThouse, I think I'll go nuts."

I elected not to comment on that last phrase. Baccaliprati was completely oblivious to the irony of it.

"Michael, please sit down. Let's try to discuss this calmly if we can." I paused in the hope that he would be able to collect himself. He took a couple of lab wipes, blew his nose, and sat down. "I can't promise you anything, but I will see what I can do. I think there would have to be some indication that the kinds of errors in judgment that caused this situation can be corrected. Is there any reason to think that that's the case?"

"They were all accidents, Dean McTavish, and I am certainly willing to promise to try to do better."

"Well, as I said, all I can offer you now is a commitment to look into it."

"Thanks a lot, Dean McTavish. I guess that's the best I can hope for. Thank you for seeing me."

"Good-bye, Michael."

Unbelievable!

If the first three hadn't been enough, there was still Da Vinci left, and I was already exhausted. But as I should have expected, he was in the waiting area outside my office when I finished with Baccaliprati. He and Baccaliprati ignored each other as they passed. I wasn't surprised. It was clear that the NUTS regarded (or in this case disregarded) each other with profound contempt. Da Vinci was about sixty and was a few inches shorter than me, which would have put him at about five feet nine or five feet ten. He was dressed in shorts and a T-shirt that had "You Don't Know Me" written on its front, and he wore sandals and mismatched socks, one blue and one black. Jarvis had told me that Da Vinci, or should I say Nicholas Baldwin, had been an all-American linebacker in his college days. He hadn't attended a major college, so he made his mark at one of the lower division schools; but still, All-American was All-American. Even at sixty, he was lean and seemed to be quite fit. Despite his eccentricities, he apparently took care of himself. I envied his full head of hair since I was already beginning to lose some of mine. My dad's genes were finally beginning to kick in.

I opened the door and invited him in, extending my hand to shake his. He brushed right by me, sat down, behind *my* desk, pulled a pair of glasses from the pocket of his shorts, and balanced them on his nose.

"I'll bet you're wondering why my first name is Leonard and not Leonardo, aren't you?"

"I admit, the thought has crossed my mind," I replied.

"You know, what I'd really like to have is a chain saw."

"And what would you do with a chain saw?" I said, smiling. This meeting might be strange, but it might be more fun than the other three.

"That's a stupid question. I'd cut things down of course."

"What things?"

"Street signs, fences, domed sports stadiums, college presidents, field-goal kickers."

"No deans?"

"Probably not. Deans aren't worth the effort. You know, I really like old TV sitcoms.

Have you ever tried to see how far you can spit? I have. My record is ten feet six inches. And I sprained a throat muscle to do that. I'm still gonna try to break that record though."

"Professor Da Vinci," I began, trying to move the conversation along, "I—"

"Call me Leo. My friends call me Leo. Of course, I don't have many friends."

"I wonder why," I mumbled.

"What was that? Okay, let's get down to business, McTavish. You know why I'm here, don't you?"

"I don't have a clue, Professor Da Vinci, uh, Leo, but based on my meetings with your colleagues, I suspect it has something to do with getting you out of the Department of Nuclear, Uranial, and Theocratic Studies."

Everybody else wanted out. I presumed that he did too.

"Wrong. I'm perfectly happy with the NUTS. In fact, I'm there by design, by my own design. You probably haven't noticed, McTavish, but I've been watching you. I went to the meetings where you spoke to faculty while you were being considered for this job. I even went to one of the meetings you had with students. I've asked people about you, at least those that will still talk to me. And I like what I've found out. I've decided that I like you, McTavish. I think you have the potential to shake this place up a bit, so I'm going to give you the benefit of my wisdom about it. So what I'm actually here for is to help *you*, McTavish."

I'm thinking to myself, *Do I take this guy seriously, or is he so seriously deranged that nothing he says will be worth the spit he used to set his record?* I had to think fast, of course, because Leo paused only briefly before continuing this harangue—or whatever it was.

"I'm not really crazy, McTavish. How in hell did you get a name like McTavish? Ah, who gives a shit anyway. Anyway, I'm not really crazy. At least I'm not completely crazy, at least I don't think I am, but that doesn't really matter either. The point is that I can help you. You see, I really *am* in the Department of NUTS by design. That's right. I made a specific effort to be put there. I decided a few years back that I didn't want to work anymore. I just didn't. I didn't want to teach. My research wasn't worth shit anyway. I just wanted to be left alone. But I didn't relish the thought of having to eat Kentucky Fried Chicken, or worse, every day and to beg for the money to get that. I also like to have a draught of single malt scotch on occasion and a draught of Guinness more often than that. So I had to come up with a way to get paid for not working. The tenure system provided me with the ideal solution to my problem. So I pretended to be a semipsycho. At least most of it was pretending. I did just enough to cause concern but not enough to get me thrown in jail, or worse, fired. I knew that if I stayed far enough away from the border line, the university would have to keep me. I am, after all, a tenured full professor with ten years of distinguished service to the university."

"Haven't you been here for twenty-five years, Professor Da Vinci?" I was actually beginning to enjoy this.

"Leo! Leo! It's Leo! And don't be a wise ass. After they put those other wackos in the Department of NUTS, I knew that was the place for me. So I did just enough shit to get people's attention but not enough to get me kicked out. And sure enough, two years ago, I became the lockjaw professor of Uranial Studies. Urania is the muse of astronomy, you know, and because astronomy had been my field, it seemed only fitting that my newfound discipline should have a department of its own. I also take some pride in knowing that the department wouldn't have had a name if I hadn't been added to it. It would have been the NTS Department, or worse, the NATS Department. What the hell kind of name would that be? So I still draw a monthly paycheck from this university, and I don't have to do anything but stay away from everybody. And that's fine with me. In fact, it worked out just the way I planned it."

"That's quite a story, Leo, and I must confess that I'm impressed, if it's all true. But why exactly are you telling me this?"

"Because I like you, McTavish, like I said, didn't I? I've watched you, and I like you. With my help, I think you have a chance to be a halfway decent dean, and we've had precious few of them around this place since I've been here. And for that reason, and because I like to do things that really piss off the big brass, I am going to help you."

Do I really need help, I thought, *from a man who calls himself Leonard Da Vinci?*

"Exactly what kind of help are you offering, Leo?"

"Well, Ty, I have been here for twenty-five years as you so cleverly pointed out. I know where a lot of the bodies are buried. I also know the Arts and Sciences faculty and the present administration pretty well. I think you may find that knowledge useful. I know you were some assistant big-ass wig at your former institution, McTavish, but this is a different ball game. First of all, this is a private institution. We don't answer to the public in the way they did at HUT. Second, there's a lot of money connected to this university that is waiting to see how the wind blows before it is actually spent here. At least some of what you do will affect whether that money comes here or goes elsewhere. I'm still a few years away from retirement, so what you do affects me.

"Finally, you're black, in case you haven't noticed. That will be an advantage for you in some arenas. There are probably still some people around who think you carry a straight razor or a switchblade in your sock or a Nation of Islam membership card in your pocket. You don't, do you? In other cases, though, your race will be a hazard. In many instances, I will be able to tell you which situations are which."

"I don't want to sound unappreciative, Leo, but exactly why are you offering me this service? What's in it for you?"

"I already said, I like you, asshole, and I meant that. I like the way you handled yourself during the search process, and I like what I've heard about you since you've been on campus. Even though I'm in the NUThouse, I keep my ear to the ground, and I hear things. I like what I've heard about you, although it's true that you haven't really been here long enough to really screw up. I like the way you handled the other nuts too. Even though you just saw them today, I'd know by now if you'd given in to any of them. But that's not all of it. As I said, for the foreseeable future, my fortunes are tied to the fortunes of this university. I'm in a good situation here, and I don't want to lose that. If I help you, maybe you'll see your way clear to conclude that I *am* contributing to the success of the enterprise in my own special way, and you'll leave me alone. That's really all I want."

"I can't make you that promise, Leo, but if you're serious about your offer (and I thought but didn't say, *If you're really not a psycho*), I accept it gladly. I will certainly need help to do my job here successfully and well."

"Fair enough. And to prove that I've made my offer to you in good faith, I'm going to give you this initial bit of advice essentially for free. So listen, and listen good. Nobody ever gets fired around here because they've pissed off the president or the provost, and that will be even more the case with Sligh and Asskisser in those jobs. If you don't succeed here, Ty, it will be because you pissed off some faculty, not some administrators. There's an old, or maybe not so old, adage that says that leading faculty is like herding cats. If only it were that easy. Leading faculty, Ty, is like trying to tie snakes together. They wiggle and squirm, so it's hard to tie them up or down in the first place. Once you think you have them tied securely, they wiggle and squirm, and the knots come loose. More importantly, snakes can bite, and some of the bites can be poisonous. It's those poisonous snake bites that will get you fired here, Ty, and I know every viper on this campus.

"Don't get me wrong. Most of the faculty here are hardworking, conscientious, really good people. They make this university what it is. Of the rest, most are harmless. Take my three colleagues in NUTS, for example. Harmless, strange but harmless. Baccaliprati didn't blow up the Physics Building on purpose. Hell, he probably did the university a favor by destroying that piece of shit. Urgek is a nebbish. Ebola-Shalaka, well, the jury is still out on her. But there *are* some true reptiles out there, Ty, and they will bite your balls right off and leave their venom running through your veins. As I said, that's some free advice that you can use or not as you see fit. And there's more where that came from."

"Whew. Well, I must say, Leo, that this conversation has not been anything like what I expected. I was actually dreading the prospect of having to meet another member of your department, and although I concluded a while back that our chat might be amusing, I still expected it to be a waste of my time. I'm beginning to think I was wrong."

"I can see you're a cautious man, Ty. I like that. Take your time. You can seek my advice when you feel you need or want it and judge for yourself whether it's of any use. But I warn you now, I'm going to want something in return. Fair enough?"

"Fair enough. May I have my desk back now?"

"Sure. It's been nice chatting with you." He rose and headed toward the door to my office. "By the way, I'm not really crazy, but in my next life, I do intend to have nuclear capability. It will make getting my way a hell of a lot easier."

"Well, thanks for stopping by, Leo. You are certainly more than you appear to be."

"You're not as dumb as you look either, Ty."

CHAPTER IV

ALTHOUGH I DID THINK about it a bit, I was never able to decide which one of the NUTS called Jarvis the dirty name, not that it really mattered. It could have been any one of them. In fact, as I thought about it, I was surprised that it was *only* one of them.

Life settled into near normalcy for the next few weeks after my meeting with the NUTS. There was the usual round of meetings and only a few very minor crises to handle, so I was able to spend most of my time getting to know people and learning the university. I was beginning to think that my first term, perhaps even my first year as dean, would pass relatively smoothly and that I might not need to take Leo Da Vinci up on his offer to be my assistant dean. But then, only a few weeks after my arrival, the crisis developed that was to color essentially all of the rest of that year. It began with a late-night phone call. I'm a pretty light sleeper. But that doesn't make the sound of the telephone ringing in the middle of the night any less jarring.

"'Lo, this is Ty McTavish," I said after I gained control of the receiver.

"Ty, this is Hermione Bull."

Hermione Bull. Director of the SNAF-U Office of Statistics, History, and Institutional Trends (I think you can come up with the appropriate acronym for this office without any help from me). Hermione had been at the U for about ten years, having come here after holding a similar position at the University of the Yukon (or some such institution) for the previous two years of her career. Hermione had a doctoral degree in Botanical Anthropology and had written her dissertation on the effects of different types of pollen on the development of aggressive tendencies in certain aboriginal tribes in Ecuador. Obviously, she was eminently qualified for her position at SNAF-U.

"Hermione, it's three o'clock in the morning. I hope this is important."

"It is important, Dean McTavish. I wouldn't have called you otherwise."

There was obvious distress in her voice, and although I couldn't be sure, the occasional little gasps she made between words seemed to suggest that she had been crying. As I was soon to learn, she had been.

"Something terrible has happened," she said, and then she did indeed begin crying softly. "I'm not even sure how to tell you this."

It's funny how the mind never waits for information in situations like these but starts racing off on its own instead. Both Hermione's tone and the fact that she had awakened me in the middle of the night had to mean that something especially serious had transpired. Had President Sligh had a heart attack or, worse, committed suicide or been murdered by a student or more likely by one of the NUTS? Was it the chair of the board of trustees? Had the campus burned to the ground? Had the Earth been invaded by Martians? Had my favorite restaurant closed forever?

"Try to calm yourself, Hermione," I said, trying to be as soothing as I could over the phone. "Slow down and tell me what happened."

"We've been…" Sob. "We've been…" Sob. We've been…" Sob.

"We've been what, Hermione?"

"We've been…" Sob. "We've been…" Sob. We've been…" Sob.

"Hermione, please calm down and tell me what has happened." I was trying to remain calm myself, but her inability to come to the point was starting to exasperate me. I suppose I could have tried to be sympathetic, at least to her obvious distress, but I was beginning to suspect that whatever the problem was, it wasn't likely to be worth a middle-of-the-night phone call.

"Hermione, Hermione?"

"I… I'm sorry, Dean McTavish. I'm so sorry, but I just can't bring myself to say the words again." Sniff… sob. "They just stick in my throat each time I try to say them."

Sob.

"What you surely do need to know is that I just got off the phone with President Sligh, and he has called an emergency meeting of the executive staff for eight thirty this morning. And he wants you to attend that meeting as well. This is a development that affects us all, Dean McTavish. I'm sure you'll understand when you learn what has happened."

Sob. Sob.

"Good -bye!"

Sob.

"Oh, one more thing, Dean McTavish. President Sligh wants us all to wear black to the meeting."

"Good -bye!"

So it looked like someone important had died, but who? The chairman of the board? Some faculty member? Some student? This year's Oscar winner for Best Supporting Actor? Or horror of horrors, was I the one who had died, and was I going to find that out by going to a SNAF-U staff meeting? There was no point in trying to figure it out right then, so I hung up the phone, and although it took me a while, I went back to sleep.

Jarvis canceled all my appointments for that morning, and I reported dutifully for the executive staff meeting. The president's executive staff at SNAF-U normally met about once every two weeks. The group was composed of the president, the provost, and the other senior vice presidents of the institution, namely, the vice president for Biomedical Practice, the VP for Student Affairs, the VP for External Affairs, the VP for Internal Affairs, the VP for Business Affairs, the VP for Legal Affairs (no double entendres are intended here, but more about "affairs" later), the VP for Personnel, and the secretary of the university. The associate vice presidents who reported to each of the VPs were also included in the meeting. There was one other attendee who very interestingly was not a vice president—the director of Systems, Lands, Operations, and Physical Plant (SLOPP), Buster Dukes. More about him below too. As you can see from the list of participants, academic deans were excluded from the president's executive staff. Nevertheless, President Sligh had asked me to attend a couple of meetings shortly after my arrival on campus. He thought they would provide me with some insight into the workings of the university. He was right, but not perhaps in the way he intended.

Executive staff meetings were held in the president's conference room. To my knowledge, those meetings and certain special conclaves convened by the president were the only gatherings held in that room. The room was impressive. There were wood paneling on all four walls and a large mahogany (I guessed) table with lushly padded leather chairs for the conferees. The executive staff meetings were scheduled to begin at 8:30 a.m., and this special one was no exception. As I was the new kid on the block, I arrived a few minutes early. The associate VP for External Affairs and one or two others were already present. As I'd had occasion to speak with her on several occasions since my arrival at SNAF-U, I took the seat next to her. Her distinguishing physical characteristic, or the lack of one in this case, was that she had no lips whatsoever. Nevertheless, there was an oval of lipstick in the area below her nose.

"Good morning, Charity," I said, smiling. Her name was Charity

Butler. I knew immediately that my cheerful greeting was inappropriate. Like Hermione Bull, she had been crying.

"You can't sit there," she scowled. "That's Vice President Plodter's seat."

"Oh, I'm sorry," I replied. "I had no way of knowing that there was assigned seating for this meeting." I hadn't been aware of assigned seats at any of the other meetings I'd attended, but perhaps that was because I had been a guest at those meetings. Of course, I was a guest at this meeting too.

"Well, there is." President Sligh sits at the head of the table and Provost Azkizur sits at the opposite end. The other vice presidents are then positioned around the table in a specific order with their associates seated next to them."

"Interesting. Perhaps then you can point me to a seat that won't be occupied."

She started counting the chairs around the table.

"I don't think there will be any vacant seats at the table. What are *you* doing here anyway?"

I ignored her.

"Well, then, I'll just pull up an extra chair for myself."

"No," she said, her voice rising. "That will mess up the arrangement. It's all symmetrical. If you add another chair, it will, it will…"

"Charity," I said, determined to bring this matter to a conclusion (translate: determined to prevail in this confrontation), "I'm here at the invitation of President Sligh, and I don't believe he intends for me to stand during this entire meeting."

She frowned but didn't say anything more. I took the seat next to her. Over the next few minutes, the rest of the cast members came in. The president and the provost arrived together at exactly eight-thirty and took their assigned seats. The somber faces around the table let me know quickly that whatever was wrong, whoever had died, the SNAF-

Ugees obviously took it very seriously. Everyone around the table but me was dressed in black, black suits, black dresses, black skirts and blouses. I wore a gray suit with a black tie. Sligh acknowledged my presence with a nod, folded his hands in front of him on the table, and began to speak.

"My friends, this is a dark, dark day for SNAF-U as I'm sure you're all aware. A dark, dark day. I can recall no time during my presidency when the day was as dark as this one is. As you know, we have had suicides on this campus in the past…"

So that was it.

"But even those incidents, as chilling as they were, can't compare to what happened to us last night. We've had financial crises, and of course, there was the scandal involving our former board chair and the pig farmer. And I'm sure you all remember the year when the Admissions Office made that mistake and only admitted two students to the freshman class. But none of those situations compare at all to the straits in which we find ourselves today. And I'm ashamed and embarrassed that this happened on my watch. I've spoken with the board of trustees, with each member in fact; and while they all feel that the buck always stops at the feet of the commander in chief, they do intend to allow me to stay on as president, at least for now. I'm grateful for that, and I must be honest and say that it's probably more than I deserve. After I got the news last night, I fully expected that someone else would convene this meeting and would be sitting before you right now. I certainly wouldn't have blamed them if they had relieved me of duty. I must say too that in all candor and honesty, I still find it hard to believe that this has really happened. After all that we've done. After all the efforts we've made. After so much energy, expense, after…" He paused. "I have to be honest with you and admit that, for a very brief moment this morning, I considered suicide myself."

There were audible gasps from all at the table including me. I was at a complete loss to imagine what could possibly have happened to occasion such a passionate response.

"But life must go on," Sligh continued. "Before *we* go on, though, I have a note I'd like to read to you. It's from Barnabus Chuttlewood, chair of our board of trustees. Barney was vacationing at Olan's condo in Florida when I called him last night with the tragic news. He flew back this morning, and this message was delivered by special courier just a few minutes ago.

Sligh unfolded a sheet of paper and began reading.

"Dear Robert. Please be assured that my wife and I and all of the members of the board of trustees sympathize and empathize with you in this time of such great tragedy and loss. I want you to know that we were just as stunned as you were to hear the news. Neither Meribeth nor I slept a wink last night. And we're not likely to be able to sleep tonight either. But be assured as well that we will stand with you as we work to recover from this heinous calamity. SNAF-U has faced adversity before. We have endured the Great Depression, two World Wars, and the loss of Division I football. We survived those tragedies, and we will survive this one. SNAF-U will survive!"

Hermione Bull and Charity Butler began to cry, and I could see a tear beginning to form at the corner of Dick Brohwknoz's eye. Dick was the vice president for Student Affairs and was the only male member of the executive staff who had worn a black suit, black tie, *and* a black shirt. Sligh rose, walked over to Hermione, and put his hand on her shoulder.

"Hermione, will you give us the background to this tragedy? Oh, before you begin," Sligh looked down at Hermione Bull and smiled warmly, "I'd like to thank you for your diligence and loyalty during this crisis. Your continued good work has been the one ray of sunshine in this darkest of hours." He squeezed her shoulders, and she smiled weakly. "Would you now please give us the information you have available?"

"Thank you very much, President Sligh." Hermione's eyes were red and swollen. She arranged a sheaf of papers in front of her as she spoke. "As all of you know, the national news magazine, *National Opinion on the News, Science, Education, Nature, Sports, and Everything*, annually produces a list of the top twenty-five colleges and universities in the country. You all also know that for as long as we can remember, SNAF-U has been on the list of the top twenty-five schools. In order to ensure that SNAF-U was always up to date regarding requirements for inclusion in *NONSENSE*'s top twenty-five, I have maintained personal contact with Douglas O. Little, the *NONSENSE* executive responsible for the survey and the rankings. Because of that relationship, Mr. Little emailed me a copy of this year's ranking last night. I asked him to provide me with that information as soon as possible prior to its release to the public, and that's why he sent me the email. I received the message at about ten last night, and I'm sorry, President Sligh, but I just couldn't believe it. So I sat at my desk at home for at least two hours just staring at the page before I called you. I just couldn't believe it."

Hermione hesitated and her lower lip began to quiver.

"And then, of course, after talking with the president, I called all of you to give you the horrible news. For the first time since anyone can remember and despite all of our efforts, *SNAF-U is not on the list of this year's top twenty-five schools!*"

Even though everyone around the table but me had already heard that news, there was another audible gasp when she finished that sentence. Tears began to stream down Dick Brohwknoz's face, and I could hear him murmuring softly, "Oh no, oh, please no, no, no, no."

For her part, Hermione was quite clearly holding back what would have otherwise been a flood of tears.

"As you all also know, I think *NONSENSE* doesn't publish a rank ordered list beyond the top twenty-five schools," she continued, "but I was able to persuade Doug Little to tell me where SNAF-U was ranked among the top fifty. We are number twenty-eight."

Several around the table, shook their heads in disbelief. Hermione started crying softly as did Imajean Plodter, the VP for External Affairs.

"Thank you, Hermione. I know we all appreciate your efforts on our behalf and on behalf of the institution. But I think you also know that heads will have to roll because of this."

"Yes, I do, Mr. President. I'm just so grateful to you and to the board that one of those heads won't have to be mine."

I could hardly believe what I was hearing. SNAF-U had surprised me in plenty of ways in two months, but this was clearly a new high (or low, depending on your point of view). Falling out of the *NONSENSE* top twenty-five wasn't a good thing, but it wasn't the end of the world either. At least not in my opinion. And being number twenty-eight was far from a terrible ranking. But that was clearly a minority view around this table. The one thing I *had* learned in two months was to keep my mouth shut, at least for now.

Sligh was silent for a moment as he looked around the table. Then he banged his fist on the tabletop.

"By heaven we're not going to take this lying down! It's too late to do anything about this year's ranking. But we're going to start right here this morning to make damned sure that we will be well within the top twenty-five next year. We're going to start right here and now! Hermione, do you have the list of criteria that *NONSENSE* uses to generate its rankings?

She nodded.

"Please read the list to the group."

Hermione wiped her eyes with a tissue. "As I think most of you know, there are several major criteria that go into the *NONSENSE* ranking of schools. Those criteria include Tuitional Aggrandizement Originality,

Instructional Workforce–Baccalaureal Relativity, Baccalaureal Persistence Index, Cosmic Placement Perception, Baccalaureal Selection Stringency, Fiduciary Positional Quotient, Quadrennial Baccalaureal Efficiency, Altruistic Pecuniary Indicators. There are a few others, but those are the major ones. We were below the top twenty-five schools in nearly everyone of those categories."

All around the table (except guess who) nodded as if they actually knew what the hell Hermione was talking about and what those categories actually were. I didn't have a clue, so I kept my mouth shut.

"Thank you, Hermione." Sligh leaned forward, folded his hands, and fastened a determined gaze on each of us at the table in turn.

"Now here's what I propose we do. We can sit here on our asses, or we can take the bull by the horns. Hermione has the fax copy of the top twenty-five ranking. That ranking includes information on each of those schools in each of the categories she listed as well as the others that she didn't mention. We'll get to those later. As I said, we need to be well within the top twenty-five next year, so I would argue that we should ignore the data from the lower half of the top twenty-five and concentrate only on the upper half. In fact, I suggest we look only at the top ten schools on the list. Let's see what they did and then decide what we need to do to match that, okay?"

There was a communal nodding of heads.

"Good. Let's begin at the beginning, with Tuitional Aggrandizement Originality. That was the first category, wasn't it? I think that has to do with the amount of tuition each institution charges. Hermione, what was the average annual tuition charged by the top ten schools in the ranking?"

Hermione pulled a calculator from her attaché case.

"Let me see. It'll only take me a minute. Hhmm... Uh, seventy-nine thousand dollars."

"No, Hermione," Sligh replied, sounding somewhat annoyed. "I mean the average annual tuition not the highest tuition charged by an institution."

"Seventy-nine thousand dollars," Hermione said with determination.

"You mean to say that the top ten schools on the list charge seventy-nine thousand dollars a year just in tuition? Are you sure you calculated the average correctly?"

"Well, let me do it again." A pause. "Yes, the average is $78,988 for the top ten schools."

"And that's just tuition?" Sligh asked. "It doesn't include fees?"

"That's correct, sir," Hermione responded, "just tuition."

"Well, that's a problem we can certainly correct. Let's move into the big leagues. Our tuition is only twenty-eight thousand a year. Clark, announce immediately that next year our undergraduate tuition will be increased to $70,000. Let's not try to do too much in one year."

"Yes, sir," Clark replied briskly. Clark Bunghall, VP for Business Affairs.

"Good. This may be easier than I thought. Give us the next set of data, Hermione."

"Just a second, Mr. President," Hermione said softly. "We have to have a reason for the tuition increase. That's where the issue of originality comes in. At one of the HUT's in the top twenty-five, for example, they raised tuition last year so that they could increase the number of their football scholarships each year from 300 to 450. We have to do something clever like that. We can't just raise the number."

"I have an idea, Mr. President." It was Olan Azkizur. "Given that we've just started a scholarship fund for students from towns in Alaska that can't be reached by road, we could raise tuition and justify the increase based on the need to use the money for that scholarship fund."

"Excellent idea, Olan." Everyone nodded; that is everyone but one. "Write that down Hermione. *NONSENSE* will have to agree that that's a worthy cause and that it more than justifies an increase in tuition. Terrific, Olan! Just terrific! What's the next category, Hermione?"

"Instructional Workforce–Baccalaureal Relativity. That category has to do with faculty/student ratios. Give me a second, I'm just finishing the calculations. The average faculty/student ratio reported by the top ten institutions was two to one."

"You mean one to two, don't you, Hermione? Either that or the ratio must be students to faculty."

"President Sligh, I've double-checked the calculations. The average ratio of faculty to students reported by the top ten schools was two faculty to one student."

"That's impossible," I said, unable to hold my peace any longer. "No legitimate institution in this country has twice as many regular faculty as students."

"And that may be our problem, Ty. Maybe you've hit the nail on the head. Hermione, do the *NONSENSE* guidelines say anything about regular faculty?"

"Why, no, they don't, President Sligh. Under the category of Instructional Workforce–Baccalaureal Relativity, they simply ask for the ratio of faculty to students in the undergraduate college."

"Then that's it!" Sligh said, smiling. "We simply add anyone who can even remotely be defined as faculty to our list, starting with our lecturers and instructors, anyone who's not tenure track but who teaches undergraduates. That would include graduate students too. And, Buster, don't you have undergraduate students working in various offices in SLOPP?"

"Why yes, Bob, I do."

"And don't those students receive instructions from SLOPP personnel on how to do their jobs?"

"Absolutely!" Buster smiled.

"Then that's instruction, and those instructors can be counted as faculty. Buster, give Hermione a list of all your personnel who provide any instruction of any kind to undergraduate students. The rest of you, do the same."

"My staff trains undergraduates in all sorts of things all the time." It was Ima Plodter, clearly becoming more cheerful.

"Good, Ima, give the data to Hermione. The rest of you, do the same. Once she's compiled the information, we'll see where we are. If necessary, I know there are others around here who can be defined as faculty."

"Wait a minute," I interjected, "we can't just—"

Sligh ignored me. "What's next on the list, Hermione?"

"Baccalaureal Persistence Index, or what most of us refer to as student retention rates. The top ten schools claim that on average, 95 percent of their students are retained after their freshman year, 100 percent after the sophomore year, and 100 percent after the junior year. Our figures are 85 percent after the freshman year and about 90 percent after the next two years. At least those are the figures we reported."

"Okay. What can be done about this one? What exactly do those numbers mean? It's the number of students enrolled in any given year who are also enrolled the following year. Is that right, Hermione?"

"Precisely, President Sligh."

"What about this idea?" It was Dick Brohwknoz (pronounced as *BRONE-noz*, by the way, although as with other administrative surnames on this campus, there were many for whom that was not the preferred pronunciation). "Suppose we try to get as many of our dropouts as possible to enroll in SNAF-U distance learning courses. They could enroll in classes for one or two credit hours, and then, I don't need to tell you, we could count them as SNAF-U students even if they're not on campus. We could offer them scholarships and use that as an additional justification for our tuition increase."

"Brilliant idea, Dick!" Sligh beamed. "Ima, get on that right away.

You and Hermione can determine how many students we'd need to sign up each year in order to raise our retention rate, say, five to ten points each year."

"Here's something else we could do, Mr. President." Brohwknoz was clearly on a roll now. "Suppose we change our enrollment policy so that at the beginning of an academic year, students enroll for two years rather than one. I don't need to tell you that that would mean that even if they left campus after the first of those years, we could count them as students since they would have already enrolled for the second year."

"Dick, I don't pay you nearly enough. Oops, forget I said that. Did you get that all down Hermione? Brilliant, Dick! Just brilliant! I can't believe that the combination of these two strategies won't allow us to move right up there with the big boys. What's the next category, Hermione?"

"I think Cosmic Placement Perception was next, Mr. President. That may be a tough one. The way the system works is that the magazine polls the presidents of the schools that were in the top twenty-five the previous year and asks them what they think about the schools the magazine is ranking in the current year. The presidents are asked to rate those schools on a scale of one to ten. The top ten schools in this year's ranking all got ratings of 9.95 or higher. The number one, PERU, got a 9.99. Our ranking was 8.11. We had a 9.1 last year. So we slipped a whole point in reputation between this year and last. It's certainly hard to know what might have caused people who thought highly of us a year ago to change that opinion."

"Well, maybe we should put that category aside and come back to it at the end of the meeting if there is time."

There were looks of surprise from some around the table. Why was the president deferring consideration of this issue? Although I hadn't seen this detour coming, I did have an idea why it had. It was because Sligh had pissed off a significant fraction of the people who cast votes in this year's *NONSENSE* ranking.

According to Leo Da Vinci, who as you will see, was becoming something of a guru for me, it happened at the annual meeting of an organization of universities known as the Hallowed Old Temples of Self-satisfaction, Hubris, and Irrelevant Traditions (HOTSHITs). The way these meetings work, in case you don't know, is that the presidents and provosts from HOTSHITs get together once a year, usually at some exotic location, and spend three or four days telling each other how great they all are. They have what are called plenary sessions, where one person tells everybody else how great they all are; and they have panel discussions, where four or five people, sometimes more, tell everybody else how great they all are. The previous year's meeting had been held in Paris (France) in the spring. Ah, April in Paris. Of course, there isn't a single member of HOTSHITs in Paris, France, or any place else in Europe for that matter. All the HOTSHITs members are American universities. Still, they had to have the meeting someplace.

Anyway, because SNAF-U is indeed a Small but National, Aspiring to be Famous University, Sligh was asked to moderate two panel discussions. Moderate, mind you. This usually means that the moderator sets the stage for the presentations of the other panelists. Sets the stage, mind you. The moderator is usually expected to make only brief remarks and to keep the process moving in a timely manner. Sligh's first panel was composed of six presidents, including him, four of whom were from institutions that traditionally appeared in the top ten in the *NONSENSE* rankings and all of whom were from top twenty-five schools. Needless to say, those guys had a lot to say about how great they all were. Or at least they thought they did. But they never got the chance. The panel discussion was supposed to last an hour with an additional fifteen minutes for questions and answers, but Sligh talked for fifty-five minutes. The other panelists had to try to cram their remarks into the remaining twenty, and there was no time left for Q and A. All of the other panelists and most of the audience were pissed, especially since Sligh's monologue had by all accounts been pretty much unintelligible.

The second panel was pretty much like the first. The theme of the first panel had been "How Great We All Are," and the theme of the second "Why We're All So Great?" Same format—six presidents, including Sligh, an hour for the panel, and Sligh as moderator. The initial result was the same too. Sligh went on for thirty minutes, giving pretty much the same spiel as he had in the previous panel discussion. According to Leo—and I have no idea where he got this information, but then he always amazed me with what he knew—after thirty minutes, everybody, panelists and audience, was starting to squirm. It was then that one of the other panelists, the president of the number two rated, PERU, got up, took the microphone that was sitting in front of Sligh at the table, and told him to shut up. Which, interestingly enough, he did. The remainder of the panel discussion, while truncated because of the amount of time Sligh had taken, proceeded pretty much normally. Sligh is reported to have turned several shades of red as he sat and listened to the other panelists, and when it came time for questions and answers and to summarize the proceedings and bring things to a close, Sligh said not a word.

Leo surmised—and I suspect that his surmise is correct—that the whole episode left a bad taste in the HOTSHITs mouths, at least in terms of their attitudes toward SNAF-U. And since the *NONSENSE* Cosmic Placement Perception ranking was indeed a survey of what people think, the rankest form of subjective critique, in fact, nothing more than a beauty contest, it should not have been surprising that Sligh's performance at the HOTSHITs meeting lowered SNAF-U in the opinions of some. Maybe many. Sure, they should have been objective and considered the institution in its entirety or at least what they knew of it. But presidents *are* human, aren't they? In any case and for whatever reason, we were skipping Cosmic Placement Perception, at least for now.

"What's next, Hermione?"

Sligh's voice interrupted my reflections, and I hoped the staffers missed the slight smile that crossed my face as I thought about Leo's rendering of the HOTSHITs story.

"Baccalaureal Selection Stringency, Mr. President. For those of you who may not be familiar with what that means, it means what fraction of applicants is actually admitted to the Literary College. For the top ten institutions, it's about 20 percent. We've gotten the figure down to 44 percent in recent years, but that's the best we've been able to do so far, so we have a ways to go before we can compete with the big guys. Any suggestions?"

Hands on chins, fingers through hair. Then Dick Brohwknoz spoke up again.

"I have an idea, President Sligh. If selectivity is the number of applicants we admit, then we can either increase the number of applicants or decrease the number of admits. Right?"

Dick had obviously graduated elementary school.

"That's right, Dick." This time, Sligh sounded skeptical.

"Well, why don't we just change our definition of 'applicant.' I don't need to tell you that how we define the term is up to us. We can say that it's someone who submits a complete or even a partially completed application, or we can define it another way. What if we say that an applicant is any person not enrolled at SNAF-U who inquires about attending here either in writing or by telephone or in person when they're visiting the campus? I don't need to tell you that that would almost certainly increase the number of applicants, and it would have no effect on the number of students we admit."

A huge grin covered Brohwknoz's face. Sligh actually got up from his chair, walked around to Brohwknoz's seat, and shook his hand. Plodter, Dukes, and Bunghall began to applaud.

"Dick, you've done it again. I don't know what we would have done here today without you. Hermione, get on this, will you? Check with the Admissions Office and determine whether they keep records of such inquiries. If they don't, tell them to start doing so yesterday. And make sure that it's written down somewhere, if only in the minutes of this meeting—as a matter of fact, that's probably the only place it should be written down—that from this point forward, an applicant is anyone who inquires about admission to the Literary College by letter, phone, in person, email, whatever. And make absolutely sure that we're recording the number of hits on our website. I know we get a ton of those."

By this time, you can imagine that I was aghast at all of this. As dean of Arts and Sciences I was responsible for the workings of the Literary College, and I was not at all comfortable with the use of these subterfuges just to improve our rankings in a commercial publication. I knew, though, that expressing my opinion at this point would have no significant effect. But how much longer could I keep quiet?

"This is really going quite well, all. Fiduciary Positional Quotient is next as I remember. Is that correct, Hermione?"

"Yes, President Sligh. Again, the top ten institutions all have endowments of at least a billion dollars. While our endowment is growing, we're only up to six hundred million at last count. At its current rate of growth and given what's happening to the economy, we won't make a billion by the time of next year's survey. Isn't that right, Clark?"

Clark Bunghall nodded assent.

"This will be a tough one. Maybe we can approach this one too from the standpoint of the definition of the criterion. Hermione, how does *NONSENSE* define 'resources'?

Hermione pulled another document from her attaché case.

"According to Doug Little, 'financial resources' refers to the financial assets of an institution that can be used to support its faculty, students, and programs."

"So we can count our buildings as financial resources. Do we do that?"

"Yes, sir."

"Then there are no gains to be made in that regard. 'Assets that can be used to support its faculty, students, and programs.' It doesn't say what support means, does it?"

"No, it doesn't, Mr. President."

"Does it define what 'students' means?

"No, it doesn't, Mr. President."

Where was he going with this?

"Then anything that we want to define as supporting our faculty, students, and programs counts as resources, and we can define SNAF-U students in any way we think is reasonable. Now let me see. SNAF-U has about seventy thousand living alumni, and all of them were students here, at least at one point. Let's see. I think it's a safe estimate that on average, each of those alumni is probably worth say, at least ten thousand dollars. No, make it twenty thousand. That seems reasonable, doesn't it? That's money that supports our students, at least our former students, right? And the guidelines don't say that we can't include them. They clearly need that money to live on, and that's support. I don't see why we can't count that. Let's see, that would be seventy thousand alumni times twenty thousand dollars each. Why, that's a hundred and forty million dollars!"

"Actually, it's 1.4 billion dollars, Mr. President." Clark Bunghall.

"That's even better, Clark. In fact, that's just super! Add that to our total. There's no reason that can't count as financial resources. Don't you all agree?"

Nods and smiles again from everyone but me.

"What else can we do? Come on. Think, people!"

Ima Plodter. "Well, President Sligh, is there any reason why we can't simply add our annual operating budget to the total pool of resources we report? After all, that money goes to support our faculty, students, and programs."

"Excellent idea, Ima. That's just what I was thinking. Why shouldn't we count those funds since some of that money comes from sources other than the endowment in any case. So that's what we'll do. From now on, Hermione, the financial resources category will include the value of our endowment, our capital and other resources, our estimate of the resources of our alumni, plus every cent we spend annually to run the university. That last figure itself comes to well over five hundred million dollars, and the sum of those last two will take us easily over the one billion mark, maybe over two billion. Sometimes I even amaze myself. The end is in sight! Good work, people, good work! What's next, Hermione?"

"Altruistic Pecuniary Indicators. We're way short of the top ten schools in this category. Some of them bring in millions of dollar each year from alumni gifts. We only bring in less than a million. I really don't know what to suggest about this."

"Well, let's put our thinking caps on. This definition approach has worked for us so far. Maybe we can do something with the definition of giving. Ima, how much money do we bring in each year from our fee-for-service alumni programs?"

"I don't have the exact figures, Mr. President, but if you include the alumni events, homecoming, alumni weekend, alumni use of university facilities, alumni purchases of SNAF-U memorabilia, the alumni continuing education programs, all the things like that, I'll bet it comes to several hundred thousand dollars."

"Good. Starting now, all those moneys will be counted as alumni giving. Hermione, another thought occurs to me. We've got a bunch of

SNAF-U alumni on the faculty here, and many of those faculty have grants to support their research and teaching. Tally up as much of that money as you can identify. From now on, those funds count as alumni giving. Any alumnus who has a research grant of any kind from any source has made that grant a gift to the university."

"In that same vein, President Sligh..." Dick Brohwknoz. "I don't need to tell you that our alumni spend lots of money on campus for various goods and services. They all have to eat, so they buy lunches here, they buy stuff from the gift store and snack bars, some of them go to sporting events and other activities. It would be hard to determine an exact figure, but we could probably make an estimate of what they spend in a year and use that figure. Maybe we could even do a questionnaire and ask them what they think they spend. I don't need to tell you that that would probably come to a significant amount."

"Excellent, Dick. Get on it right away. We'll lick this thing yet. Any other suggestions?"

"Do the rules say that the alumni have to be alumni of the Literary College?

"I'm afraid they do, Buster," Hermione replied. "That's one issue on which the guidelines are specific."

"But do they say that only money given to the college by those alumni can count?"

"I'm not sure what you mean, Buster," Hermione replied.

"Neither am I," Sligh added. "Go on, Buster."

"Well, suppose a person who graduated from the Literary College gives a thousand dollars to the medical school. That's still a gift from a college alumnus, isn't it?"

"Damn if it isn't," Sligh said brightly. "Look into that, Hermione. Any other ideas?"

There were none.

"Okay, I think that whittles the list down to one final item.

Quadrennial Baccalaureal Efficiency. Hermione, fill us in on how the big boys are doing."

Maybe if I ask an innocent question here, I thought, *I can bring some sanity to this exercise.*

"Hermione," I ventured, "I have a quick question before you proceed. If what *NONSENSE* wants is the graduation rates for the schools they rank, why don't they just call this category Graduation Rates instead of Quadrennial Baccalaureal Efficiency? I don't think 'baccalaureal' is even a real word."

"Well, Dean McTavish, I actually asked Doug Little that same question," Hermione replied. "He says they name their categories to make them more interesting to their readers. The people at *NONSENSE* have decided that fewer people would be interested in the rankings if they used ordinary names for the categories. They think that Quadrennial Baccalaureal Efficiency is catchier than Graduation Rates. He also claims that 'baccalaureal' is a real word."

"Thanks for that clarification, Hermione," Sligh said, obviously annoyed that I'd asked the question. "Let's get on with it."

"Well, Mr. President, as I said, all the top ten schools have very high retention rates, so they have very high graduation rates as well. In fact, some of them report graduation rates that are higher than 100 percent."

"How can that be? How can you graduate more students than you have?"

"Well, Mr. President, as best I can figure, what those schools do is to argue that a significant number of the students who drop out in their freshman years ultimately come back to finish their degrees. So then, at least according to the way they keep their books, in a given year, they graduate the remainder of the original entering class, plus all the students that have come back in the intervening three years, plus any transfer students, so since they calculate the graduation rate based on the number of students who entered four years earlier, their graduation rate is sometimes actually higher than 100 percent."

"Have we been doing that?"

"No, we haven't, Mr. President, we didn't think it was, well... honest."

"Well, we *can* do that, can't we? If they can do it, we can do it. And if it's honest for them, it's honest for us. That should be a relatively simple solution to the problem. Get on it, Hermione."

"There is one problem, President Sligh. It's not clear how many of our dropouts actually come back here and finish their degrees."

"Is there any way to determine whether they graduate from some other school? We might still be able to count them as graduates."

"That would be difficult."

"Well, there's got to be an angle we can use here. Think, people! Hermione, give us the *NONSENSE* definition word for word."

"Graduation rate is the percentage of students admitted as freshmen who graduate with a bachelor's degree in no more than four years from the date of admission."

"So it doesn't say that they have to graduate from the same school."

"No, it doesn't, Mr. President, but I'm sure that's what they intended."

"Who gives a fu... Who cares what they intended? We're fighting for our lives here! So we will count students who graduate from other schools if we can identify them as long as they enrolled at SNAF-U for say, one semester. Who else can we count? Damn, this is a toughie."

Brohwknoz raised his hand then lowered it again.

"Wait a second." Sligh had hit on a ploy. "A significant number of our students are dual majors, aren't they, Ty?"

I wanted no part of this exercise but could think of no diplomatic way to avoid answering a direct question.

"Yes, President Sligh. In fact, over 50 percent of our students are dual majors, some are even triple majors." For what it's worth, I have never really seen the value of dual majors, especially when the requirements for one or the other or both are watered down to allow students to do two. But that hardly mattered here."

"Great. Then that's it. What we'll do is to award those students two degrees. Then we can count them as graduating twice. Get on it, Hermione. Okay, let's see now. We've dealt with the tuition issue. In fact, raising our tuition should also help us in several other categories. It should increase our selectivity and should also increase our financial resources. We've solved the faculty/student ratio problem. Has anyone thought of any other categories of employees we can count as faculty? No? Well, I have. Ima mentioned our continuing education programs a few moments ago. Ima, determine whether any of those programs enroll college students. I'll bet some of them do. I know that at least some of them want to learn how to juggle and how to change diapers and how to find wives and husbands and stuff like that. And we'll count the instructors in any of those courses that enroll college students as college faculty. And, Clark, make sure that the proceeds from that program count as both alumni giving and financial resources.

"Okay, so that's faculty/student ratio. We talked about retention. Anyone have any additional thoughts about that? Student selectivity, yep, we dealt with that. Alumni giving rate and graduation rate. What have I left out, Hermione?"

Hermione blushed. She was clearly hesitant to mention the remaining rating category again.

"Uh… Cosmic Placement Perception, Mr. President."

"Ahhh. I had almost forgotten about that one."

Read: I *wanted* to forget about that one.

"As I said earlier, we slipped ten points in the survey this year, and that put us well below the figure that the top ten schools received."

"Mr. President, if I may ask a question." After this spectacle, I was feeling malicious. "Do we have any idea why we fell ten points in the space of just twelve months?"

Sligh frowned at me. I wasn't sure whether he knew that I knew what I knew or whether he was just annoyed by the question. Not that it mattered.

"No, I don't, Dean McTavish. In any event, I'm open to suggestion. Since we were in the top twenty-five last year, I received a ballot for this year and voted my conscience as I was instructed to do by the magazine. The problem is, of course, that while we have some control over the numbers we provide in the other categories, because they reflect things that happen here at home, we have no control over what the other presidents *think* about us. I'm not sure what we can do about that."

"Maybe there is something." Buster Dukes again. "Why don't you invite the guys in the top twenty-five down to Azkizur's condo? You could host several visits between now and the time for the next survey. Wine them, dine them, let them bring their wives or husbands or whatever and generally show them a good ol' time. Bring 'em around to our way of thinking. Get 'em on our side. After all, these guys are human, aren't they?"

"Terrific idea, Buster! Hermione, get me the office numbers and the home phone numbers if you can of all the presidents of the top twenty-five schools in the rankings. And Babylonia..."

Babylonia Pendergrass was Sligh's administrative assistant.

"Check my calendar to see when I can get away to Florida. I will probably need at least three or four weekends. And we should probably try to schedule the dates as close to next year's balloting as possible.

"Olan," he said, turning to Azkizur, "I presume the condo will be at our disposal as usual." And without giving him a chance to respond, he said, "Good. It's settled then."

"I want to thank all of you for your assistance this morning. We still have a few other *NONSENSE* categories to deal with, but we've made an excellent start. It was indeed a dark day when it began, but rays of bright sunshine have burst through the clouds. I am supremely confident that the ideas and suggestions that have hatched here this morning will stand us in good stead, and if we implement them efficiently and effectively, I have no doubt but that we will find ourselves well placed within the *NONSENSE* top twenty-five next year. I can't say enough about how proud I am of all of you. I would wager that there is no other institution in the country that could have responded to this challenge as quickly and effectively as we have. And that is in large part because of all of you. This has to be the best administrative team at any institution in the entire country. You're the best!"

And as you might well have predicted, the executive staffers burst into applause. And then it happened. I hadn't believed Leo when he had told me about this, but as had almost always been the case, as difficult as it was to believe, he had been right. The SNAF-Ugees burst into a cheer for Sligh, with the two of them alternating the phrases in a fashion that made it clear that this routine had been well rehearsed.

"*Who's the boss?*"

"*You's the boss!*" Fists were pumping the air.

"*Who's the boss?*"

"*You's the boss!*"

"*Who's the boss?*"

"*You's the boss!*"

And with that, Sligh strode triumphantly from the room.

So now you know how most universities make us think they're great when they really aren't.

As I said, they cheat.

CHAPTER V

I T DIDN'T TAKE LONG for the word to spread across the campus that SNAF-U had been trashed by *NONSENSE*. There were articles in the student and faculty newspapers and ongoing commentary on the campus radio station. Even the local news media carried the story. To my amazement, dismay, and disgust, Sligh even ordered that formal classes be canceled one afternoon; and instead of meeting with those classes, the faculty were instructed to convene small groups of students to get ideas from them about dealing with the crisis. Although I wasn't nearly as distressed by the situation as most of the SNAF-Ugees seemed to be, I did feel that it was my responsibility to do what I could to get us back on the list. After all, even I had to admit that it was better to be in the top twenty-five than not to be.

In the weeks immediately following the announcement, many of the faculty in the Literary College made appointments to see me, ostensibly to share their thoughts about our readmission to the gang of twenty-five. More about some of them later. But those one-on-one chats suggested to me that one way to gather information on a larger scale would be to get as many of the faculty together at once to discuss the problem. It also occurred to me that that expedient might decrease the number of individual meetings that I'd need to have. So I decided to honor one of the most venerable and venerated of faculty traditions. I scheduled a faculty meeting.

We hadn't had one to that point, and it was about time to do so. The *NONSENSE* issue was as good a reason as any. We convened at four o'clock in the afternoon of what, to that point, had been a pretty good day. I'd had to deal with only two complaints, neither of which had to do with *NONSENSE* and its hit list. The meeting was held in the auditorium of the Social Sciences Building and, to my surprise, was quite well attended. I wondered if they'd come to see whether the black guy could walk and chew gum at the same time.

"Good afternoon all," I began, "and welcome to the first faculty meeting of this academic year and the first at which it has been my honor and pleasure to preside as dean of Arts and Sciences. I'm Tyrone McTavish. I've been here at SNAF-U since the beginning of the term, as I'm sure you all know, and I'm delighted to be a member of the SNAF-U family. And thanks to all of you who have helped to make my transition to administration here a smooth one.

"I'm sure that I don't need to apprise any of you of the recent developments regarding the *NONSENSE* list of the top twenty-five universities in the US. I suspect that most of you have read President Sligh's thirty-one-page special report on the matter that has been circulated around the campus and the forty-page commentary provided by Provost Azkizur. Both the president and the provost are interested in your thoughts on the situation and especially on strategies that you can suggest that might facilitate our return to the *NONSENSE* list. No matter how we feel about such rankings, it's better to be in the top tier than not to be. Thus, the major, in fact the only item of business on today's agenda, is the *NONSENSE* list, our current absence from it, and our desire to return to it. So with that preamble, the floor is now open for discussion of—"

"Excuse me, Dean McTavish." The voice came from the rear of the auditorium. "I'm Garfield Goobler from the Department of Metafunctional Psychophilosopy. I hate to interrupt you, but the bylaws of the Literary College specify that the first item of business in any faculty meeting must be the approval of the minutes of the last meeting. As secretary of the faculty, I circulated those minutes at the beginning of the term. I presume the faculty have had the chance to peruse them and that, in accordance with the college bylaws, they can be approved at this time. Then we can move on to other business."

I thought to myself, *Does anyone really gives a shit about the minutes of a meeting that took place months ago? Does anyone even remember that meeting?* As I was soon to learn, apparently, they did.

"Thank you for calling this matter to my attention, Dr. Goobler. I'm still pretty new here and haven't digested all the details of the college bylaws yet. I trust, as Dr. Goobler suggests, that you all have had time to digest the minutes. If there are amendments or corrections that anyone wishes to offer, I'm sure Dr. Goobler will be happy to incorporate them into the final document? Are there any?"

Several hands were raised. I acknowledged the one farthest from me.

"Uh, Casper Diggitz, Program in Indochinese Literature and Culture," Professor Diggitz said, lowering his hand and rising. "My name is spelled incorrectly in the minutes, Dean McTavish. There are two g's in my surname, not one. Thank you."

"Thank you, Professor Diggitz. We'll make that change." I had to be polite even when I thought the comment was trivial, self-serving, and stupid. "Do you have that, Dr. Goobler?" He nodded. "Are there other corrections?"

"Yes, Dean McTavish, I have one." It was Delilah Doofa, from the Program in Psychiatric Epistemology. Dr. Doofa stood, holding her copy of the minutes at arm's length, her glasses dangling from a cord around her neck. "In the second line of the third paragraph, about halfway down the page, in the section describing the discussion of the nominations for faculty committees, approximately five words in on that line, I would like to have the comma at the end of that phrase replaced with a semicolon."

You can't be serious. That's what I thought. Of course, what I said was "Thank you, Professor Doofa. Are there any objections to that change?"

One of my colleagues stood to address the group.

"Yes, Dean McTavish. Mark McChunkler, Program in Molecular Endocrinology. Dr. Doofa's analysis notwithstanding, I see no reason to place a semicolon at the end of that phrase. I agree that the comma is probably inappropriate but would suggest that if any change is to be made, a full stop should be placed there and what is now the next phrase should become the next full sentence. The following sentence should then begin the next full paragraph. I think those changes will tighten up the document considerably."

Professor McChunkler took his seat, smiling broadly in Doofa's direction.

"Professor Doofa, is that suggestion acceptable to you?"

My brain was screaming. *Help me, please help me! Is there any way I can take a toilet break right now?*

"No, it isn't," Doofa replied, somewhat angrily, "but in the interest of moving the meeting along, I'll accept it anyway."

"Thank you, Professor Doofa." And thank the gods.

"Are there any other amendments to the minutes?"

I crossed my fingers behind my back. It didn't work.

"I have an additional correction to make, Dean. Morris Folder, Program in Historical Microbiology." He was sitting near the front of the auditorium, so he turned to face the rest of the faculty. "You will recall that there was a discussion of the new faculty leave proposal at the last faculty meeting, and I made several extensive comments about that proposal. I note, with some concern, that my comments are not reported in the minutes, nor is there any reference to my having made them. To rectify that situation, I have brought a printed copy of those comments and move that they be incorporated into the minutes. In case any of you have forgotten my comments, I'll be happy to read them for you now."

I had to move quickly.

"Is there a second to Dr. Folder's motion?" I asked while Folder was putting on his glasses. "Hearing none," I said, as I looked around the room, "the motion fails."

"But, but, wait just a minute," Folder sputtered.

Folder frowned, glared at me, muttered to himself, tore up the sheet of paper he'd been waving around, and sat down.

"Is there a motion to accept the minutes as amended?" There was, and we laid that bit of trivia, at least, to rest. Unfortunately, there was a lot more trivia to come.

"To repeat my earlier comments then, the major item I'd like to have you discuss today is the *NONSENSE* list of the twenty-five top institutions. Perhaps I can get the discussion rolling by reviewing the criteria used by—"

"Uh, excuse me, Dean McTavish." Goobler again. "But the bylaws state that before we can discuss any new business, we need to conclude our discussion of any remaining old business. And as the minutes indicate, we did not conclude our discussion of the freshman seminar program in the last meeting."

At this point, I should have simply seized control of the meeting and told all and sundry that I didn't give a flying fig what the bylaws said. But I didn't. I was still the new kid on the block, and I just didn't think I'd gotten to the point yet where even a semidictatorial posture was appropriate. So instead—

"Thank you again, Dr. Goobler," I said with as much composure as

I could muster. "Will you please review the freshman seminar proposal for me and the rest of the group?"

"With pleasure, Dean McTavish." He cleared his throat. "As you all know, last spring, the Faculty Executive Committee proposed a relatively minor change in the existing freshman seminar program. Their proposal reads as follows: During their freshman year, all college students will take a seminar course in either the fall or the winter term. Two hours of course credit will be awarded for these seminars, and the credit may be used to satisfy the credit hour requirements for graduation but may not be used to satisfy concentration requirements. These seminars will be taught by tenure-stream faculty."

Goobler continued, "The change from the existing system was to increase the number of credit hours awarded from one to two. As you all know quite well, a credit hour is the equivalent of one hour of class time per week, per semester. So a four-credit-hour course will meet for four hours a week, a two-hour course will meet twice a week, etc., throughout the semester. The college rules specify, again, as most of you should know, that while the executive committee can propose a curricular change like this, it does not have the power to implement it. Implementation requires that the college faculty approve the proposal by a vote taken at a faculty meeting. In accordance with the bylaws, I distributed copies of the proposal to the faculty last spring, and according to the rules, you have the right to propose amendments to the document before it is brought to a faculty meeting for final consideration and for approval or rejection. As secretary of the faculty, it was my responsibility not only to distribute the proposal but also to solicit written amendments to it, which I did. By the closing date for submission of amendments, twenty-four hours after the solicitation was begun, I had received a total of 257 amendments to the proposal. It was curious but perhaps not unexpected that although there are nearly 500 faculty in the Literary College, those 257 amendments were sponsored by fewer than 30. Indeed, 7 faculty submitted at least 25 amendments each, and one of our number submitted all of 31. The next step, Dean McTavish, is to call upon the sponsors of those amendments to present them to the group for discussion."

"Thank you, Dr. Goobler." For nothing. "Can you suggest an appropriate starting point?"

"Yes, I think I can. I suggest we begin with what is really not an amendment at all but was nevertheless proposed by one of our number, Dr. Galvan."

Clive Galvan rose, cleared his throat, and turned to face his audience.

"Clive Galvan, Department of Statistical Theology. Thank you, Dean McTavish, Dr. Goobler. As you all know, many of the traditions of the academy have existed since the creation of the first universities in Europe. Even in those days, some administrative structures were presumably necessary to ensure the smooth day-to-day operation of the university. But even in those days, it was the faculty who were at the heart of the academic and intellectual enterprise. It was and is the quality of the faculty that draws students to an institution like SNAF-U. It is the faculty who bring attention, nay fame, to an institution as a result of the strength of their scholarship and the quality of the instruction they provide. It is the faculty who are ultimately responsible for establishing the values of the institution and ensuring that those values become a part of the institutional fabric. One of the most important values of the academy is academic freedom. I must say that while I applaud the concept of freshman seminars, I find the current proposal completely unacceptable. Because it did not originate from the faculty itself, I think it is a violation of our academic freedom, and I am offended by its presentation for consideration here. I move that this proposal be rejected out of hand for that reason."

There was a smattering of applause, but his motion received no second.

"Dr. Galvan," I said as patiently as possible, "I don't quite understand the basis for your argument. The Literary College Executive Committee is a representative body of college faculty elected by the college faculty. So in point of fact, this proposal did originate from the faculty. In any case, all of you as faculty members have the opportunity to modify it now."

Galvan sputtered and seemed confused. Apparently, he didn't know that the executive committee was an elected body. Maybe he didn't even know that it was composed of college faculty.

"Oh. Well, I guess if you look at it that way. But I don't recall that I voted for any of the members of the committee." And he sat down.

"Thank you for your input, Dr. Galvan. Let's move on, if we can. Dr. Bicker."

Boris Bicker of the Department of Sociological Thermodynamics stood and cleared his throat. Throat clearing has always been a prerequisite to any comments made by a faculty member in a faculty meeting.

"Boris Bicker, Sociological Thermodynamics. I have several amendments to propose. The first deals with the awarding of credit for these seminars. As you all know, we currently require that students take a total of 120 credit hours in order to graduate from the Literary College. As I see it, the seminar proposal, as it is written, will undermine the objectives of our current graduation requirements since students will be required to take a total of 122 hours in order to graduate. Under our current system, a student could theoretically take 30 four-credit hour courses in order to reach the required total of 120. If we institute this two-credit-hour seminar program, that will no longer be possible. I think this change will be unfair to our students and will make it extremely difficult for them to plan their schedules easily and without confusion. Moreover, it will work against the didactic and pedagogical objectives of a unified curriculum. I'm sure I speak for us all when I say that those objectives comprise the heart of the curricular changes we made three years ago and to undermine those objectives will lay waste to the five years of hard work it took to put the revised curriculum together. So I propose that we lower the number of credit hours required for graduation to 118 credit hours. That way, students could take twenty-five four-credit-hour courses and six three-hour courses and one of these two-hour seminars and still have a total of 120 hours."

Dr. Bicker smiled a self-satisfied smile and sat down. Again, there was a smattering of applause, which for the life of me, I am still unable to come up with a reason for. One of the members of the executive committee stood to respond to Bicker's argument. He looked as confused as I did.

"Dr. Bicker, I'm afraid you've missed the point. Our proposal won't affect the number of credit hours required for graduation. That number will still be 120. Students will simply take the two-hour freshman seminar, which they can count toward graduation if they need it. For example, they might take twenty-nine four-hour courses and two two-hour courses including the seminar. That would still make a total of 120. If they don't need the seminar credits for graduation, it will still show up on their transcripts, and they will have satisfied the seminar requirement."

"Oh. Uh. Well, okay," Bicker responded. "I'm not quite sure that I follow your reasoning, but I'll withdraw that amendment. But I'd still like to propose a different one. Again, in keeping with the spirit of the revised curriculum that we worked so hard to construct and adopt, I propose that the number of credit hours required for graduation be increased from 120 to 126. That way, students can take thirty-one four-hour courses and the two-hour seminar and still have a total of 120 hours for graduation."

Quite obviously, Bicker didn't get the point, and I was rapidly becoming pretty sure that he never would. I had no reason to believe, though, that he was about to give up, especially since he had just pulled a pile of papers from his briefcase. *Time to do the deanly thing*, I thought. I missed my chance once. I wasn't going to do so again.

"Let's think about that one for a while, Boris, and come back to it if you don't mind. In the meantime, I believe Dr. Stargell has an amendment or two to propose."

Bicker sat down, still rummaging through the sheaf of papers he'd extracted from his case. *Gimme shelter*, I thought.

"Cloris Stargell, Program in Literary Linguotherapy. I have two amendments to propose. I propose that we change the phrase 'students will take' to 'students shall take' in the first sentence of the proposal. That's my first amendment. And I propose that we change the wording of the last sentence from 'seminars will be taught' to 'seminars shall be taught.' That's my second amendment. And finally, I propose that we change the wording of the second to last sentence from 'but may not be used' to 'and may not be used.' That's my second amendment."

Yes, she did offer two different second amendments.

"Would you like to give us your reasons for making those suggested changes, Dr. Stargell."

Dr. Stargell cleared her throat.

"I think they sound better."

"Is there any support for or discussion of Dr. Stargell's proposed amendments?"

There was none.

"Those amendments die then for lack of support. Do you have other amendments, Dr. Stargell?"

"I do," she said somewhat hesitantly. Then she looked around at her faculty colleagues, some of whom were glaring pretty menacingly at her, and sat down.

Without waiting for me to call on her, Maneata Femzilla stood and introduced herself.

"Femzilla, associate professor of Militancy Theory. I demand that we remove the degrading and sexist term 'freshman' from this proposal and replace it with 'first-year students.'"

To my amazement, Femzilla then sat down. I was sure that she would either (a) offer a raft of additional amendments attacking the sexist, gender-repressive, male-dominated seminar proposal or (b) launch a completely unrelated attack on me, SNAF-U, Walmart, or the New England Patriots. I breathed a sigh of relief when she did not but held my breath when Leo Da Vinci rather than a member of the executive committee rose to respond to her.

"The term 'first-year students' would not necessarily apply only to freshman, Dr. Femzilla. As you know, the college admits a significant number of transfer students each year. Technically, any such student would also be a first-year student."

Thanks, Leo.

"But as long as we're on the subject of first-year students, I do have a modification of Dr. Femzilla's amendment that I'd like to propose."

I should have known that Leo would never let me off that easily.

"I would like to propose that all faculty in Uranial Studies in the Department of Nuclear, Uranial, and Theocratic Studies be immediately awarded a 50 percent pay increase."

"Thank you for your input, Dr. Da Vinci. Let's move on, shall we? Is there any support for Dr. Femzilla's proposal?"

About a dozen hands were raised.

"Then we'll put it to a vote."

The amendment was defeated overwhelmingly. Femzilla scowled and folded her arms across her chest.

"Are there other amendments that anyone would like to raise for discussion?" I knew that there were many still remaining to be discussed, but I hoped that the fates of those that had been raised would discourage the sponsors of the remaining ones. My hope was in vain.

"Why, yes, Professor McTavish. Fong Wu, assistant professor of Macromolecular Biochemistry. Let me begin by saying that I think the idea of a freshman seminar is an excellent one. It will provide an opportunity for faculty to work with students in small groups and should represent a valuable learning experience for the students. However, as we all know, all of us already have quite busy schedules. So I propose the following: First, I suggest that all the freshman seminars be scheduled for Sunday afternoons. We all know that our students don't do anything worthwhile on Sunday afternoons. They watch sports on TV, play Frisbee on the quad, go to movies, and so forth. Moreover, to increase the value of the freshman seminars to our students, I further propose that all the seminars be conducted in a language other than English. That way, students can satisfy the seminar and language requirements simultaneously."

Wu smiled broadly and sat down. I could hardly believe my ears. But my duty was clear.

"Is there any discussion of Dr. Wu's proposal?" There was none. "Does anyone wish to offer a motion regarding that proposal?" No one did. "Dr. Wu, do you wish to offer a motion?"

Wu started to stand but thought better of it. He shook his head and folded his hands across his chest. Maybe that's the faculty I-lost-the-battle-but-I-still-think-I'll-win-the-war position.

As the meeting progressed (if that's the term to use), about a dozen other amendments were offered, discussed, and rejected in turn. At five fifteen, I decided that it was time again for me to take control.

"Colleagues, it's after five o'clock. I know it is your tradition to hold these meetings to no more than an hour and a half, and I'd like to honor that tradition. However, we haven't even touched on what I hoped would be the major agenda item for the meeting—the NONSENSE top twenty-five list. I would like to at least talk a little about that. So let me start by reviewing the *NONSENSE* ranking criteria. As you know, there are several, including—"

"Dean McTavish," another voice from the back of the room said, "Keefer Vandenbosch, Department of Deconstructive Aquatic Engineering. I move that the meeting be adjourned."

A chorus of seconds followed, almost before Vandenbosch finished his sentence.

"But we need to talk about the *NONSENSE* list!"

"Call the question!"

Which I did.

"All in favor say aye. Opposed? The meeting is adjourned!"

Well, I had learned one thing—SNAF-Ugees believe in ending their meetings on time.

CHAPTER VI

A FEW DAYS LATER, Jarvis informed me that there were several faculty members who wished to speak with me about the *NONSENSE* list. I was delighted. Finally, I thought I can get some faculty input on this issue. Boy, was I wrong. I realized that very shortly after the beginning of my first meeting with Maurice Tormouth PhD, assistant professor of Geochemistry at SNAF-U. He had been an assistant professor for eight years. Normally, junior faculty are reviewed for promotion to associate professor in their sixth year and are either promoted or terminated after that review, but Tormouth had been given two extra years to get his act together. He didn't and had been notified that his promotion had been denied a few weeks before he came to see me. As dean of Arts and Sciences, I was informed of the departmental decision immediately, so I knew that he'd come knocking on my door sooner or later. I expected him, and I expected the conversation to be a difficult one, but not for the reason it turned out to be, especially since the reason he gave for the meeting was to discuss the *NONSENSE* list.

"Come in, Dr. Tormouth," I said. "Please make yourself comfortable."

"Thank you, Dean McTavish," he replied, "and you can call me Mo if you like. Most of my colleagues do."

"Fine, Mo. I believe you want to discuss the top twenty-five list, and I'm delighted to have the chance to speak with you about it. If you were at the faculty meeting the other day, you know that we missed the chance to discuss that matter in that meeting. So I'm especially anxious now to know what the faculty think about it."

"Well, I'm afraid I missed the faculty meeting, Dean McTavish. I had meetings with students that day, I had experiments going on in my lab, and I had to prepare my lecture for my next class. In spite of my situation, I'm still trying to be a conscientious faculty member. And I'm just as delighted to have the chance to talk with you about that situation and about how it relates to the *NONSENSE* rankings, Dean McTavish. I'd like specifically to talk about the Instructional Workforce–Baccalaureal Relativity criteria. I have a specific suggestion that I think will help the university tremendously in meeting that criteria. As you know, Dean," he continued, "the Geology Department has refused to put my name forward for promotion to associate professor, and I think this decision was completely unjustified, unfair, and downright wrong, of course, and before filing a formal appeal of that decision, I decided it would be a good idea for me to speak to you about it."

"Well, Mo," I interjected, "I'm not sure what your personal situation has to do with the *NONSENSE* rankings, and in any case the appeals process requires—"

He didn't allow me to finish my sentence. Indeed, I'm not at all sure he even knew that I had said anything. The "break" in the conversation that I thought I detected was apparently just an opportunity for Mo to catch his breath.

"I'm here to talk to you about the specifics of my case, Dean McTavish, and for you to understand what's going on, I want you to know about me, my family, and the background I had before I came to SNAF-U and to the Geology Department. So let me begin by telling you about my grandfather who received the first PhD in physics from PNEU-A in 1900, and after that, he did postdoctoral work at the Ausgezeichnetes Institut für Physik in Berlin and then took a job as an assistant professor at PERU-B, where he rose quickly through the ranks to full professor and chairman of the department. I can remember sitting on his knee with my dog, Archimedes, at my feet, listening to his stories about his experiences as a physicist and university professor, and I can tell you, Dean McTavish, those were exciting times, which brings me to my father who followed in his father's footsteps and got his PhD in physics from PNEU-A, did postdoctoral work in Germany, although at a different institute, and he took a job at PERU-C, where he quickly rose through the ranks to full professor and chairman of the department, and I can remember sitting on my father's knee with my dog, Archimedes, at my feet, listening to his stories about his experiences as a physicist and university professor. Those were exciting times, I can tell you, Dean McTavish, so it was pretty much a given that I would follow in my grandfather's and my father's footsteps and although my grandfather had already passed on by the time I made the decision, but my father was somewhat disappointed when I decided not to become a physicist, but geology is a hard science, and my specialty requires a thorough grounding in physics and math, so he didn't take it too hard when I decided to go into geochemistry, and I was accepted by a PNEU for college and did well enough to get into another PNEU for graduate work, and since I did my graduate work at the same PNEU that my father and grandfather did, my father was obviously very pleased and that negated any ill feelings he might have had about my not going into physics especially since I did a lot of course work in physics and math as an undergraduate and as a graduate student which I had to do, of course, because geochemistry requires—especially the area of geochemistry that I chose to study, geochemical astronautics—requires a strong background in math and physics as well as chemistry, some astronomy, and even a little biology, so I took all those courses when I was in college and grad school because I knew that I needed to be well prepared not only to be a good scientist but because I knew from sitting on my grandfather's knee, with my dog, Archimedes, at my feet, and sitting on my father's knee, with my dog, Archimedes, at my feet, those were exciting times, Dean McTavish, and I named my dog, Archimedes, because I was interested in science even as a child, and I knew I'd be following in my grandfather's footsteps and my father's footsteps, and I knew that I would have to go to a good college and a good graduate school and that I would have to publish papers and that I would someday rise through the ranks at a good university like SNAF-U to full professor and ultimately to chairman of the department since both my grandfather and my father were not only full professors, Dean McTavish, but they also became chairmen of their departments at two of the most well known and most prestigious and strongest institutions in the country, even in the world, since clearly in most areas, not all, of course, and I don't know very much about the social sciences and humanities, but I do know quite a lot about science, not only geology and geochemistry but also physics and math, since I had to take many courses in those fields as an undergraduate and a graduate student because even for geochemistry, a thorough grounding in math and physics is absolutely necessary, although there are some other areas of geology that don't require as much math and physics as I took, and of course, I had to take some biology too, since my specialty is Geochemical Astronautics, and most of the best universities in the world, at least in the sciences, I don't know much about the social sciences and arts, the best universities are right here in the United States, and I went to two of those universities, Dean McTavish, one for my graduate work and one for my undergraduate work. Now, of course, I took courses other than science courses when I was an undergraduate at least, not only because I had to but also because I knew that it was important for me to be a well-rounded student because I had learned from sitting on my grandfather's knee, with my dog, Archimedes, at my feet and from sitting on my father's knee, with my dog, Archimedes, at my feet, that it was important for me to know about subjects other than physics and math and geology and geochemistry and astronomy and biology and that I needed to take some courses in literature and politics and history and philosophy and economics, and I did but I didn't like any of those classes very much except for economics, and I think the only reason I liked that was because it had some math in it, but I did well in those classes, even though I didn't like them because I had learned from my father and my grandfather, with my dog, Archimedes, at my feet that it was important to be a well-rounded student and that I had to do well if I was going to get into a good graduate school and get a good postdoctoral position and a good job at a school like SNAF-U and rise through the ranks to become a full professor and chairman of my department, so I studied hard, Dean McTavish, I got good grades, and I got into a good PNEU for college and graduated with honors and got into the same PNEU that my father and grandfather had gone to and wrote a good thesis and got my degree and went to Denmark for a postdoc and came to SNAF-U eight years ago as an assistant professor and began my independent studies on the geology of space travel…"

At this point, I thought to myself, if I put my head down on my desk and press my ear really close to the surface, maybe I can hear the electrons moving around in their orbits. Any sound would be better than this. Mo Tormouth was clearly planning to regale me with every detail of his career since his college days, and if I let him, he might even be tempted to try to recall his impressions of his mother's womb. I assumed, of course, that he had had a normal birth, but so far, I had only heard about his beloved father and grandfather and his dog, Archimedes, of course. I certainly wasn't going to ask him about his mother. In fact, I wasn't going to ask him about anything if I could avoid it. I was trying to think of a way to shut him up and get him out of my office. Very undeanly of me, I suppose.

"So when I got to SNAF-U eight years ago I had a very clear idea of what was required to be a successful university professor since both my father and my grandfather had very successful careers, and I had every intention of following in their footsteps, so I talked with other faculty and with the chair of the department, and I not only asked about faculty who had been given tenure and promotion, I asked them to tell me about some of the losers who hadn't been good enough to get tenure so I would be able to avoid making the mistakes they made. Not that I ever thought I was going to be a loser, I was sure from the time that I set foot on campus that I would rise to the rank of full professor and become chairman of my department because my father and grandfather had both risen through the ranks to full professor and had become chairmen of their departments, and both of them were at schools that were at least as good as SNAF-U, maybe even better, but the chair wasn't really willing to give me much information about the losers although he did tell me what I needed to do in order to get tenure myself, that I had to publish some papers and not screw around in the classroom and serve on some committees and not make an asshole of myself and don't impregnate any coeds and get some grants to support my research and publish some papers and like that, and I think I did all those things, Dean McTavish. I have published three papers in the eight years I've been here, and they are all in the top journals in Geochemical Astronautics, and I did have a grant from the Society for Labyrinthine Undertakings in Geochemical Sciences, and although that grant expired five years ago, I did what the chair and the other faculty said I had to do, and I published three papers, and I taught all the courses they told me I had to teach, and I served on the committee to choose upholstery for the new seats in the Geology Auditorium, and I had a grant, and I didn't get any coeds pregnant, so I don't understand why I wasn't promoted to associate professor."

I waited for about thirty seconds before I said anything. I was not at all sure that Mo had finished, and although I had no desire to hear a single additional word from his mouth, I had already concluded that until he had completely vented his spleen, anything I had to say would simply bounce right off him. The question was, how could I respond without setting him off again?

It may again have been undeanly of me, but I rose, walked to the door of my office, opened it, and extended my hand to indicate my desire to shake his.

"Mo, thank you for coming by. I'll consider what you've said and let you know what I decide. One final question, though, before you go. Can you tell me how any of this relates to the *NONSENSE* top twenty-five list?"

"I thought it was obvious, Dean McTavish, the Instructional Workforce–Baccalaureal Relativity criteria. If I don't get tenure, our IWBR ratio will decrease by one. That's sure to keep us out of the top twenty-five, don't you think? Well, thank you, Dean McTavish." He shook my hand and left.

The next discussant of the *NONSENSE* problem was Thayer Avery Ware, associate professor of Tibetan Genetics. I was out of the office when he arrived but got back about five minutes after the time scheduled for our appointment. When I walked in, he was pacing up and down in front of my office door.

"Good afternoon, Dr. Ware." I extended my hand. He wiped his on his jacket before shaking mine. He said nothing. "If you'll give me a minute or two to collect myself before we begin?"

Ware nodded nervously. He sat down on the couch in the outer office and immediately began wringing his hands and casting darting glances from side to side. Ware was short and thin. I guessed that he was in his early to midforties. He was dressed in blue suit, shirt, and tie, and although everything matched, it appeared that none of the components of his wardrobe had ever been pressed. After a couple of minutes, I ushered him into the office and directed him to the seat next to my desk. He sat and immediately began chewing his fingernails. I wasn't looking forward to this.

"Dr. Ware," I said as brightly as possible, "what exactly can I do for you?"

"Quite honestly, Dean McTavish," he replied somewhat sheepishly, "I'm not really sure that you can do anything for me. But I wasn't sure where else to turn. At least, you may be able to advise me about what I should do next. I don't know if there's a faculty security criterion on the list of the *NONSENSE* criteria, but if there isn't, there should be. And if you can help me, I'm certain that it will strengthen our position vis-à-vis the *NONSENSE* rankings."

"Well, I'm not sure exactly what you have in mind, Dr. Ware, but I'm willing to help in any way I can, especially if it helps with *NONSENSE*. What exactly is it that you're concerned about?"

"About the conspiracy!" he answered, his voice rising. "About the conspiracy, that's what!" At that, he stood up and began pacing around the room, wringing his hands and mumbling to himself, "About the conspiracy, about the conspiracy, the conspiracy."

"Please try to calm yourself, Dr. Ware. Sit down and tell me about this conspiracy."

He sat but continued the hand-wringing and the initially occasional but increasingly frequent furtive glances around the room.

"Before I say anything more, I need you to give me your assurance about some things."

"And what might those be, Dr. Ware?"

"First, I need your absolute assurance that everything I say to you will be held in strictest confidence."

"You have that assurance, of course, Dr. Ware."

That assurance seemed to relax him a bit.

"Second, I need your assurance that you will never repeat anything I say to anyone else."

"Dr. Ware, I just said that I would keep our conversation strictly confidential, and I will."

He apparently wasn't listening.

"Third, I'd like you to sign this document." He pulled a piece of paper from his coat pocket and handed it over to me. It read, "I, _____, promise and affirm that any and all elements of my conversation with Dr. Thayer Avery Ware, associate professor of Tibetan Genetics, will be kept strictly confidential and will never, under any circumstances, be revealed to any third party." The paper was clearly a photocopy, so there was every reason to believe that he had lots of other copies. "Please sign and date this statement of assurance, Dean McTavish."

"Dr. Ware, I will do nothing of the sort," I replied calmly, "I have given you my assurance that I will keep our conversation confidential. I can and will do no more than that."

Ware got up and began pacing again.

"Oh, all right," he demurred. "I didn't really expect you to sign it anyway. Nobody ever does. Except my wife. Occasionally."

As I said, I knew he had more than one copy of his assurance.

"Now let's not waste any more time, Dr. Ware. Please sit down and tell me what the problem is. Exactly."

"It's the conspiracy, Dean McTavish. The conspiracy!"

"What conspiracy?" This was getting us nowhere. "You've got to give me more information, Dr. Ware."

He settled back in the chair, started the hand-wringing again, but seemed resigned to the fact that he was going to have to give me at least some details.

"I think… I think there is a conspiracy to try to force me to resign from the university or to be fired from the university or to drive me crazy, which I guess would accomplish the same thing."

He clearly wanted to get up and start the pacing again, but I glared at him, and he stayed in his seat.

"Dean McTavish, can you be absolutely sure that your office isn't bugged? I mean, you can give me your word, but that still—"

"Dr. Ware." It was becoming increasingly difficult for me to be patient with this guy. Why wasn't he in the NUThouse? "Just tell me about this conspiracy. Why do you think there is one, and who do you think is behind it?"

"Well…" I could tell it was a real strain for him to stay seated. I was almost ready to let him stand up and pace if that would get him out of my office any quicker.

"Things keep happening. I mean, things that don't happen to anybody else, at least I can't imagine that they do. Things like this, for example. I got a letter last week from a colleague at another university, and the flap of the envelope had been taped closed. I think someone had opened the letter, and that's not the first time they've read my mail."

"But there could be a simple and innocent explanation for that, Dr. Ware. Did you think to call your colleague and ask if he had taped the letter shut himself?"

"Uh, no. Why didn't I think of that? But wait minute. Even if I did and even if he had said yes, that wouldn't prove that somebody hadn't read it before it got to me. In fact, that might make it even more likely because since it had already been taped shut, no one would know that they had opened it and then taped it back again. But that's not the only thing, anyway. Faculty from my department have been sitting in on my classes. I didn't invite them, so why are they there?"

"Dr. Ware, my guess is that there is a simple and equally innocent explanation for that too. I'm sure you know well that all the departments in the college have implemented programs to help faculty to improve their teaching and that as one element of those programs, senior faculty visit the classes of junior faculty. Those visits are sometimes announced and sometimes unannounced. I suspect that's the explanation for the faculty who have visited your classes."

"But they've already come twice, Dean McTavish. And it wasn't the same people each time. If it had been the same people each time, your explanation might be plausible, but it wasn't the same people each time. But that's not the only thing anyway. One day, a few weeks ago, when I got to my office in the morning, I found that my computer was turned on. I always turn my computer off when I leave in the evening. Always. So the only explanation for it being on that morning was that they had broken into my office and were trying to access my computer files."

"Was there any sign of forced entry, Dr. Ware?"

"No, there wasn't, but I'm sure they have a key. And that's not the only thing, anyway. They've been sending students to spy on me. Over the last few months, I've had probably a dozen students make appointments to see me outside of my regular scheduled office hours."

"Were these students in your classes, Dr. Ware?"

"Well, yes, they were, but why didn't they just come to see me during office hours? I make myself available for at least fifteen minutes every week. They could come to see me then, except that no one ever comes to see me during my office hours either, which makes it even more strange. Why would they need to come to see me at any other time if they hadn't been put up to it? Oh, sure, they ask me questions about the lectures and the reading and such, but I know they're really there to try to read my mail and my other correspondence and to see what may be on my computer screen and to listen in on my phone calls. That's what they tell them to do. I know. And that's not the only thing either. I think my phone is tapped."

"Well, let me ask another question, Dr. Ware. Who exactly do you think is responsible for all this?"

"How can you even ask that question, Dean McTavish? The answer is obvious! *They* are responsible!"

"But who are they, Dr.Ware?"

"*They, Them*, the ones who want to make me leave or get me fired or drive me crazy or all of those things! *They're* the ones responsible!"

And he was out of his chair once again, pacing and wringing, wringing and pacing.

"Can you give me any names, any specifics, Dr. Ware?"

"Well, no… but I know who they are. I know who they are. I *do* know who they are! And I'll bet you know who they are too. You just won't admit it. Are you trying to protect them?"

"Dr. Ware," I said, rising from my seat, "thank you for coming in to see me. I will look into your concerns, and *if* I find anything, I will certainly let you know." That last conditional phrase was, of course, deliberately designed to take me off the hook. What I really planned to do was to see whether I could add another resident to the NUThouse.

Ware started for the door. A little voice inside my head told me that he wasn't quite finished. Not yet.

"I do have one final request of you, Dean McTavish," he said as he headed for the door. "In spite of what you said, I do know that you're taping this conversation, so if you don't mind, I'd appreciate it very, very much if you would destroy the tape or at least provide me with a copy of it. Thank you."

A couple of weeks later, I was sitting in my office, with, believe it or not, nothing in particular to do. I'd handled all of the day's pressing business and finally had a few minutes to myself to sit, think, read, whatever. Or so I thought. Jarvis interrupted my reverie before I was able to settle in to it.

"Sorry to bother you, Dean McTavish, but there's a faculty member here to see you. She says she doesn't have an appointment, but she hopes you'll be able to meet with her anyway. She says it's about the *NONSENSE* poll."

Sigh.

"Okay, Jarvis, send her in."

Dr. Margaret O. Lomaneak was a professor of psychology. She was already a full professor and had established an international reputation in her field which had something to do with why adults don't like spiders and snakes and kids do. As I was soon to discover, the problem was not with Dr. Lomaneak's national and international reputation. The problem was with her opinion of herself.

"Come, in Dr. Lomaneak," Blah. Blah. Blah. You know the routine by now.

"Thank you for seeing me, Dean McTavish, and please call me Meg."

"Fine, Meg." Blah. Blah. Blah.

"I'll get right to the point. I know that you and many others here at SNAF-U are devastated by the failure of the university to make the *NONSENSE* top twenty-five list as am I. I know too that one of the criteria used to determine the occupants of that list is Cosmic Placement Perception. I have a suggestion that I believe will greatly increase our reputation in not only the national but also the international community and will almost certainly vault us back onto the list. Indeed, I think there's a good chance that if you implement my suggestion, it will move us into the top ten."

"Wow, I'm all ears, Meg."

"As you know, Ty, my research deals with the differential responses of children and adults to specific environmental stimuli. I suspect you're also aware that I have achieved significant prominence in my field, both nationally and internationally, as a result of my studies of the responses of children and adults to insects, especially spiders, and to reptiles, especially snakes."

I decided not to point out to her that spiders aren't insects.

"I've received numerous awards for my research from various psychological associations, both in this country and abroad, and again, as you may be aware, I have research grants from both governmental agencies and private foundations. I am on the editorial board of several prestigious psychological journals, and I am the founding editor of one of those journals. I think all of my colleagues, and even you, Ty, though you've only been here for a short time, would have to agree that my reputation has enhanced the reputation of SNAF-U, not only in psychology, but also more generally as a top-flight research university."

"I admit, Meg, that your reputation has preceded you. I have heard nothing but good things about the quality of your scholarship and the quality and magnitude of your scholarly contributions to the Psychology Department and to the university."

"Good, then," she said in a tone that suggested that she thought she was going to get what she wanted from me. "That should make this discussion go even more smoothly than I anticipated. What I want is this, Ty. Psychology, like so many other disciplines, is expanding. We as an institution have to be able to expand with it. It is no longer possible, in my opinion, for SNAF-U or any other respectable institution in this country or the world to respond to that challenge within the context of the traditional departmental organizational structure. We need to move beyond that paradigm and begin to think in larger terms. I have already begun to think in those terms, and I'm here to propose a new paradigm for SNAF-U and to enlist your assistance in implementing that proposal.

"What I have in mind is this—a College of Psychology that would have the same status in the institutional academic hierarchy as the other schools and colleges of the university. The college could then be divided into various departments that would correspond appropriately to the major subdivisions of modern psychology. The college would, of course, be headed by a dean, and I can think of no one better qualified for that position than myself. In addition, I would also be willing, initially at least, to serve as chair of one of the departments, the one dealing with my subspecialty, of course. My appointment as dean would, as I'm sure you can appreciate, require that my salary be significantly increased, and I would also expect an additional adjustment during the time I serve as chair of the department. I would also expect a research allowance to permit me to hire assistants to facilitate my research while I am discharging my administrative responsibilities. And a year's paid leave every other year.

"As dean of the College of Psychology, I would also expect to be able to hire faculty, and I estimate that during the first few years of its existence, we would need to hire at least sixteen new faculty members, eight of them at the level of associate professor or above. As dean, I would expect to play the major role in determining what areas of the new college require additional staffing and in choosing the candidates to fill those positions. Of course, budgetary authority for the existing faculty in psychology at SNAF-U would be transferred to me, and the college will need to have budgetary support beyond that required for faculty salaries and the like. I would think that an initial budget of around twenty million dollars would be appropriate. Over the longer term, I would hope to establish several institutes within the college, and those will require additional funding, but we can worry about the budget for those entities when the time comes. I have outlined all of these ideas in writing."

She removed a manila folder from her briefcase and placed it on my desk.

"As I said, Ty, I think this plan will provide an immediate and significant boost to our reputation. In fact, I think it could help us in other areas related to the *NONSENSE* survey as well—Baccalaureal

Selection Stringency, Fiduciary Positional Quotient, Altruistic Pecuniary Indicators. Maybe even others. I thought it would be best to speak with you before broaching my idea to the provost and the president. What do you think of the idea?"

I leaned back in my chair and realized that I had been holding my breath for some seconds. During my years as an academic administrator, faculty had come to see me for lots of reasons. Sometimes I knew enough about the individuals to anticipate their motives. Sometimes I didn't. I had no idea why Meg A. Lomaneak wanted to see me before she came and accepted at face value her claim that it had to do with the *NONSENSE* ranking. So once again, I was taken completely by surprise by her "plan." But I had been in this situation enough already to know how to respond.

I rose, walked to the door of my office, opened it, and extended my hand to shake hers.

"Meg," I said jovially, "you've given me a lot to think about. I'll get back to you when I've had a chance to mull it all over. Please leave your documents with me."

I took the papers from her hand.

"But… ," she began but didn't finish. "Well, thank you, Ty. I'll look forward to hearing from you."

And with that, she left.

I saw Meg on numerous occasions during my tenure as dean at SNAF-U. I never mentioned her proposal again. Interestingly enough, neither did she. At least not to me.

Maybe she discussed it with her dog, Sigmund.

You may remember Maneata Femzilla from the faculty meeting. Dr. Femzilla was associate professor of Militancy Theory, with tenure in the Department of Philosophy. She was apparently in her late forties; thus, a bit younger than me, and had been at SNAF-U for about fifteen years. She was due to be promoted to full professor in a year or two, and from what I had heard, there were no impediments to that promotion, at least not in terms of her teaching or her research. She did have a reputation for being something of a troublemaker, though. Although I neglected to check with Leo Da Vinci about her when I learned she had made an appointment to see me, it didn't take me long to understand the basis for that reputation. I was also sure that Maneata Femzilla was not the name she was born with.

"Please, come in Dr. Femzilla…" Blah. Ditto. Blah. Ditto.

Femzilla was dressed stylishly but not at all extravagantly. She flashed a brief and quite a winning smile at me as we shook hands. I suspected that because of her politics, the world saw that smile only infrequently.

"It's a pleasure to finally meet you, Dean McTavish. I've been looking forward to this meeting, and I must say that I'm delighted to see a new face around here, although I should tell you that my first choice for this job would have been a woman, but at least they didn't hire a white male. Too bad that faculty diversity isn't one of the *NONSENSE* criteria. Then we'd have a lot more faculty around here who look like you and me."

"I can certainly appreciate your point of view, Dr. Femzilla, and I can assure you that I intend to be as sensitive as I can to the needs and the agendas of all the members of the SNAF-U family. And by the way, please call me Ty."

"I'm very pleased to hear you say that, Dean McTavish," she replied without humor, "since my reasons for coming to see you have precisely to do with those needs and agendas and will provide you with the opportunity to show exactly how sensitive you are. And although I'm vehemently opposed to ranking systems like the *NONSENSE* listing, I'm practical enough to understand that such rankings are important to many people, especially to students and their parents… And you may feel free to call me Dr. Femzilla."

The clunk I heard was the gauntlet hitting the floor.

"Then perhaps you should tell me exactly what's on your mind, Dr. Femzilla."

"There are lots of changes that need to be made around here, Dean McTavish, if this institution is to be transformed from the sexist, gender-repressive, male-dominated bastion that it currently is. And you are at least one of the people in position to facilitate such a transformation. I know we can't do everything at once, so I've made a list of the changes that I think can be accomplished immediately."

Great, I thought. This should *really* be fun. Would this conversation have anything at all to do with the *NONSENSE* top twenty-five?

"First of all, I want the signage changed on all of the lavatories on campus, from 'Women' and 'Men' to 'Feminine' and 'Masculine.' And take those stupid pictures off the doors. Most women I know haven't worn A-line dresses since they were kids. And the last time I checked, most of us had two legs, just like you do. Second, I want the sexist last syllable removed from the name of the Political Science Building."

"You mean Madison Hall?"

"That's correct. Call it Madikid Hall or Madichild hall or whatever else you want, but the male-specific reference of the last syllable is offensive."

"But the building is named after one of SNAF-U's presidents, Dr. Femzilla." Why did I say that?

"Exactly! One of SNAF-U's *male* presidents. Thirdly, I want the chair of the French Department to either be removed or to be forced to change his first name."

The chair of French was Guy LaForge.

"Dr. Femzilla, this is ridiculous. There can't be any sexist connotations associated with his first name since it isn't even pronounced 'guy,' and to be offended by a person's name in the first place seems to me to be just plain silly."

"I might have expected that you would respond that way, Dean

McTavish, though I had hoped for better from you. Nevertheless, I intend to complete my list of demands. Fourth, I want you to institute or to at least support a policy that employees of the masculine gender named Richard, at any level in this institution, should never be referred to as Dick."

I suppressed a groan, but I'm sure my facial expression conveyed my feelings. Femzilla frowned but continued her harangue.

"Fifth. You are well aware, Dean McTavish, that there is a significantly lower fraction of faculty of the feminine gender in the Literary College than faculty of the masculine gender. I believe the breakdown is something like 30/70."

She had a point there, and that was an issue I was determined to address as dean.

"You are right there, Dr. Femzilla, and that's a situation I hope to do something about." It was an unkind thought, but I figured that if perhaps I threw her a bone, I might at least thin the atmosphere a little bit. No such luck.

"Good. I can tell you exactly what you need to do. You should fire enough male faculty and replace them with women so that the final ratio is 55/45, women to men. After all, that ratio is much closer to the overall ratio in the general population. Indeed, if you are really committed to equality for women on this campus, you should resign your job and insist that it be filled by a woman.

"And lastly, at least for now, you absolutely must get the institution to change the ridiculous name of its sports teams."

I have to admit, Femzilla had a point there too. And here was one issue that related directly to one of the *NONSENSE* criteria, one that we had talked about, albeit briefly, in a subsequent executive staff meeting— Mascot/Nickname Cute-ivity. Like many institutions, PNEUs and PERUs as well as HUTs, SNAF-U had fielded athletic teams, men's and women's, for many years. Until relatively recently, the men's teams had been called the Husbandmen and the mascot had been this guy dressed up as a sharecropper or something like that. This may have worked just fine in 1920, but ninety years later, not only wasn't this picture very energizing (Go Husbandmen?) but no one could also agree on what to call the women's teams (Husbandwomen? Husbandchicks? Husbandbabes? Femi-Husbandmen? Lady Husbandmen? Husbandettes?). So a few years before I arrived at SNAF-U, the students were given the opportunity to choose a new nickname for the sports teams and their mascot. As you might imagine, some of the names were pretty grotty, but to their credit, the students rejected such possibilities as the Fever Blisters, the Landmines, the Coliform Bacteria, the Beerhunters, and the crudest of the lot and incidentally the second highest vote getter, the Bodacious Rat Turds. The ultimate winner, for reasons absolutely no one could fathom or explain, not even the students themselves, was the Screech Owls. Not great but better than the Husbandmen.

Or so everyone thought at first. Things were fine for a while. The men's teams were referred to as the Screechers, Screeches, Owls, Birds, Screech Owls, etc., and except for the odd noises produced by the spectators at SNAF-U sporting events, everyone was reasonably happy. The women seemed satisfied too as their teams were usually referred to in pretty much the same terms. There had been no move to call them the Lady Owls, Owlettes, Birdettes, or Screechettes. But then some (presumably) male SNAF-Ugee had (what I'm sure he thought was) a bright idea, and he and some of his cronies elected to try it out at a women's basketball game. Unfortunately, the notion caught on very quickly, and from that point on, essentially all the male SNAF-U students and even a significant fraction of the female student population referred to the women's teams as the Hooters. Needless to say, that didn't sit very well with any of the female faculty or administrators or with the women athletes either. And although I have no specific information on this point, it's my guess that the *NONSENSE* Mascot/Nickname Cute-ivity judges weren't too thrilled with our mascot name or the mascot himself, some guy running around in a seedy owl suit. So Femzilla was right, a change was in order. We learned from Doug Little, Hermione Bull's contact at *NONSENSE*, that those involved in the survey liked mascot names that didn't end in the letter *s*. Maybe husbandmen wasn't so terrible after all.

"You're on target again, Dr. Femzilla. I agree that the popular nickname for our women's teams is degrading and that we need to do something about it."

"And what exactly do you plan to do about all this, Dean McTavish?"

As I said, by now you should know the routine.

CHAPTER VII

ABOUT TWO MONTHS HAD now passed since our fall from *NONSENSE* grace. Some of the furor had subsided. At least the level of wailing and gnashing of teeth had decreased considerably. Even Hermione Bull and Charity Butler were now seen to smile on occasion. We hadn't had another faculty meeting although I still thought a faculty discussion of the *NONSENSE* rankings would be useful. But given my experience the first time around, I held little hope that a second try would turn out any differently. Faculty had also stopped coming to see me in lame attempts to use the *NONSENSE* business to get something for themselves. Yet I knew that the *NONSENSE* crisis would be with us until the next fall, when the new rankings would be released. So it was no surprise when I received a call from Olan Azkizur, requesting my assistance with a *NONSENSE*-related matter.

"Ty, this is Olan. Have you got a minute?"

"Sure, Olan, what's on your mind?"

"I've just received a phone call regarding one of our graduate students. It seems that she's have some significant difficulties with her doctoral thesis advisor. She has cleared all the necessary hurdles and has written her dissertation, but her advisor has apparently decided that it is not acceptable. I'd like for you to look into the matter if you don't mind."

"Well, of course, I'll be happy to look into it, Olan, although I'll only be able to intervene if there has been some impropriety. You know as well as I do that the thesis advisor and the dissertation committee pretty much have the last word as far as the acceptability of the thesis is concerned. Academic freedom and all that. But I can at least inquire and see what's going on. What's the student's name?"

"Muffy Torkelson-Little," Olan replied. "Does that name ring a bell?"

"No, Olan, I'm afraid it doesn't. Should it?"

"Well, yes, Ty, it should. Ms. Torkelson-Little is the niece of Douglas O. Little, the *NONSENSE* executive who is in charge of the top twenty-five listing. I think it goes without saying that we don't want to do anything, *anything*, that is likely to jeopardize our return to the rankings next year. So I hope that you can resolve the matter regarding her doctoral dissertation in a satisfactory manner. One that is satisfactory for her, for her uncle, and for us."

"I will look into it, Olan. I'll see what I can do."

This was clearly going to be a tricky situation to handle. On the one hand, I couldn't infringe on the prerogatives of the graduate faculty. I knew that I would certainly be pissed if some dean tried to tell me whose dissertation I should accept and whose I shouldn't. But on the other hand, I needed to be a good soldier. If the truth were told, in spite of my feelings about the *NONSENSE* poll, I didn't much like the idea of being at school that wasn't in the top twenty-five. All the other schools I'd been at had been and were never in any jeopardy of falling out of that group. I needed some advice. It was time to give Leo Da Vinci a call.

"Leo? This is Ty McTavish. How are things?"

"I'm in the middle of playing a video game right now, McTavish, and when I finish, I want to look for some porn on the Internet. Can you call back later?"

"This won't take long, Leo. I need your advice about a couple of things, one of which relates to an appointment I have later this afternoon. So if you can tear yourself away from your computer, just for a minute, I'd appreciate it."

"Shit! Now look what you did! You made me screw up the game! Now I'll have to clear my scores and start all over again. I was up to 468 consecutive wins, on my way to 500. You're not off to a very good start with me today, McTavish. All right, what's the deal?"

"First of all, Leo, I have to bow to your wisdom and knowledge. I sat in on the executive staff meeting that was held the day the NONSENSE ratings were released. The meeting was bizarre, to say the least, and as I said, when we talked the day before, I did not believe for a minute your story about the staff cheering the president at those meetings. But... you were right! Damn! You were exactly right. I couldn't believe it."

Da Vinci chuckled in spite of his frustration with me.

"At the end of the meeting, Sligh stood up and yelled, 'Who's the boss?' And his minions dutifully respond, 'You's the boss!' And on and on. 'Who's the boss? You's the boss! Who's the boss? You's the boss!'" And then he leaves the meeting. I could not believe it."

"Well, Ty, as I said, I'd never seen it myself, but more than one person had told me that it was true. They say that some of the staff members sometimes refuse to participate, but from what I hear, the head of Physical Plant Operations and a few others even seem to enjoy it."

"Interesting place, this SNAF-U... but I need to move on. I got a call from Olan Azkizur yesterday about a graduate student, and I have an appointment to see her this afternoon. So I have another question for you. What can you tell me about the Department of Uruguayan Language and Literature?"

"Aha, DULL. Well, you probably know that the department has only one more faculty member than NUTS. And four of them are married to each other... I mean two of them, ahh, you know what I mean. DULL was originally a component of the Division of Cultural Studies. But it was hived off a few years ago. The woman who's now the chair and her husband somehow conned some Texas cattle rancher into donating two million dollars. Can you believe that? Two million dollars to support the study of Uruguayan Language and Literature. Apparently, the guy's mother married a Uruguayan rodeo cowboy or something like that. Because of that gift, the woman who's now chair was able to convince the provost and then the president that ULL should be a department. Chair studies twentieth-century Uruguayan philosophy or some shit like that. I didn't know there was such a thing."

"What about the other faculty?"

"They all had pretty good credentials when they were part of Cultural Studies. My take on it is that the chairman's husband was pretty much bound to follow her to DULL. The female half of the other couple was one of the chairman's cronies in Cultural Studies, so it made sense that she would come along, and she presumably brought her husband with her. The fifth guy is a relatively new assistant professor, probably the only recent PhD in Uruguayan Language and Literature in the country, maybe even the world."

"It's one of their grad students who's coming to see me this afternoon, so can you tell me anything about their graduate program?"

"You mean besides the fact that they shouldn't have one? No, I can't tell you much except I think their next PhD will be their first PhD, first that is since DULL was created."

"Well, thanks, Leo. Oh, don't hang up yet. I have one more question. I noticed, because I suspect that you intended for me to, that you never refer to the chair of DULL by name. Why is that?"

"Simple. Because every time I say her name, it cracks me up.

"What's so hilarious about Bye-TIM-mie?"

"That's not how I pronounce her name, Ty, and you know it. Good-bye."

My appointment that afternoon was with the DULL graduate student, the eminent Ms. Muffy Torkelson-Little. I looked into her background a bit before she arrived so that I would be prepared for our meeting. In addition to being D.O. Little's niece, Muffy graduated from one of the Seven Sisters Colleges with a degree in Romance Languages and immediately enrolled in graduate school at SNAF-U. That was a dozen years ago, almost to the day. It was no surprise to find that she hadn't completed her degree even after twelve years. The average time to degree in the humanities graduate programs at SNAF-U was 13.5 years, so Muffy, at least at this point, was still well below the average. As Uruguayan Language and Literature was far removed from my own sphere of professional interests, I took a look at Muffy's academic record to get some sense of the kinds of courses that were elected by graduate students in that area. Among others, Muffy had taken Linguistics 576; Theoretical Aspects of Poesic Metaphysics, in which she received an A+; Music 780; Liturgy in the Early Compositions of Chuck Berry, also an A+; and Philosophy 6348B, John Wayne… Prophet or Pariah? She only got an A- in that one.

Like many students in the Humanities and Social Sciences, once Muffy completed her coursework, she left the university to finish her research and write her dissertation. She took a job teaching algebra at a community college in Biloxi, Mississippi. She was right on time for our appointment, and I greeted her in the waiting area and ushered her in. As I expected Muffy was in her early thirties, and she was actually quite an attractive young woman.

"Good afternoon, Ms. Torkelson-Little." I had learned long ago to use "Ms." with *any* woman, at least at first. My experience had been that if she wanted to be "Miss," or "Mrs.," or something else, she would tell me. "Please sit down."

Muffy was one of the tiniest women I'd ever seen. She couldn't have been more than four feet tall. If I hadn't seen her record and known that she was in her thirties, I would surely have thought she was a child. She took a seat near my desk. It was exactly the same seat that Michael Baccaliprati had sat in when he came to visit me several months earlier. The pose she assumed was much like that Baccaliprati had adopted when he sat down. Except for the difference in gender between the two of them, this could have been the beginning of the Baccaliprati meeting, because as soon as she sat down, Muffy Torkelson-Little burst into tears. Déjà vu all over again. I passed her the lab wipes.

"I'm sorry, Dean McTavish," she said, trying her best to compose herself. "I promised myself that I wouldn't do this. It's certainly not the way I wanted to start this meeting. But I just don't know what to do."

"There, there, Ms. Torkelson-Little," I said in my most solicitous and, I hoped, comforting tone. "Please try to calm yourself." I certainly did not want a repeat of the Baccaliprati debacle. "What exactly is the problem?"

"It's my dissertation. Dr. Bytemie is my major advisor, as you may know. I gave her a copy of my thesis a few days ago, and well, she says it's not acceptable, at least not in its present form. I had planned to graduate at the end of this term, Dean McTavish, and I really wanted to finish in less than the average time for humanities students at SNAF-U, but it's obvious that I won't graduate if Dr. Bytemie won't accept my thesis. And won't that hurt our *NONSENSE* ratings if I don't graduate? Won't that decrease our Quadrennial Baccalaureal Efficiency if I don't graduate?"

"Well, actually, no it won't, Ms. Torkelson-Little. You see, the Quadrennial Baccalaureal Efficiency criterion only applies to undergraduates."

But I knew that her failure to graduate would affect our DPODL (Don't Piss Off Doug Little) criterion, and that could have a more significant impact on our *NONSENSE* ranking than our QBE.

I had a copy of her dissertation in front of me. I hadn't looked at it carefully, but one thing about it that was impossible to miss was its length. It was 781 pages long, and my understanding was that Muffy still hadn't written a concluding chapter. By way of comparison, my doctoral dissertation was less than a hundred pages long, and as I think I've mentioned already, I published three papers from that work in what was arguably the best biophysical journal in the world. Obviously, things were different in the humanities.

"Well, perhaps you can tell me a bit about your thesis, Ms. Torkelson-Little." If I can get her talking, I thought maybe she'll stop crying. "Let me see. The title is 'An Hyperbolic and Heuristic Deconstruction of the Commodification of Anti-intellectualism and Postmodernism Represented in Metaphysical Treatises Published in Montevideo, Uruguay, between August 1 and December 15, 1988.' Is that correct?"

"Yes, that is its title, Dean McTavish."

"Tell me a little bit more about it, please."

"What I've tried to do is to briefly but concisely deconstruct the commodification of anti-intellectualism and postmodernism during the period in question, using hyperbolic and heuristic approaches to that deconstruction."

"Yes… but what exactly does that mean, Ms. Torkelson-Little?"

"Well, anti-intellectualism and postmodernism were commodified in Montevideo, Uruguay, during the period August 1 to December 15, 1988, to an extent that had not been observed before that time and has not been observed since. In fact, the only other example of that degree of commodification of anti-intellectualism and postmodernism, at least the only example we know about that even comes close to what happened in Uruguay took place in the late third century in Mongolia. I have, I hope successfully, deconstructed that most recent commodification using hyperbolic and heuristic symbolism in my dissertation."

"How did you happen to choose that topic, that time period, your approach, et cetera?"

"By all appropriate measures, Dean McTavish, this time period is perhaps the most important in the whole history of twentieth-century Uruguayan philosophy. The attempt at commodification by the anti-intellectuals and postmodernists in Montevideo almost turned Uruguayan philosophy upside down and had an impact on the use of metaphor and anachronism in the phenomenology of that period that remains to this day."

I had no reason but to believe that Muffy Torkelson-Little was trying her best to explain her thesis work to me. It wasn't working. I hadn't understood a word of what she had said. It was time to try a different tack.

"Well, thank you for that exposition, Ms. Torkelson-Little. Let's move on, if you don't mind. What exactly does Dr. Bytemie say are the problems with your dissertation?"

At this, Muffy began crying again, although not as pitifully as before.

"Well, Dean McTavish," she said between tears, "first of all, she's says it's not heavy enough."

Rather a crude way for a dissertation advisor to make that point, I thought.

"I can see how that might be somewhat upsetting, Ms. Torkelson-Little. She might have put it a bit more delicately. Clearly erudition and sophistication are expected in an acceptable doctoral dissertation, but there are ways of communicating that to a candidate without appearing insensitive."

"No, Dean McTavish, you don't understand. She didn't mean that it wasn't sufficiently sophisticated or erudite. She meant that it didn't *weigh* enough. When I gave it to her, the first thing she did was to put it on a scale she had on her desk. She said it was light by about a hundred grams. How many pages is a hundred grams, Dean McTavish?" And Muffy was crying again.

"There, there, Ms. Torkelson-Little, please try to calm yourself. I have to say that I'm astounded at this. I have heard of dissertation advisors who have wanted theses to be shortened and occasionally even lengthened, sometimes with justification, but I've never heard of anyone who estimated the appropriate length or content by *weighing* it."

"Well, that's exactly what she did. She said that she had seen enough good dissertations in this field to know that mine was too light—by about a hundred grams. How many pages is a hundred grams, Dean McTavish?"

"I don't know, Ms. Torkelson-Little, but before we deal with that question, let's discuss some of Dr. Bytemie's other criticisms of your thesis. What else did she say was wrong."

"She said that some of the passages in it were too easy to understand."

"You mean, of course, too hard to understand."

I assumed that she simply misspoke because she was so stressed.

"No, Dean McTavish, she said it was too *easy* to understand."

"Too *easy* to understand? Is that the language she used? Too *easy* to understand? Did she mean that you needed to add a bit more sophistication to your arguments and analysis?"

"I don't think so, Dean McTavish, and that is exactly what she said. Some of the passages were too easy to understand."

"Can you give me an example."

"May I?" She took the copy of her dissertation that was sitting on my desk and turned to a page about halfway through. She began reading.

"'This tension between the anti-intellectuals, the postmodernists, and their competitors had a serious negative impact on the development of philosophical thought in Montevideo during this period.' That's an example of a passage that Dr. Bytemie says is not written in a fashion that is sufficiently complex."

Muffy pulled a crumpled piece of paper from her backpack.

"Dr. Bytemie says that the passage should sound something like this: 'This anti-Platonic illusion suggests a conflict between form and substance, between art and science, between philosophy and imperialism, that transcends traditional anthropomorphic interpretations of chaos and induces the automatonization of the anti-intellectual, the postmodernist, the aesthete, and the career military officer.'"

"Is that what the passage you read from your dissertation is intended to say, Ms. Torkelson-Little?

"I don't know, Dean McTavish. Dr. Bytemie thinks it is. To be honest, I have no idea what the sentence that Dr. Bytemie wrote actually means."

"Well, let's move on. What other criticisms were there?"

"She said I didn't cite enough work by what she considers to be the two leading authorities on the subject of my dissertation."

"And who might those two leading authorities be, Ms. Torkelson-Little?" As if I didn't already know.

"Her and her husband."

"Anything else?"

"Nothing really major, sir. Most of the other criticisms were pretty minor. But don't you think those are enough? How many pages is a hundred grams, Dean McTavish?"

"I don't know, Ms. Torkelson-Little." I paused. "But the question really is, what exactly would you like me to do about all this?"

"Well, I've thought of several possibilities, Dean McTavish. Maybe you could become my thesis advisor and approve my dissertation so that I wouldn't need Dr. Bytemie's approval."

"I couldn't do that, Ms. Torkelson-Little. While I have some authority to override faculty decisions and while it's possible that I may ultimately need to do so in this case, I couldn't simply assume responsibility for your dissertation myself."

"Well, then, could you just fire Dr. Bytemie and her husband?"

"No, I can't do that either, Ms. Torkelson-Little, at least not because of this situation. Does the other Dr. Bytemie have some role in all of this?"

"He's sort of the cochair of my dissertation committee. Mrs. Dr. Bytemie is the official chair."

"Have you spoken with him?"

"He was there in the meeting I had with his wife. If you can't be my advisor, can you get me an advisor from another department?"

"That is a distinct possibility, Ms. Torkelson-Little, and I'll look into it, but I can't promise you anything specific. Have you thought of any other options?"

"Would the university give me money to transfer to another school so I could finish my dissertation someplace else?"

"I seriously doubt it, Ms. Torkelson-Little," I said as I rose from my desk. It was time to end this conversation. "I will look into the situation, that's all I can promise you at this point."

"Thank you, Dean, McTavish. I appreciate your listening to me, and I'm sorry about the crying and stuff. One more thing," she said over her shoulder as she was leaving the office, "would I be dismissed from the graduate school if I were to kill the Bytemie doctors?"

At least she still had her sense of humor. Or was she being serious? You never know with those Uruguayan philosophers.

Dr. Wanda Bytemie was an imposing woman. She cut a very different figure than her colleague, Ola Hyphen-Shalaka. Bytemie was nearly six feet tall and must have weighed at least two hundred pounds. Still, I had an inch or two and (unfortunately) about ten pounds on her if it came to that. She wore a dress with patterns of some sort in red, yellow, and green; but she complemented it with a scarf that was purple and orange.

I'm certainly no slave to fashion, but even I do a better job of matching my colors than that. From what I knew about her, I guessed that she was in her mid to late forties, although like many of the woman I'd met here, she looked older. SNAF-U did have a reputation for treating its senior women rather badly, at least in some cases. Of course, some of them bore significant responsibility themselves for the way they were treated here. Wanda Bytemie's manner as she came into my office let me know that this was not going to be an easy meeting.

"I want you to know, Dean McTavish," she began without invitation, "that I consider this meeting to be an infringement of my academic freedom."

Academics invoke "academic freedom" anytime they think that they're not going to get their way.

"Please sit down, Dr. Bytemie. I'm sorry you think your academic freedom is in jeopardy here, especially since I've done nothing to suggest that you have any reason for concern about that."

"Well, isn't the purpose of this meeting to get me and my husband to change our decisions about Muffy Torkelson-Little's dissertation?"

"No, Dr. Bytemie, the purpose of this meeting is to give me a better understanding of the nature of your criticisms of the dissertation and to see if there is anything I can do to help move the situation along."

"Oh," she said in somewhat lower dudgeon, "then what exactly would you like to know?"

"To begin with, Dr. Bytemie, according to Ms. Torkelson-Little, you judged the appropriateness of the length of her thesis by weighing it. Isn't that a somewhat unorthodox way to make that judgment?"

"That question is an infringement of my academic freedom, Dean McTavish, but I will answer it anyway. I've had years of experience in assessing the quality of doctoral dissertations in my field. That experience has taught me that there is a minimum length and, therefore, a minimum weight that is acceptable if a dissertation has worth, has sufficient scholarly merit, contains the relevant amount of information, references the appropriate sources, analyzes and interprets the references aptly, and is to ultimately be published in book form. Ms. Torkelson-Little's dissertation is a hundred grams underweight."

"Exactly how many pages is a hundred grams, Dr. Bytemie?" I couldn't resist asking that question.

"I'll ignore that attempt at sarcasm, Dean McTavish. Ultimately, Ms. Torkelson-Little's dissertation will sink or swim on its content, but there is no law that says I can't determine whether it's long or good enough by how much it weighs."

"No, there isn't, but this isn't about law, Dr. Bytemie, it's about what is reasonable and proper and what is not. But perhaps we can return to this issue a bit later. Ms. Torkelson-Little also claims that you feel that some sections of her thesis are too easy to understand. Why wouldn't you want her thesis to be intelligible, especially to someone who is not an expert in your field?"

"That question too infringes on my academic freedom, but again, I will attempt to answer it. Assuming Ms. Torkelson-Little ultimately produces a dissertation that is worthy of publication, and I must say that I very much doubt that she will, the most significant measure of the value, the moment, and the impact of that book will be the size of the audience that reads it. Therefore—"

"Exactly my point," I interrupted, "it would seem to me that Ms. Torkelson-Little's attempt to make her dissertation intelligible should accomplish exactly that purpose. Assuming that her dissertation is published, wouldn't you and she want to ensure that her readership is a large as possible?"

"You *miss* the point, Dean McTavish, as I was sure you would. The point is *not* to produce a volume that everyone can understand and interpret. Even you could do that. No. The point is to produce a book that can *only* be understood by the specialist, by the expert, by the initiated, by those who shape the field. The fewer the people who can understand it, the greater will be its impact on the field. My most important work, for example, can only really be appreciated by two people in the field of Uruguayan Languages and Literature—my husband and me—and I'm not sure that he can really understand all of it."

Why did that not surprise me? As you might well imagine, I had pretty much determined by this time that this conversation was extremely unlikely to lead to any resolution of the situation. But as I was into it this far, I thought, *I might as well see it through to some conclusion.*

"Is that one of the books that you feel Ms. Torkelson-Little gave insufficient consideration in her thesis?"

"Yes, as a matter of fact, it is."

"But if only two people in the world can really understand and interpret it, and Muffy Torkelson-Little is not one of those two people, how can she be expected to include material from it in her dissertation since that would clearly require such understanding and interpretation?"

I thought I had her there, but she didn't even blink.

"What we expect her to do, Dean McTavish, is to acknowledge those areas of my work that are relevant to the subject of her dissertation—she can do that whether she understands my work or not—and then to further acknowledge that she is not yet sufficiently well schooled to do more than acknowledge the significance of my contributions. You may be interested in knowing in this regard that my work is cited with some frequency in journals like the Yearbook of International Paradigmatic and Epistemological Studies and the Archives of Research in Gravimetric Hermeneutics. Of course, most of the people who cite it don't understand it either."

"Now let me get all of this straight, Dr. Bytemie. There are only two people in the world who can truly be said to understand your work, yet it is routinely cited in, let me see, YIPES and ARGH, presumably by people who *don't* understand it. What you want Muffy Torkelson-Little to do is to say something like, 'Dr. Bytemie has written extensively on this subject and her, uhhm, contributions are cited frequently, and even though I don't understand what she has written, I know it must be important because she and her husband say it is, so I mention it here.'"

"That's *not* what I said."

"Perhaps it isn't at that, Dr. Bytemie. In any case, although we can or could continue this conversation, I don't have any real sense that it will lead to a meeting of the minds. I'm afraid I have to conclude that there are issues here that bear looking into, and I would be remiss in fulfilling my responsibilities to students not to do so. I have no desire to infringe on your prerogatives as a faculty member, Dr. Bytemie, or on your academic freedom, but I do intend to see that Ms. Torkelson-Little is treated fairly."

"As you wish, Dean McTavish. I agree that we have nothing further to discuss. No, that's not true. There is one thing," she added over her shoulder as she was leaving my office, "I am afraid that Ms. Torkelson-Little may be suicidal. I hope you won't be tempted to award a degree to her posthumously should she be inclined to succumb to those urges. Good day."

Uneffingbelievable!

A couple of days passed during which I thought a lot about but didn't actually do anything about *L'affaire* Torkelson-Little. One afternoon, toward the end of the week, Jarvis came into my office to tell me that Mr. Dr. Bytemie was in the outer office. He knew he didn't have an appointment but wished to see me if I could spare the time. I was between meetings at the time, and even though I had had enough of the Bytemies for a while, I agreed to see him. I was curious to see what the other half of the Mrs. Dr. Bytemie was like.

One look at him told me that they were truly the odd couple. And for more reasons than one, apparently. Willard Bytemie was about six inches shorter and at least fifty pounds lighter than his wife. While Wanda had been rather primly (if anyone who weighs two hundred pounds can ever be thought of as prim) and professionally dressed, Willard was dressed in blue jeans, a sweatshirt, leather jacket, and Adidas.

"Please come in, Dr. Bytemie, make yourself comfortable."

"Thanks for seeing me on such short notice, Dean McTavish, and please call me Will."

"And I'm Ty," I added.

"Let me first apologize for Wanda. She told me about the meeting. I'm afraid she tends to take all of this a bit more seriously than she should."

"Thanks, Will, but no apology is necessary. She's obviously a person who feels strongly about her discipline."

"That she does. We both do for that matter. I just tend to express my commitment to my scholarship in a somewhat less energetic, and to be honest, a less defensive fashion than she does."

And I thought, *Apparently in a less inflammatory fashion as well.*

"I can tell you," I continued, "that I have thought a lot about the Torkelson-Little business over the last few days, but I haven't come to any resolution of it yet. It's a complex situation. On the one hand, there are Ms. Torkelson-Little's legitimate concerns. I would think that both the Drs. Bytemie would have to ultimately agree that weighing dissertations is somewhat unorthodox, at least it's a practice that I'd never heard of before. And while I am aware that some social scientists and humanists, and yes, perhaps even some scientists believe that for a person's scholarship to be distinctive, it must also be obscure. I think that's a philosophy that should be discouraged. And while I'm not even close to being an expert in your field or your wife's, I do have broad interests and would genuinely like to be able to read and understand your work. If it's deliberately intended to be unintelligible to the uninitiated, I can have no hope of doing that and neither can Muffy, someone who is trying to become an expert in the field herself."

"I can't argue with any of that, Dean McTavish, and I hate to interrupt your train of thought here because your arguments are undeniably compelling. I have tried and will continue to try to get Wanda to see that point of view. But I guess your secretary didn't make it clear. I didn't come here to talk about the Torkelson-Little business."

"Oh, you didn't? Then why are you here, Will?"

"I was hoping you might help me get a better parking space."

CHAPTER VIII

A S IF SNAF-U HADN'T already pitched enough curves to me, a new set of surprises began first thing on a Monday morning, about a week into my second semester there.

"Dean McTavish?" Jarvis peeked around the edge of the door to my office. "President Sligh is on the phone for you."

"Put him through, Jarvis."

"Good morning, President Sligh," I said cheerily. It was a bright sunny morning. My first semester at SNAF-U had gone pretty well, all things considered, and I was in an expansive mood. Sligh wasn't.

"Dean McTavish, you'll be getting a phone call soon from the father of one of our students, Mr. Burleigh Bier. He wants to make an appointment to see you. I want you to meet with him as soon as possible. I can't understand how something like this could happen, Ty. You know how hard we're trying to get back onto the NONSENSE list. You know that we were weak in the Quadrennial Baccalaureal Efficiency and the Altruistic Pecuniary Indicators categories. We can't afford to do anything that will further weaken our position in those categories. You should know that, Ty. And besides, we're an educational institution. We're here to build and support, to develop, to teach, and to train. We're *not* in the business of ruining students' lives, Dean McTavish. So please talk to Mr. Bier when he phones. Good-bye."

Now what in hell was that all about? I hardly had time to consider the possible answers to that question before Jarvis appeared in my doorway again.

"Dean McTavish, it's Provost Azkizur on the phone. Can you take the call?"

"Please put him through, Jarvis." Maybe Asskisser could explain why Sligh was so pissed off.

"Good morning, Olan, what's on your mind?" I was determined not to let Sligh's mood affect mine.

"Ty, you'll be getting a phone call soon from the parents of one of our students, young Bucky Bier. His parents want to see you, and I think you should meet with them if it is at all possible. They have a serious concern they want to raise with you, and I think you should listen to what they have to say. If I may say so, Ty, I expected more from you than this. You know how hard we're trying to raise our *NONSENSE* ranking. We work and struggle, and then something like this happens. You need to be much more careful in the future, Ty, and you need to be much more on top of things. We're not out of the woods yet. And what's more, even if we were still on the *NONSENSE* list, that doesn't give us the right to ruin any student's life. We're not in the business of ruining students' lives, Ty."

"Whoa, hold on just a damn minute, Olan! First of all, I'll be happy to meet with the Biers, and I would have been even without phone calls from you and the president. And I certainly agree with you that we're not in the business of ruining students' lives. And for that and lots of other reasons, I think I'm entitled to know what this is all about, especially since both you and the president seem to think I'm responsible. What exactly is going on here?"

"I think you need to hear that from Mr. and Mrs. Bier. Good-bye, Ty."

Damn! What in the…

"Dean McTavish, it's me again." Jarvis. "Vice President Brohwknoz is on the phone for you. Shall I put him through?"

Why not?

"Ty, this is Dick Brohwknoz. I'm sorry to bother you because I don't need to tell you how busy I know you are. I have a favor to ask of you. I've been contacted by the parents of one of our students, Bucky Bier. Fine young man, good student, involved in several campus organizations, doing volunteer work at a local nightclub. I don't need to tell you that we need more students like him. Bucky's parents need to speak with you, Ty, and I hope you'll agree to meet with them. I don't need to tell you that we need to be responsive to the concerns of our students and to the parents of our students. I don't need to tell you. I don't need to tell you that as vice president for Student Affairs, I've always considered that to be one of my highest priorities. In these trying times, what with our omission from the *NONSENSE* list, I don't need to tell you that we have to be especially responsive to the concerns of our students and their parents. Don't you agree, Ty? After all, I don't need to tell you that we're not in the business of ruining students' lives, Ty. Don't you agree?"

"Dick, you're the third person to call about the Bier situation in the last fifteen minutes. I've been called by the president, by the provost, and now by you. Of course, I agree that we're not in the business of ruining students' lives. How could any right-thinking person feel otherwise? My problem is that I haven't the slightest idea what any of this is about. It would really help a lot if you would enlighten me."

"Well… I think you should probably hear that from Mr. and Mrs. Bier, Ty. Thank you for taking my call and agreeing to meet with the Biers and… well, I think I'll let it go at that. I don't need to tell you how busy I know you are. Good-bye, Ty."

Within five minutes of the end of my call from Brohwknoz, Jarvis informed me that Mr. Burleigh Bier had phoned for an appointment. He and his wife were coming to town that very day and hoped to see me first thing the next morning. Since there was a space on my calendar, I instructed Jarvis to pencil them in. I also asked him to get me some background information on Young Bucky. Jarvis brought in Bucky's file, and I learned that he was a junior in SNAF-U College and was majoring in Acoustical Pyrobiology. He was a premed and had performed exceptionally in his coursework up to that point. His grade point average was 3.98 out of a possible 4.0.

Mixed emotions. That's an accurate description of my feelings about the meeting with the Biers. On the one hand, I just had to find out why Sligh, Azkizur, Brohwknoz, and presumably the Biers, including Bucky himself, had concluded that SNAF-U had ruined or at least was ruining Bucky's life. I certainly needed to find out what the hell I had to do with it. At the same time, given my experience with the SNAF-Ugees to that point, I couldn't help but believe that it was bound to be something really odd.

The Biers, Burleigh and Calpurnia, showed up as scheduled first thing the following morning. They came from a large city in the upper Midwest where Burleigh served as a tax consultant. Whatever that is. Burleigh wasn't burly, but he was stockily built, several inches shorter than me. He was probably about fifty, balding, and his girth suggested that he and Calpurnia lived pretty well. She was taller than he but was also on the heavy side. Burleigh's expression was stern as he entered the office. Calpurnia's eyes were red and swollen. She had obviously been crying a lot. I was beginning to wonder just how many SNAF-Ugees believed that crying like a seven-year-old was the best way to get what they wanted.

I escorted them into my office, directed them to the couch, and took a seat in a chair in front of them. Calpurnia took a tissue from her purse, wiped her eyes, and blew her nose rather loudly. I resisted the temptation to offer her a lab wipe. Since I had no idea what this meeting was about, I was completely in the dark as to what approach to take. I decided on the cheerful, solicitous one.

"Well, it's a pleasure to meet you, Mr. and Mrs. Bier. Thank you for coming to see me. I don't have many chances to meet with the parents of our students, but I'm always interested in the perspective parents can provide about what we're doing and how well we're doing it. So I'm glad to have this opportunity to chat with you."

Bad idea.

"You can dispense with the pleasantries, Dean McTavish," Burleigh spat. "This is a serious matter, and neither my wife nor I have time for any small talk. You and your colleagues have put my son's future in serious jeopardy. We put his life and his future in your hands when we sent him to college here. We now find that you have betrayed him, betrayed us, and have very likely ended any chance he had of making something of himself."

"Mr. Bier, I apologize if I offended you. I was simply trying to break the ice. You are obviously aware that the president called me to let me know that you wanted to meet with me. What you may not know is that neither he nor the provost, who also called me, nor the vice president for Student Affairs, who *also* called, gave me even the slightest indication of what this meeting would be about. I am completely in the dark. In a word, I have no idea why you're here."

"Harrumph." Or a word to that effect. "We're here, Dean McTavish, to insist that you undo the harm that has been done to our son, Bucky. As I suspect you know, Bucky is a junior in SNAF-U College, an Acoustical Pyrobiology major and a premed student. Since he was just a baby, our family has had a dream. That dream was shared not only by my wife and me but by her parents, my parents, Bucky's uncles and aunts, by all of our family, and by many of our friends and neighbors. It has been our dream that Bucky would finish college, enter medical school, finish that, and go into practice as an acoustical pyrophysician. We've worked hard, McTavish, all his life, to ensure that he'd be able to fulfill our dream for him. He was a straight-A student in high school, Dean McTavish. We looked carefully at about two hundred colleges and universities before deciding on SNAF-U. We finally decided to send him here because we thought this was a school where he would be given the kinds of grades that would be required to get him into the best medical schools. We thought that he would be taken care of here, that you and your faculty would understand and support his dream and ours, and that you would give him the kind of grades he needed to go to a top medical school. We thought you would give him straight As because that's what it takes. And he was a straight-A student here at SNAF-U too, Dean McTavish, until last semester."

Once again, I resisted a strong temptation. This time, it was the temptation to say that students aren't given grades, they *earn* them. Or at least that's the way it should be. But it was clear that Burleigh wasn't finished.

"Day before yesterday, we got a copy of Bucky's grades for last semester. When we looked at those grades, we were absolutely astounded, Dean McTavish. Astounded! Bucky got As in three of the four courses he took last semester. But in one course, Advanced Ghanaian and Uzbek Theophilology, he didn't get an A, Dean McTavish. He didn't get an A."

Burleigh paused, Calpurnia blew her nose again.

"What was his grade in that course, Mr. Bier?"

"They gave him... *an A-.*" Burleigh shook his head in disbelief, and Calpurnia began sobbing softly.

"His future is almost certainly ruined, Dean McTavish, unless something can be done to change that grade. He'll never get into a reputable medical school with an A- on his record, and neither his mother nor I want him to go to some second-rate state school. Neither does he. So unless you change his grade, you and this university will have to live with the knowledge that you have ruined the life of an outstanding young man and an aspiring acoustical pyrophysician, and you will have dashed the hopes and dreams of an entire community. What we want to know is what you intend to do about this, this travesty. What we want to know, Dean McTavish, is, are you prepared to give us our son's future back?"

Wug! Here I'm thinking that Bucky has started using drugs or gotten some coed pregnant or gotten drunk and trashed a fraternity house or pissed on some faculty member's desk (although that was perhaps still a possibility if the grade wasn't changed) or something like that. In my wildest dreams, I would never have imagined that this distraught couple had come halfway across the country to complain because their son's GPA had dropped from 4.00 to 3.98 and that the grade that caused that drop was in a course that would almost certainly have no bearing at all on his acceptance by a medical school. Of course, it didn't matter a damn what I was or wasn't expecting. It was time, as usual, to react. I took a deep breath.

"First of all, Mr. Bier and Mrs. Bier, let me say that I can easily imagine how important your son's future is to all three of you and to your community. I would be astounded if it were any other way. I know too how much work and sacrifice go into raising a child and preparing him or her to ultimately take on the world on their own."

What in the hell was I trying to say to these people? What in the hell was I going to say next?

"Although I wasn't given any details of this situation by the president, the provost or by Vice President Brohwknoz, I know they assured you that SNAF-U is indeed not in the business of ruining students' lives. Let me add my assurance to theirs. I can't make any promises, Mr. and Mrs. Bier, except that I will look carefully into the situation. I will speak to the instructor in the course, and I will speak to Bucky. To the extent that I am then able, I will inform you of what I learn and what disposition, if any, will be made regarding the situation. I'm afraid that's all I can do, at least at this point."

Burleigh Bier leaned toward me with a look on his face that I can only describe as a combination of contempt and determination.

"We had hoped for more than that, Dean McTavish, a lot more. We *want* a lot more than that. We *demand* a lot more than that! As I said quite clearly, I think what we came here for is to convince you to change his grade. We know you have the power to do that. President Sligh told us that you did. What we want to know is will you do it?"

I considered my response. It had to be one that assured the Biers that I would pursue the matter but, if possible, one that convinced them simultaneously that they should not.

"It is true, Mr. Bier, that I have the power to change a student's grade. But I don't have the power to do so arbitrarily. I have only heard your side of the story. Not only haven't I heard what the instructor in the course in question has to say, but I haven't heard from Bucky either. As I said, I will look further into the matter. And that is all I can and will promise at this point. I can and will make no further commitment no matter how vigorously you may be prepared to press your case."

The Biers exchanged a glance. As if on cue, they stood up, and each of them shook my hand. I must admit I was caught off guard. I certainly didn't expect anything approaching a cordial end to this conversation.

"Well, thank you for seeing us, Dean McTavish. We'll look forward to hearing from you. Oh, one more thing. I don't want to appear heavy-handed, and I certainly don't like to kick a man when he's down, but like most of the rest of the civilized world, we're well aware that SNAF-U was dropped from the *NONSENSE* list of the top twenty-five schools in the country. We didn't raise our son to go to a school that wasn't in the top twenty-five, Dean McTavish. And we certainly don't see how this wanton and malicious attempt to lower our son's GPA to 3.98 will help the university's chance of getting back on that list. In fact, unless something is done about our son's situation, it seems to us that your chances of getting back into the top twenty-five are somewhere between slim and none because we know that there are other students here who have received A- grades as well. So since this situation seems to be an indication of how students are treated here generally, there may not be much chance that SNAF-U will ever crack the top twenty-five again. We trust that you feel the same way. Oh, one more thing. My wife and I subscribed to *NONSENSE* so we have a stake in this beyond what happens to Bucky. Thank you again."

And with that, the Biers were gone. Except for hello, Calpurnia Bier hadn't said a word.

My first move in dealing with the Bier business was to schedule a meeting with Zephram Gangle, professor of Intercontinental Theophilology and instructor of the course in question, Advanced Ghanaian and Uzbek Theophilology. I knew that the principle of academic freedom prohibited me from requesting that he arbitrarily change Bucky's grade, nor would I have made such a request in any case. I simply wanted to learn more about the situation and, in particular, to determine the factors that led to the assignment of the grade in the course. Before meeting with him, I thought it might be smart to give him a call to let him know why. I certainly didn't want to put him in the situation that Sligh et al. had put me in. I was relieved to learn that Gangle would be happy to provide me with information about the situation, so I had Jarvis schedule an appointment. Gangle came to see me the following day.

"Dr. Gangle, thanks for coming in. I think you know why I asked to see you. It's about Bucky Bier, who was a student in one of your courses. This is a tricky situation for me, Dr. Gangle. On the one hand, I want to help the Biers and Bucky, but on the other—and I want to be certain that you understand this—I don't want to do nor do I intend to do anything that infringes on your prerogatives as a faculty member and as the instructor of AGUT. Between you and me, I think the Biers have overreacted, and that's an understatement. But I told them I'd look into the matter, and so I will. What I'd like to hear from you is a little bit about the grading system used in the course and how Bucky's grade was determined."

"Certainly, Dean McTavish, I'm happy to oblige. And let me say that I do appreciate your assurance with regard to my academic freedom. As you know, the course deals with intercontinental theophilological concepts, concentrating specifically on an African country, Ghana, and a Central Asian country, Uzbekistan. Grades in the course are determined based on student performance in five or six different areas. So there are four exams, each worth a hundred points, four quizzes worth twenty-five points each, four take-home assignments worth twenty-five points each, and a term paper worth a hundred points. Oh, and students get fifty points for in-class participation and fifty points just for showing up for 60 percent of the classes. I think that should total eight hundred points. Any student who gets six hundred or more points of the total gets an A in the course. If you get five hundred to five hundred ninety-nine points, you get an A-, four fifty to four hundred ninety-nine, B+, and so on down the line. That's pretty much it."

"Let me make sure I understand. It's possible to get as few as five hundred points out of eight hundred, the equivalent of a, let's see, roughly 60 percent average, and still get an A- in AGUT. Is that correct?"

"Why, yes, Dean McTavish. Do you have a problem with that?"

I ignored the question even though I did have a *serious* problem with it.

"And how many students in the class got grades of A or A- last term, Dr. Gangle?"

"Let's see. I brought my class register along with me just in case." He removed a red notebook from his briefcase. "Hhmmm. There were fifty-seven A's, forty-six A-'s, and... uh, all of the students in the class last term got either an A or an A-. Of course, that was unusual. I usually give at least two or three B+s, and two years ago, I even gave two B's."

At this point, I'm thinking, *Do da term "grade inflation" ring a bell, Kingfish?*

"Okay, Dr. Gangle, let's talk about Bucky Bier's grade specifically. How did he perform in the various course assignments?"

"Well, let me check. Let's see, he got a total of three hundred three on the exams, seventy-seven on the quizzes, fifty-four on the take-home assignments, and sixty-seven on the term paper. He never said anything in class, so he didn't get any points for in-class participation, and according to my records, he missed almost half the classes, so he didn't get those points either. That gave him a total of 501, so he got an A- in the course. You haven't asked me, Dean McTavish, but I don't see any way I could raise that grade to an A. Bucky did come by to see me about his term paper, and I raised his grade from fifty-seven to sixty-seven, but that wasn't nearly enough to bring him up to an A. I brought the term paper along with me in case you wanted to see a sample of his work."

Why not, I thought. *Might as well.*

"Yes, maybe a look at his term paper will give me some additional insight into the situation. Let's have a look."

Gangle passed the paper to me. I leafed through it quickly and noticed that it was literally covered with his comments handwritten in red ink. The title of the paper was "Humor in the Mystical Writings of Idi Amin: A Theophilological (sic) Treatiss (sic) by Buckminister Bier." I read the first paragraph of the paper.

"What is humor? Humor is swett (sic) on the face of the muse. Humor is cheeze (sic) in the mousetrap of life. Humor is the cleft in the clevage (sic) of the bosom of love. Humor is golf-ball sized halestones (sic). And so it is fitting that we consider the humor that appears in the mhystical (sic) writings of one of America (sic), ney (sic) the world's gratest (sic) theophilologians (sic, although maybe this should be the correct spelling of that word)."

Next page.

"And so humor and mhysticism (sic) form an integeral (sic) part of the theology of this unscrutable clerk (sic). And so it should, because those emotions, feelings, thoughts are (sic) whatever it is appropiate (sic) to refer to them, are relevent (sic) components of theophilological (sic, but see above) theory. And when we see in context, the way those elements of theophilology fit aptly together."

And so it went. Fifteen pages of what was probably the worst piece of narrative prose that I have ever read. Sentence after sentence, paragraph after paragraph of incomplete sentences, misspelled words, improper grammar, incredible syntax, and fuzzy, I mean really fuzzy, thinking. Muffy Torkelson-Little's thesis was most assuredly obscure. But it was written in proper English. Bucky's paper was obscure *and* illiterate. And with all of that, he had gotten a final grade of 67 on that paper and a grade of A- in AGUT. But was there anything that I could do about it? Probably not. If I couldn't raise Bucky's grade—which possibility never ever entered my mind—I couldn't lower it either. Especially since Bucky's performance was presumably not any different from that of half the students in AGUT—the half that got A-'s. So as had been the case in far too many of my encounters with various SNAF-Ugees, there seemed nothing left to do but to bid farewell to Dr. Zephram Gangle.

"Is there anything else you think I should know about the course or about Bucky's performance in it, Dr. Gangle?"

"No, I don't think so," Gangle replied, scratching head. "I think that about covers it. Is there any additional information you need from me?"

I avoided the temptation to ask how he managed to keep his job here. Although my guess was that with the exception of the Biers, his students and their parents probably loved him. They had to love the way he assigned grades in his course.

"No. Thanks for coming in, Dr. Gangle." Et cetera. Et cetera.

The ball was clearly in my court at this point, and fortunately, my course was clear. There was no way I was going to suggest that Bucky's grade in AGUT be changed. I would simply have to take the heat that would undoubtedly redound to that decision, and I was fully prepared to do so. I called Sligh to inform him of my decision. He didn't try to dissuade me but concluded the conversation by offering that he hoped I'd be able to live with myself, especially if SNAF-U didn't make the *NONSENSE* top twenty-five the following year. The Biers were big donors, you know. I didn't bother to say anything to Azkizur or Brohwknoz since I was pretty sure that Sligh would raise the issue at the next executive staff meeting, one which I hadn't been invited to attend. I learned later, from Leo Da Vinci, of all people, that I was right. Sligh did raise the matter there and charged Azkizur with setting up a committee to review the grading systems used by faculty in all of the SNAF-U schools. For whatever reason, though, he never did so.

I then called the Biers. I dreaded doing so but clearly had to. I informed Burleigh of my decision and explained my reasons for it as thoroughly as I could. He would have none of it. He offered as how this was typical of the assholes who run American universities and American government, called me a name that was considerably stronger than asshole, but stopped just short of qualifying as a racial slur, and slammed down the phone. All of that was pretty much what I expected, and I assumed that the matter was now closed. I was wrong.

About a week after my conversations with Sligh and Bier, Jarvis came into my office to inform me that there was a commotion of some sort on the lawn of the quadrangle in front of the building. It was a demonstration of some kind. I could hear chanting in the background but had no idea what was going on. I went to the front of the building and saw then that there were about a dozen students manning a picket line, marching in front of the building. They carried signs that said "Free Bier!" and were chanting that slogan and another which sounded like "Saps support Bier." I later discovered that Saps was really SAPS, the Society of Associated Premedical Students. They had organized to support the changing of Bucky Bier's grade in AGUT and had decided to bring their protest to the front of my building. Off to the side, not marching with the rest of the group but carrying a "Free Bier" sign and with a baseball cap pulled down over his eyes, was Richard Brohwknoz. If I hadn't already been convinced about how to respond to this situation, his presence there certainly convinced me. I decided to ignore them.

And I was reasonably successful in doing so until later than afternoon. I had pretty much managed to relegate the chants of the protestors to the category of background noise when quite suddenly, the noise level increased significantly. And the nature of chants changed as well. "Free Bier" and "SAPS Support Bier" were still there, but now there was something different in the mix. I went to the front of the building once again. Now in addition to the dozen or so SAPS, there were about twenty additional protestors apparently involved in a counterdemonstration since many of them were carrying signs reading "SAPS SUCK!" What was this all about?

Well, I learned again later that day that the counterprotestors were members of a campus fraternity, NuNuNu. They had heard the "Free Bier" chants earlier in the day, had thought that what they were actually chanting was "Free *Beer*," and had come over to the quadrangle to get some of the same, only to be sorely disappointed. They decided not to let this deception go unpunished, thus the counterdemonstration. I'm not a fan of Greek organizations, but the members of NuNuNu certainly endeared themselves to me that afternoon.

There was only one thing left to do to bring this matter to closure and that was to talk to Bucky Bier himself. I had Jarvis make the necessary appointment.

Bucky didn't look much like his mother or his father. Maybe that's why his mother had been crying. He was tall and very thin, but that may have been, in part at least, the result of his distress over his terrible grade in AGUT. Although my building and all the buildings on campus were nonsmoking facilities, Bucky was smoking a cigarette when I went to the outer office to collect him. Jarvis told me later that Bucky looked so pitiful when he came into the office that he just didn't have the heart to make him put the cigarette out. I did. He stubbed the cigarette out, came into my office, and sat down. I launched into my routine.

"Bucky, let me say first that I understand your distress. We all want to do well in everything we do, and I know you had hoped to get an A in AGUT. But A- is not a bad grade."

I was tempted to say that based on what I had read from his paper, it was a grade that he was damned lucky to have gotten.

"But I've spoken with Dr. Gangle, and I'm convinced that the grade you received in the class was an appropriate one under the circumstances. I know that's not what you wanted to hear, but that's the way it is."

"Well, if that's what you've decided, I guess there's nothing I can do," he said with some resignation in his voice. "I never thought there was any chance that you'd give me a better grade, even though my folks did. But I want you to know, Dean McTavish, that because of this, my life is ruined! My life is crap! I'll never get into a respectable medical school with an A- on my record. Once again, the power structure has squashed the little man into crap."

"Bucky," I responded, "I'm not at all sure that your fears about getting into medical school are justified. If you continue to do well in your classes here, I would think you would have a very good chance of getting into just about any medical school in the country. A GPA of 3.98

is a darned good GPA. And I'm sure you know that grades aren't the only factor that medical schools take into consideration."

"That just shows that you don't know how it works," he said, scowling. "With an A- on my transcript, I could only get into some state school or some school in the Bahamas or Guatemala or England or someplace like that. I could never get into a really good school with my grades. And it's all because of that bastard Gangle. He could have given me an A if he wanted to. He didn't like me. I know that was it. I had a hard enough time getting an A in his other course."

Beginning Ghanaian and Uzbek Theophilology.

"Recriminations against Dr. Gangle will do no good, Bucky. What's done is done. You will simply have to make the best of it."

"You could change the grade if you wanted to."

"Perhaps I could, Bucky. But within the context of Dr. Gangle's grading system, you got the grade you deserved in AGUT."

In fact, you got a grade way, way better than you deserved.

Bucky pulled a cigarette from a pack in his shirt pocket. I advised him sternly that he couldn't smoke in my office. To my considerable surprise, he then crumpled the cigarette up, put it in his mouth, chewed it, and swallowed it.

"Well, what am I supposed to do now?" he asked, wiping a shred of tobacco from his mouth.

I suppressed a grimace and answered, "I've already given you my suggestion, Bucky. You should continue your studies, do your best, and retain your aspirations to go to medical school. Despite what you may now believe, Bucky, getting an A- is not the end of the world. For one thing, no matter what grade you got, you'll always have the knowledge you gained from your work in the course."

What in hell was I thinking? Why did I say that?

"Knowledge?" he screamed. "Who cares about knowledge? I didn't come here to learn anything! I came here to get good grades so that I could get into medical school, be a practicing acoustical pyrophysician, make a lot of money, and buy a Jaguar or a Ferrari or a BMW. Well, no, maybe not a BMW. I got a BMW for my sixteenth birthday. Now I'll never be able to do any of those things. My life is crap! And it's all your fault. You could change my grade if you wanted to. You know that SNAF-U will never ever get back into the *NONSENSE* top twenty-five if you keep treating students the way I've been treated."

"I'm sorry you feel that way, Bucky. As I've said, I've given you my best advice. What happens from here on is up to you and your parents."

And I could have added but didn't, there is nothing more that I have to say or that I intend to do about this matter, whether or not we ever got back into the top twenty-five. Bucky must have sensed my resolve because he got up and walked toward the door, avoiding, perhaps by design, the customary parting handshake. He did have a parting request of me, though.

"Well, if you won't change my grade, there is one thing you could do for me. Would you give me a couple of bucks. I need to buy some condoms. No, make it five bucks. I'd like to get something to eat too."

CHAPTER IX

A COUPLE OF WEEKS after the meeting with Bucky, I got a memo from the president's office, requesting my presence at the next meeting of the executive staff. As I mentioned, I hadn't been invited to the previous one for some reason, and I concluded that probably because of the Bier situation, I was in the president's doghouse. I was favored with an invitation this time. So here I was again, meeting with that august body. I arrived just before eight thirty, as I had in the past, and took the first seat I got to. Charity scowled at me but said nothing.

"Good morning everyone," President Sligh said, smiling broadly as he entered the room. "I'm delighted to see you all here."

What, no cheer?

"This morning, as has frequently been the case in the past, especially during this academic year, we will have a couple of guests meeting with us. One of them you know well, Dean Ty McTavish. Welcome back, Ty."

"Thanks, President Sligh."

Hmmmh. Maybe I hadn't been in the doghouse after all.

"We have a full agenda today, folks, so let's get busy. Olan, will you pass out the copies of today's agenda please? As you all know, although we were eminently successful in addressing our deficiencies in a number of the *NONSENSE* categories in an earlier meeting, we didn't have time to consider all of the categories. We will address at least some of the remaining categories in this meeting. The first of those categories is... what's it called, Hermione?"

"Vehicular Placement Initiative, Mr. President."

Vehicular Placement Initiative? Why don't they just say parking, and what the hell does that have to do with how good a school is anyway? Once again, though, I kept my mouth shut.

"Ah, yes. Well, I'm pleased to announce that we've already developed a plan to deal with that criterion."

And Sligh looked toward the vice president for Internal Affairs, Anthony Atherton-Sparks. Another hyphenated last name. At least he was born with his. Sparks was apparently in his early thirties, and he looked much younger than that. He was at least a couple of inches taller than me, which made him far and away the tallest administrator at SNAF-U. Not that that mattered, of course, but except for Atherton-Sparks and me, SNAF-U administrators were mostly short guys. I suspect that he was considered quite handsome by most of the female SNAF-Ugees. His tailored suits and the British accent certainly added to his image. Even I had to admit that he had a certain flare. He had been at SNAF-U for about three years from what I understood. And from what I had heard, Sparks was a particular favorite of President Sligh. Everyone I'd spoken to about the executive staff referred to the VPIA as Anthony or Anthony Atherton-Sparks or Tony Atherton-Sparks or Tony or Atherton-Sparks or some similarly appropriate moniker. President Sligh called him Sparky.

"What have you got for us, Sparky?"

"Thank you, Mr. President," he said. Sparky was a true Brit, very proper, very precise, and very verbose. Although he had been born in England, he may have been of Scandinavian extraction as he was fair skinned and blond. He was dressed in a gray double-breasted suit, tailored of course, probably in England, and he appeared to be quite fit. He apparently took care of himself. He cleared his throat and began his presentation.

"You are all very keenly aware that we have been given an extremely challenging problem to solve because of our exclusion from the *NONSENSE* list of the top twenty-five American universities. We have marshaled the resources of several campus offices, including my own, of course, to attempt to bring some closure to our struggles with this issue. The critical element of the matter was to develop a creative, innovative, and original strategy to deal with the *NONSENSE* Vehicular Placement Initiative criterion. To do this, we had to develop an original plan to assign parking stickers to faculty, students, and staff. As you know, Parking Operations issued fifteen thousand stickers this fall to members of those three groups. Unfortunately, as we are all too painfully aware, we have fewer than four thousand parking spaces on campus. If one subtracts from this total number, those spaces that are reserved for administrators, alumni, emeritus faculty, visiting dignitaries, potential donors, contractors, and friends and relatives of President Sligh and Mr. Dukes, this leaves fewer than eight hundred available spaces for the remaining members of the SNAF-U family. And of course, we have far more faculty, staff, and students than that number.

In order to convert our present situation into a more workable one and to develop a system that will impress the *NONSENSE* evaluators, we will have to stagger the allocation and the usage of available spaces. This will create some controversy, of course, since most of us already have decals for the parking decks, but there are bound to be some chunks in the yogurt in a situation like this."

Sparky *was* British, so I should not have been surprised to see examples of British pronunciation (referred to, as I understand it, as real pronunciation by the Brits themselves) and metaphor in his speech.

He pronounced the word "controversy," *con-TROV-ersy* and "yogurt," *YAH-gurt.*

"What my staff and I are proposing is the *scheduling* (again, the British pronunciation) and allocation of spaces based on surnames, month of birth, length of service to the university, and distance of the person's primary place of residence from the campus. This is how the system will work. Persons whose surname starts with the letters *Aa* through *Hd* and who were born in a month with no Rs in it and who have been working here for at least five years and live at least ten miles away can park in deck A2 on Mondays and Wednesdays, from 8 AM until 4 PM. If one's surname starts with the letters *He* through *Rf* and his or her birthday is in a month that ends in *y,* and he or she has been on the job for less than five years, and he or she lives at least fifteen miles from campus, he or she can park in deck A2 on Tuesdays and Thursdays, from nine to three and all day on Sunday. If the surname starts with the letters *Rg* through *Z,* and he or she was born in a month that has no more than four letters in it, and he or she has been working here less than a year and lives more than five but less than ten miles from campus, those persons can park in either deck A1 or deck A2 all day on Saturday and on Fridays, from midday until tea time. The same *schedule* will apply to students except that they will park in deck A3 or in lot B1. Part-time faculty and staff will also follow that schedule, but they will park in lots B2 or B3.

"Finally, individuals who don't fall into any of the foregoing categories can park in A1 or A2 or on the street any day from 9 PM until midnight unless they drive lorries rather than automobiles. Lorries will not be permitted in either parking deck at any time except for national holidays and February 29. I have summarized all this and the other information relevant to the plan in writing. Clarabel, would you pass out those summaries please? We feel confident that this *schedule* will have numerous benefits, and that it will, in particular, decrease the waiting time in the queues that form outside decks A1 and A2 each morning, from five to no more than three hours, perhaps considerably less."

"Excuse me, Tony, before you go on. I don't want to seem stupid, but can you tell me what a 'lorry' is?

"That's not a stupid question at all, Charity," Sparks replied cheerily. "In fact, I'm rather glad you asked it, because we define 'lorry' in a particular way in the context of our plan. For our purpose, the term 'lorry' refers to pickup trucks, sport utility vehicles, semitractor trailers, recreational vehicles, motorcycles and scooters, go-karts, skateboards, rollerblades, and motorized wheelchairs."

"If you will indulge me for just a moment longer, I would like to make a few additional comments about this plan. Clarabel and the other people in my office have worked very diligently to develop it. We considered many other possibilities, and they just didn't work. We all want to see a system that will do the job, so if compelled to do so, we'll start again. But I don't think we're likely to come up with a better plan than this one. And I do think that *NONSENSE* will be impressed. I've checked the sticker allocation plans at a number of this year's top twenty-five schools, and at the risk of appearing somewhat immodest, I must say that compared to ours, theirs are absolutely Byzantine."

"Thanks a lot, Sparky." Sligh was beaming. "I think we should give Sparky and his staff a round of applause for this marvelous plan. It's going to make all of our lives a whole lot easier, and I think it's guaranteed to boast our rating in the Vehicular Placement Initiative category." And those around the table began smiling broadly and applauded.

"Are there any questions?"

No one spoke, but the grins continued. Azkizur started to say something but apparently thought better (or worse) of it. Sligh looked around the table. No one said a word. Finally, Sparky himself began to smile.

I shouldn't have been surprised to find parking high on the list of

SNAF-U's problems. I suspect that it has plagued universities, their administrators, faculty, and staff since time immemorial. I'll bet that Socrates had trouble parking his chariot when he showed up at Athens U each day to teach Philosophy 101. And I'll bet he never even came to campus on gladiator weekends. Who knows? Maybe the real reason he had to take poison was because he parked in the president's space one too many times. But even so, Sparky's plan wasn't worth the recycled paper it was copied on. Nevertheless, I was pretty sure that *NONSENSE* would love it. Still, for some reason, I felt compelled to go… where angels fear to tread.

"President Sligh," I ventured, "I have a couple of questions if you don't mind."

"Uh, sure, go ahead, Dean McTavish." He gave me the go-ahead, but it was clear from the tone of his voice that he didn't approve.

"Vice President Atherton-Sparks (I refused to call him Sparky), I'm tempted to ask whether there are any people at SNAF-U whose names begin with the letters *Hf, Rf* or *Rg,* but I'll let that one pass. I guess my major question is how many people will be accommodated by your plan? How many people will actually be able to park on campus if we follow your recommendations?"

"Well, Dean, as I think should be clear from the details of my plan, the precise answer to your question depends on the day of the week, the time of day, the month, the phases of the moon, and so on, but we estimate that on the average, we can accommodate about 850 people a day. Some days a few more, some days a few less."

"And there are about eight hundred free spaces available under the existing system, is that correct?"

"Yes, Dean McTavish, that is correct."

"So if I understand it correctly, this plan will make maybe fifty more parking spaces available university-wide. Right?"

"Again, your analysis is correct, and I might add that we consider this number to represent a tremendous accomplishment and a distinct improvement over the current situation."

"Well, I certainly appreciate that parking is a significant problem on this campus," I said in what I hoped was a sympathetic tone. "I've already been visited by a faculty member who wanted some assistance from me with his parking problem. I may be in the minority here, and I apologize for saying this, but it doesn't seem to me that this plan is going to provide us with any significant relief. It seems to me that the only way to deal with the parking situation on this campus in any substantive fashion is to build more parking facilities and to come up with a plan for allocating parking spaces that not only addresses the *NONSENSE* criterion but also addresses our parking needs."

An audible and collective gasp went up from the executive staffers.

"All I can say, Dean McTavish," Atherton-Sparks offered, "is that no other plan that we considered gave us more than ten or twenty more spaces. For what it may be worth, it is my understanding that the unofficial *NONSENSE* cutoff is twenty-five for an acceptable Vehicular Placement Initiative."

"Thank you, Sparky. If there are no other questions," Sligh said, completely ignoring my input, "let's move on to the next item of business on the agenda."

"One more thing, President Sligh, if you don't mind." Sparky smiled as he fired his parting shot. "If any of you would care to discuss this plan further, please feel free to knock me up to chat about it."

"We do have one or two more *NONSENSE* criteria to deal with," Sligh said, "but there are a couple of matters that require more immediate attention. The first of those is the planning for the trustees' annual banquet and dance. Ima, would you bring us up to date please?"

The president looked toward Imajean Plodter, the vice president for External Affairs. Ima Plodter was SNAF-U through and through. Her mother had been the first SNAF-U coed many years before. Her father, who had also been a SNAF-U undergraduate, although he had done his doctoral work elsewhere, served as dean of students for some twenty-five years and was still referred to by alumni and others as Daddy Plodter. It was no surprise then to learn that Ima had done her undergraduate and doctoral work at SNAF-U, and after teaching in the History Department for a couple of years, had become associate VP for External Affairs. When her boss moved on to greener pastures, Ima was the natural choice for the job, and she got it. I didn't know exactly how old she was, but I knew she was approaching retirement. For some reason, Ima decided to stand to make her presentation, and it took her a few seconds to get to her feet. That's because Ima was at least as round as she was tall.

"Thanks, Bob," she said, smiling.

Her history at SNAF-U obviously put her on a first-name basis with the president.

"There are several issues we need to discuss regarding next week's banquet and dance. First of all, I've arranged for two dance bands so that we'll have a variety of dance music for that portion of the festivities. One of them is Geriatric Soul, the same band we had last year, or was it the year before? Anyway, we've had these guys play for us before, and you may recall that they are a particular favorite of Mrs. Halitosi. As one of our largest donors, I think it's appropriate to consider her preferences in this situation, especially considering our needs in the Altruistic Pecuniary Indicators *NONSENSE* category. We certainly can't afford to alienate one of our strongest supporters and largest donors. The second band is a group called Bellybutton Lint, recommended by my daughter. She assures me that they have some talent, that the younger members of our assembly are likely to enjoy their music a bit more than that of the old guys, and that they won't do anything to embarrass themselves or the university. So I'm prepared to give them a try."

There was some murmuring around the table, but no one raised any objection to Ima's plan.

"The second issue we need to discuss is the seating arrangement. I'm —"

"Excuse me for interrupting, Ima." It was Olan Azkizur. "But do we have a speaker for the banquet?"

"No, we don't, Olan," Ima replied curtly. "Bob made it clear to me that taking care of the band and the seating arrangement should be at the top of my list of priorities. We do, after all, still have three days to find a speaker."

Olan appeared appropriately chastened.

"Now where was I?" Ima began again. "Oh, yes, the seating arrangement. As in previous years, we will put each VP and his or her spouse and each associate VP with spouse and each dean and spouse at a separate table. President Sligh, Barnabus Chuttlewood, the chair of our board of trustees, the banquet speaker ,and Buster Dukes will sit on the platform. Here's a seating chart for each of you so you'll know where you'll be placed. Dean McTavish," she turned toward me, "it's a happy coincidence that you're here this morning because it gives you a chance to see what we've done with you. We've put you at the table with Kofi Bofi, the head of the SNAF-U Black Alumni Association, and several other prominent guests—the president of the local chapter of the NAACP, the president of the local Urban League chapter, the head of the city Croatian-American League, and the head of the National Costa Rican Scholarship Association, who it just so happens, will be visiting with us on the day of the banquet. I hope this meets with your approval."

It didn't.

"Oh, by the way," Ima added. "Charity Butler will be seated at your table too."

Aha! She's put all the token minorities at the same table, with a token white person so that the token minorities won't appear to be token minorities. I was inclined to complain, but based on what I'd seen so far,

I had no reason to believe it would do the slightest bit of good. Charity Butler presumably thought it would.

"But," Charity sputtered, "I don't want to be at the table with all those—"

"All those what?" Sligh said slowly as he peered disapprovingly over his glasses at Charity.

"Those… others."

"But you will sit at that table, and you will enjoy the evening, won't you, Charity?"

"Yes, sir. Of course, sir." Charity got the message.

"Are there any questions?" Ima asked, flashing a self-satisfied grin. "If not, I'll turn things back over to you Bob."

Sligh was smiling broadly once again. "Ima, you've outdone yourself once again, don't you all agree? Let's give Ima a round of applause."

And of course, a round of polite applause dutifully followed. Fortunately, no one seemed to notice or to care that I was not among the participants.

"What's the next item of business?" Sligh pushed his glasses up his nose. "Ah, yes, Dick, I think you have something for us."

The reference was to Richard Brohwknoz, the VP for Student Affairs. You already know of his participation in the Free Bier rally. From what I had gathered in my roughly six months at SNAF-U, those few SNAF-Ugees who had anything at all to say about him seemed to think he was doing an adequate job. But when asked for evidence to support that conclusion, the response was usually, "We haven't had any major problems with the students since he's been here." That was true, from what I was able to learn, but the primary reason seemed to be that Brohwknoz always sided with the majority of the student population no matter what the issue. A student vote recommended renaming the Student Union, the Romeo and Juliet Memorial Banana Bakery and Boogie-teria. Brohwknoz sided with the students. Fortunately, those with the authority to change the name did not. Another vote recommended paving over the central campus quadrangle so that students could skateboard and Rollerblade to and from classes. Brohwknoz supported that vote too. On the other hand, about a year ago, a small group of students staged a protest outside the administration building, a peaceful and relatively quiet one, to call attention to the fact that about a dozen students had recently developed food poisoning after eating at one of the snack bars in the Student Union. Brohwknoz was responsible for the union and its food services. He accompanied the university police when they arrived to break up the demonstration.

"Thanks, President Sligh. I do have an issue to raise with the group. You all know that the sexual behavior of our students is a matter that I am very concerned about. I don't need to tell you that one important consequence, for many of our students at least, of them being on their own in college is that they become sexually active, or in many cases, I'm afraid, more sexually active. Now I don't need to tell you that I think we have a responsibility to try to see that the consequences of this sexual activity are as benign as possible. We can't be in the dorms every minute of the day, no loco parents as they say. And even if we could, we would still have no control over student behavior when they're not in the dorms. We try to counsel and advise them to watch out and to be responsible, but that sort of approach can only go so far. I don't need to tell you that we tried to institute a compulsory class on human sexuality a few years ago, but it didn't work out. I don't need to tell you that I still have scars from that fight. So we do the best we can.

"One of the things we have been able to do is to distribute condoms to the students. I don't need to tell you that that wasn't an easy battle either. I still have scars from that fight. But we finally did succeed in having condom dispensers installed in many of the men's lavatories around the campus. I don't need to tell you that there was a campus referendum on this issue a few days ago or how it came out. I'm here to ask your permission to implement the recommendation from that referendum. I hope you all will approve the installation of condom dispensers in the women's lavatories."

Sligh jumped in immediately as soon as Brohwknoz closed his mouth. "All in favor, please say aye." Four people raised their hands, the rest said something, but it wasn't clear whether it was aye, nay, or something completely different.

"Thank you, all," Sligh said, the broad smile reappearing yet again. "And thank you, Dick. I'm sure I speak for us all when I say that we really appreciate the job you're doing. These are difficult times, no doubt about it."

"Well, thank you, Mr. President." Smiles all around. "I don't need to tell you that I'm doing my best but 'taint always easy."

"Well, thanks again, Dick."

"Thank you, President Sligh."

"You're welcome, Dick. Thank you.

"You're welcome, President Sligh. Thank you."

"You're welcome, Dick. Colleagues, let's move on. We have a couple of additional items of business to consider before we end this meeting. Let's return to the *NONSENSE* issues. There is at least one more category that I'd like for us to address today. That's Innovative Curricular Initiatives."

At last, I thought, *a NONSENSE category with a name that actually means something.*

"To help us get a handle on this one, I've invited another guest to join us. Olan, would you see if she's outside and invite her in if she's out there?"

Azkizur left the room and returned with the dean of the School of Social Work, Miranda Turquette. Miranda, I later learned, had done her undergraduate work in English at a Midwestern HUT. She got a master's degree in Feminist Theory from the same institution and a

PhD in Social Work from a university in Denmark. She had been dean of the School of Social Work for about eight years. During that time, according to what I had heard, most of the competent faculty in the school had either taken positions at other universities or had opted for early retirement. Nevertheless, the school had recently risen in rank from number 68 in one national survey of the country's top schools of social work to number 67.

"Come in, Miranda." Sligh rose and walked over to meet her, extending his hand. He ushered her to the seat next to him. "I think you know everyone here. Thank you for coming to visit with us this morning."

Miranda was wearing black pants and a red sleeveless sweater. As she shook hands with the president, I could see that, unlike many women, she didn't shave her armpits. On the contrary, the hair under her arms appeared to be tinted blue! I kid you not.

"Oh no, President Sligh, thank *you*," she gushed. "I just can't tell you how pleased and honored and flattered I am that you would allow me to share my ideas with you and your executive staff. It just confirms my feelings that SNAF-U is truly an exceptional university and you, President Sligh, are an exceptional president, and Provost Azkizur is an exceptional provost, and... well, all of you are just exceptional! You know there are so many universities in this country that seem to care only about education. They don't seem to be interested in empowering their students, their faculty, their staff, their alumni, their communities so that they will be able to overcome the truly degrading and demanizing and dewomanizing effects of disenfranchiseness. But that's not the case at SNAF-U. You, President Sligh, and you, Provost Azkizur, and you, Vice President Brohwknoz, and well, all of you are symbols that this university has been able to marriage education and enfranchiseness in ways that add empowerfulness to us all. SNAF-U is about more than knowledge and scholarship and teaching and learning. It's also about humanity, manity and womanity, and about humanness, manness, and womanness. We've been able to liaison all these various components of the educational adventure so that the rights of the individual are blended together in celebration with the interests of the displaced and disrespected, and we've been able to collectivize those interests to make SNAF-U the kind of place it is. I can't tell you how happy I am to make even the smallest contribution to getting us back on the *NONSENSE* list of top twenty-five institutionalities. I just want to say that I think I'm the most fortunate person in the world to be a part of all of this."

Miranda Turquette's eyes were actually starting to puddle. There was a moment of silence. Then Sligh smiled, and everyone around the table (again, save one) started to applaud. Miranda nodded her head to acknowledge her applause.

"Miranda," Sligh offered, "I think I can say that your inspiring words have touched us all. We are fortunate to have a person like you on our team. I've had a chance to review the curricular initiative you're proposing, and I'd like you to present it to the rest of the group now. I'm sure they'll be as pleased and impressed as I was."

"Well, President Sligh," Miranda continued, wiping her eyes with a curled forefinger, "as you know, I have an idea I have for a joint degree program, a joint program to be offered jointly by the School of Social Work and jointly with the School of Architecture. I think that it's the kind of thing that *NONSENSE* is looking for in this epoch of interdisciplinaritiness and multiculturalment. The program will offer bachelor's and PhD degrees in Psycho-Architectural Social Practice. I do hope that some of you had a chance to read my recent article in the *Record and Gazette*. It insights you into my thinking about this program."

The article in question had appeared a few days earlier in one of the campus publications, the *SNAF-U Record and Gazette*, also known as the *SNAF-U RAG*. The title of the article was "Buildings That Heal." I hadn't read it myself. I assumed, apparently incorrectly, that it was about pyramid power or some similar phenomena. As it would turn out, my assumptions may not have been so very far from the truth.

"The theme of the program," Miranda continued, "in keeping with the title of my article, will be 'Spaces That Heal.' What the program will be designed to do is to connect the relationship between physical spaces and psychological and social well-being. We want to empower and liberate our students to use nontraditional methodologies to accomplish their objectives as social workers, to bring healing to broken, disempowered, disenfranchised human beings, and to pair physical space, soul, spirit, and body in ways that are liberating and affirming and that creativize our intellects. We don't have all the details in place yet, but we have begun to objectivize our plan and to think seriously about the kinds of courses that the program will offer.

"We've divided the curriculum into four broad categories. The first of those categories will literally be titled Healing Spaces. We're thinking about offering courses such as Auditoriums That Heal, Classrooms That Heal, Lavatories That Heal, and Closets That Heal. Won't that be wonderful? The second category will be called Healing Aspects of Architectural Design, and we plan to offer courses that will help students to design spaces that will have a healing impact on the spirit, mind, body, and soul. For example, we're thinking about offering a course called Walls, Floors, and Ceilings, the Vertical and Horizontal Dimensions of Architectural Healing. We're also thinking about courses that will explore the dimensionality of architectural healing and will delve into such philosophical questions as 'Can architectural healing occur in open spaces, or to put it another way, does architectural healing require architecture?' This question, as I suspect you know, is of special importance to the architectural community, because if the answer is yes, well... I don't know what the architects or the social workers for that matter will do. But we owe to our students, our parents, and to the children that will be born in the future, and of course, to the spirit of intellectual humanitarianism, to explore questions like this. Advancing the development of psychosocial healing requires that we do. To do otherwise runs the risk of disremembering the lessons we've learned and misappyling those lessons to the human condition. Don't you agree?"

Everyone nodded in agreement. Yes, even I nodded. I had no idea what I was doing.

"The third course category will be called International Aspects of Architectural Healing, and we're thinking about courses like Western European Monuments That Heal, Eastern European Monuments That Don't Heal, Do Cathedrals Have Special Healing Powers? Does Architectural Healing Occur in Foreign Languages? and courses like that. Finally, the fourth course category will be called the Relationship between the Healing Dimensions of Social Work and Architectural Healing. We don't have any specific courses in mind for this category yet.

"I should say that we're still in the planning stages so this is just a rough outline of what our curriculum will look like. But we're oh so excited about it all! We think it's exactly the kind of program we need to meet the needs of the next generation of students and the next and succeeding generations of disempowered, disenfranchised, disaffirmed, discelebrated, dishumanized, and disprepared citizens of this country and the world. You know, we do have a responsibility to those who exist outside our borders, and we think this new joint program will help us to meet that responsibility. It will provide a very unique opportunity for students to apprenticeship with healers, builders, designers, philosophizers, and psychics and physics."

I should mention that Dean Turquette stood up when Sligh asked her to begin her presentation to the group. She stopped speaking and sat down again. There was what I can only refer to as a stunned silence. I was certainly stunned. Then, you guessed it, everyone began to applaud.

And believe it or not, before I fully realized what I was doing, I had started to clap too. Not a single word she said made any sense, but her suggestion was so downright bizarre that I must have felt that she deserved applause just for having the guts to present it. Sligh rose from his seat, extended his hands, took one of her hands in both of his, and began to shake it briskly.

"Miranda ," he said, "I said it a few minutes ago, and I'll say it again, SNAF-U is fortunate to have you here. What a wonderful idea, don't you all agree? It's programs like this one that will really put us on the map. Keep up the good work! Does anyone have any questions to Dean Turquette before we let her go?"

I know, I know. I should have kept my mouth shut here. On the one hand, I knew my question would be ignored, so there was no reason to ask it. But on the other hand, since I *knew* my question would be ignored, there was no reason *not* to ask it. So I did, as diplomatically as I could.

"Dean Turquette, you've certainly given us some things to think about, but I do have one question. If I understood you correctly (I was sure I had, of course), the programs you're proposing will be offered jointly by the School of Social Work and the School of Architecture, is that correct?"

"Yes, it is, Dean McTavish." She smiled.

"Please correct me if I'm wrong, but isn't it true that SNAF-U doesn't *have* a School of Architecture?"

Miranda Turquette left the room, not at all crestfallen because of my question.

"I believe that brings us to the final item of business on the agenda. Ollie, I think you have something for us?

"Yes, I do, President Sligh."

Oliver Wendell Broadnax III was SNAF-U's vice president for Legal Affairs, and again, from what I had heard in my short time at SNAF-U, one of the main reasons the university remained afloat. He came from a long line of lawyers as his name so obviously testified and had followed his father as chief legal counsel and VP for Legal Affairs at SNAF-U. A SNAF-U undergraduate, he had gotten his law degree from a PNEU.

"It concerns one of our faculty members, Ola Ebola-Shalaka, former director of the Department of African-American Studies. As you know, she has filed suit against the university, claiming she was unfairly and illegally stripped of her directorship. My office is handling the affair, of course, but there will certainly be some public relations fallout related to this case. That fallout might affect our *NONSENSE* standing, and I thought it might be appropriate for us to discuss that here. As she is a faculty member in the Literary College and is, therefore, well known to Dean McTavish, he might have some useful input on this matter. In particular, I'd like the thoughts of this group on—"

"Excuse me, Ollie," Sligh interrupted. "You did say that your office is handling this situation, didn't you?"

"Yes, I did, President Sligh, but this is an extremely important matter. It involves a faculty member, and it must be handled delicately. So I thought it would be a good idea—"

"Ollie, if your office is handling it, I don't see that there is anything of significance for us to discuss here. If there's nothing further, the meeting is adjourned."

One thing was for damned sure. The *S* in SNAF-U clearly did not stand for *substance*.

When I got back to my office I sat there for a while, trying to digest what I'd just seen and heard, and my mind was drawn once again to a curious feature of the composition of the executive staff. Miranda Turquette had been an invited guest at today's meeting. Although I had attended several exec staff meetings, I too was always a guest. The members were only senior executive SNAF-U staff, the president, the vice presidents, and their associate VPs, with one striking exception—Buster

Dukes, actually, Abercrombie Palomino Dukes. His parents must have been hoping for a horse. Buster was director of Systems, Lands, Operations, and Physical Plant, but you know that already. I had learned from Leo Da Vinci that Buster had been chosen for that position as a result of a national search, a search in which his competitors were folks from some of the top universities in the country with years of experience in similar positions. Before he was chosen as director of SLOPP, Buster had been an assistant clerk in the University Bookstore. Nevertheless, he was deemed the best candidate for the SLOPP position, and he became the successful candidate. Now he was not only the only non-vice president or associate VP to sit with the president's executive staff, he was also the only person other than the president, the guest speaker, and the chair of the board of trustees scheduled to sit on the platform at the trustees' banquet and dance. All that seemed rather unusual treatment for the director of Systems, Lands, Operations and Physical Plant. And he wasn't a very good director of SLOPP at that. In fact, he was downright lousy, at least from all I had heard. So how was he able to remain the apple of the president's eye, and how did he get there in the first place? I had to know. It was time to call Leo again.

"Leo, this is Ty McTavish. You know something, as much as I appreciated your offer of advice and assistance a few months ago, when you made it I didn't really think I would need to take advantage of it very often. I was wrong. I need your counsel once again."

"What is it this time?" There was more laughter than displeasure in his voice.

"It's about Buster Dukes," I replied. "I know we talked some about him a while back, but I'm still at a complete loss to explain his position in the SNAF-U hierarchy. Perhaps there's more that you can tell me about him."

"Ah, Abercrombie," Leo replied knowingly. "What is it you want to know?"

"Well, Leo, this guy is the only person on the president's executive staff who's not a vice president. He sits on the platform at the trustees' banquet. He golfs with the president and the chair of the board. From what I've heard, he entertains donors with the president at Azkizur's condo. He was the one who suggested using the condo to entertain the *NONSENSE* top twenty-five presidents to get their votes for next year. If what you told me about him before was true, that he was an assistant clerk in the bookstore before he took this job, how in hell did he get from there to here? What's the deal with this guy?"

"The short answer, Ty, is that I don't know for sure. But I'll tell you what I think and what I've heard. There're several administrators at SNAF-U who seem to get most-favored-nation treatment no matter what they do, no matter how badly they screw up, no matter how stupid their agendas may be. Dukes is at the top of the list, but he's not the only one. I'll bet you know who the others are."

Yeah, I sure do, I thought.

"There's no way in hell I can prove this, Ty, and I'm pretty sure I wouldn't want to see the evidence if it actually exists, but what I've heard is that somehow, two or three years ago, Dukes got hold of some pictures of Sligh in a compromising position with some squirrels."

CHAPTER X

SEVERAL ADDITIONAL WEEKS PASSED after the conclusion of the Bier business and that most recent meeting of the executive staff, at least the most recent one to which I was invited. And I must admit, those few weeks were pretty quiet. I was finally able to devote some effort to the responsibilities I was hired to discharge and to take off my "Ty McTavish Jr. Fireman" hat. I was even able to spend a little time in my laboratory, a responsibility that I had been pretty much forced to neglect for most of my time at SNAF-U. Fortunately, I had some good people working for me, so the research work was still being done and in fact was going pretty well. There was a good chance that we'd publish a paper or two this year in spite of all the other demands on my time.

It was the start of a brand new week, and I was feeling pretty good about myself, and, yes, even about SNAF-U. The concern about the *NONSENSE* list was waning, and as far as I knew, we had developed strategies, albeit bizarre ones, to address all the criteria required to get us back on the list. All the fires were finally out. For a while at least. I should have known that all this bliss couldn't last for long. Not at SNAF-U.

Jarvis peeked into my office.

"Dean McTavish? President Sligh is on the phone. Can you take his call?"

"Sure, Jarvis, put him through."

I picked up the phone.

"Hello, President Sligh, what can I do for you?"

"Good Morning, Ty. Olan and I are about to take a stroll across the quadrangle, and I wonder if you have time to join us. We'd like to chat with you a bit if you don't mind."

"Sure, I'll be happy to. Shall I meet you in front of the building?"

"That will be fine. In about, oh, ten minutes?"

"See you there."

Sligh and Azkizur were waiting for me when I got to the front of the building.

"Morning, Ty," Sligh offered.

I acknowledged his greeting and Olan's subsequent one, and we engaged in the obligatory round of handshakes even though we'd all seen each other earlier that morning. We began to walk toward the other end of the quad. I knew something was up, but I had no idea what. I was sure that this wasn't a pleasure cruise.

"It's good to get out and walk across the campus from time to time," Sligh mused. "Otherwise we tend to forget how really beautiful this place is. Don't you agree?"

I had to admit that I did. It was a very attractive campus, especially its quadrangle. A light snow had fallen on the city the night before. The ground was still relatively warm so that snow had only covered the grassy areas of the quad. The sidewalks were still clear. The weather pattern had passed through quickly, and the day had broken sunny and clear. The sun glistened on the roofs and marble of the buildings around the quad. As we passed the new Physics Building, Sligh finally started to make his way toward the point of our stroll.

"You know, Ty, Olan and I have had some conversations with the board of trustees about renaming the Physics Building. We're thinking of naming it after Daddy Plodter. He was a Physicist, you know, even though he spent most of his time at SNAF-U in administration, except when he was an undergraduate, of course."

Sligh chuckled, and Olan dutifully followed suit.

"Did you know that Ima is retiring at the end of this year?"

"No, I didn't," I replied. "Her departure will be a real loss to the university." I tried to sound generous without sounding false. As I thought about it, though, I realized that I had no reason to feel that Ima hadn't made real and significant contributions to SNAF-U. For that matter, there was a good chance that I hadn't seen any of the SNAF-Ugees at their best this year. At least I hoped I hadn't.

"Let me come to the point, Ty. There is a way in which Ima's retirement connects to the business that has consumed most of our energies this year. I'm sure you know exactly what I mean. There is, as it turns out, a *NONSENSE* rating category that we haven't discussed in any of the executive staff meetings that you've attended. It's called Employee Ejection Empathy, and it has to do with the way in which terminations and other departures of faculty and staff are handled by the university. It applies mostly to faculty who don't get tenure. We're required to make sure that they're given a chance to appeal the decision, that they have exit interviews, that they're read their Miranda rights, that they get to keep their parking spaces, if they have one, of course, until the day they leave, things like that. But the Employee Ejection Empathy criterion also applies to the departure of senior administrative staff, whether voluntary or involuntary. So it applies to Ima. We'll miss her, and I for one will be very sorry to see her go, but her departure does give us a chance to pick up some badly needed *NONSENSE* points, which brings me to the reason for this meeting."

Sligh stopped walking and turned to face me.

"I have a favor to ask of you. It's something of an imposition I know, as you haven't been here all that long, but I think it's a situation that could use a fresh face. I'm putting together a committee to organize a retirement party or a dinner or whatever for Ima so that we can express our gratitude in the appropriate way. I'd like you to chair that committee, Ty, if you will. She's been a real mainstay at SNAF-U for a long time, and I'm sure you can appreciate that we want to give her a suitable send-off. And while I certainly don't want to sound callous, the simple truth of the matter is that we can use the *NONSENSE* points that devising a suitable send-off for Ima will garner for us. So... will you do it?"

"Sure," I replied without really thinking about what I was saying. I should at least have gotten the names of the other committee members before I agreed to serve as chair. "Who else is on the committee?"

"Well, Miranda Turquette has agreed to serve, as has Dick Brohwknoz. I've also gotten yeses from Sparky, Charity Butler, and Clark Bunghall."

Oh great, I thought. Just great! I've agreed to chair a committee with the Turkster, Brownnose, Sparky, Lipless, and Bunghole as members. Maybe this was Sligh's way of punishing me for my behavior in executive staff meetings. What I didn't know was that there was still worse punishment to come.

"Fine," I responded, hoping he couldn't hear the apprehension in my voice. "I'll contact each of them and try to set up a meeting ASAP. I presume you want the affair to be scheduled before the official end of the semester."

"Yes, Ty, we certainly need to do it before everyone scatters for the summer. And again, I don't want to sound callous, but we also need to do it in time to submit the necessary information to *NONSENSE*. I know Ima wants us back in the top twenty-five, so I'm sure she'll be happy if we put this all together as expeditiously as possible. Thanks for agreeing to do this. It's an important responsibility, and I'm sure you'll do a bang-up job of it. Let me know if there is anything specific I can do to assist with the plans."

"I will. I'll be in touch as soon as we have some plans hammered out."

Well, what's done is done, I thought. I asked Jarvis to contact all the principals and to schedule a meeting of the committee at the first available opportunity. That turned out to be about a week after I made the mistake of agreeing to serve as chair. I got Jarvis to reserve the president's conference room, composed an agenda for the meeting, and determined not to think anymore about it until we met. But two days before the scheduled meeting date, I got a call—from Richard Brohwknoz.

"Ty, this is Dick. Thanks for taking my call."

"No problem, Dick. What's on your mind?"

"Well, it's about the committee meeting you have scheduled for day after tomorrow. I noticed that it's in the president's conference room. Is that right?"

"Yes, it is, Dick," I replied, somewhat perplexed, "is there a scheduling problem that I should know about?"

"Well, not exactly, Ty. How can I put this? I don't need to tell you that you're still sort of new here, and you don't know all the rules and regulations yet, so I don't want to appear too critical, but the president's conference room is only used for executive staff meetings and special events that the president himself convenes. I don't think he would approve at all for us to have a plain old committee meeting in that room. I don't need to tell you that we don't want to do anything to offend the president, do we Ty? I don't want to offend you either, Ty, because I know you're still fairly new here, but I have to be honest and say that I for one think it demeans the room for us to have just a plain old committee meeting there. I hope I haven't offended you, but I don't need to tell you that sometimes a person just has to say what they believe. Don't you agree?"

"Dick, please, uh, rest assured that I'm not offended at all by what you said."

I didn't say what I was really thinking, that this was just another example of Brohwknoz's brownnosing. Maybe I should have.

"You'll be pleased to know, I think, that the use of the room was cleared with the president before I had Jarvis contact you. In fact, it was the president himself who suggested that we use that room."

"Oh, wonderful, Ty," Dick spouted. He was obviously great at doing the old one eighty. "I think it will be perfect for us to meet in that room. I don't need to tell you that that way, we'll sort of have official presidential support for what we're doing. Thanks so much for doing such a bang-up job as chair of the committee. Bye now."

Asshole.

Two days later, and there we all were, in the president's conference room.

"Good afternoon everyone," I offered in my finest put-the-best-face-on-it tone of voice. "Thank you all for agreeing to serve on the committee and for making yourselves available so soon after we contacted you. I'm sure you're all well aware of why we're here, but you may not know that our efforts will have a two-fold purpose. First and foremost, of course, we want to give Ima the nicest and most memorable send-off we can. But some of you may not know that NONSENSE uses a ranking criterion called Employee Ejection Empathy in the determination of its top twenty-five schools. The criterion has to do with the way institutions handle the departures of faculty and senior administrators. So Ima's departure not only gives us a chance to do something nice for her, we should also be able to rack up some NONSENSE points if we do it well. So let's get down to business, shall we? My philosophy has always been that people in positions of leadership are expected to lead, and that applies to chairs of committees in the same way that it applies to any other leader. So I've made an outline of the issues I think we need to consider here."

I passed out a photocopy of my outline to each of the committee members.

"First of all, we need to decide what sort of celebration we want to have for Ima. Second, once that's decided, we need to decide on a date, a time, and a place. If we choose to have a luncheon or dinner, we need to make at least some tentative decisions about a menu, we must choose an appropriate gift, or perhaps even more than one gift for her, and we need to decide whom to invite. Finally, or maybe not finally, we'll just have to see how things turn out, uh… my experience has been that there is usually a written resolution that's drafted in these situations. So I've asked Tiffie Polk, in her capacity as secretary of the university, to give me some background information on Ima so that I could take a stab at drafting a resolution for you to consider. That's probably the last item of business we need to consider, so I'll wait to hand out copies of my draft. Does this outline seem reasonable to all of you?"

Nodding of heads.

"Is there anything I've omitted?"

Dick Brohwknoz. I should have known.

"Ty, forgive me for asking, but I wonder why there isn't a student member on this committee. I don't need to tell you that even in her job as VP for External Affairs, Ima had some dealings with students, and I don't need to tell you that students are very concerned that their interests are represented in the corridors of power at SNAF-U. So I think we should have a student on this committee."

"Dick, I had nothing to do with the choice of members for the committee." Although I sure as hell wished I had. "The choices were made by President Sligh without any input at all from me. So you'll need to take your idea up with him."

"Oh, I didn't know that," Dick simpered. "I thought you chose the members of the committee. If it was the president's choice, of course, I have no objection at all to the committee's composition."

"Let's move on then. Does anyone else have any additions or changes to make to my outline? Of course, as things come up in our discussion, we can modify the outline as we may need to."

Bunghole raised his hand.

"I don't have any changes to make, Ty, but I do have a question. How much is all of this going to cost? We do have some responsibilities to the university budget, y'know, as well as to Ima."

Clark Bunghall was vice president for Business Affairs and was by all accounts about as tight fisted as they come. Some claimed that he was able to squeeze a hundred and two cents out of every dollar, which probably made him a pretty valuable commodity at a place like SNAF-U. Somebody always wanted money for something. The problem was that he frequently carried his commitment to fiscal responsibility too far. For example, about two months ago, he wrote me to complain about the activities of the faculty in the Literary College. First, I got a letter from him, complaining that the faculty in the college spent too much time on research and not enough time teaching undergraduates. The next day, the very next day, mind you, I got a second letter from him that argued that the faculty should spend more time on research in order to bring in more grant money from the government. Don't get me wrong. I knew that cost would have to be a consideration in our planning for Ima's do, and I was, in any case, inclined to cut Bunghole some slack as he was the only black VP at SNAF-U. I had hoped, though, that the question of cost might not rear its ugly head quite so soon.

"There's no way that I can answer that question at this point, Bu… I mean, Clark. I think we need to decide what we want to do before we can estimate the cost."

"Well, did the president set any spending limit on this business?"

"No, he didn't, Clark, at least he didn't say anything to me."

"Well, we can't just fly out there without having some sort of checks on our spending."

"I agree completely, Clark, but let's see what we want to do. We may have to lower our sights if our plans become too extravagant, but I think we need to decide what we want to do first."

Bunghole clearly wasn't pleased, but he didn't press the matter further. At least not then.

"Okay," I said, thinking I was back in control, "let's begin at the top. What kind of affair do we want to have for Ima? Luncheon? Dinner? Reception? Some combination of the above?"

"I vote for a reception," the Turkster inserted brightly. "At a reception, you get a chance to mingle and fraternalize with all the guests. If we have a luncheon or dinner, we'll all be assigned to a table, and we'll be stuck there."

"I agree, Miranda," I replied, "we will all get a better chance to fraternalize at a reception."

I couldn't resist. Miranda was such an easy target and was absolutely clueless.

"Does anyone want to cast a vote for another format?"

All heads nodded no.

"Great. Then we're off and running. So a reception it will be. And of course, even with this format, it will be possible for us to have a sort of formal program, remarks by the president, reading the resolution, and so forth. Where should we have it?"

"How about the foyer of Madison Hall?" Sparky suggested. "It's large enough, centrally located, we've had receptions there before, and it wouldn't cost us anything to use it."

Everyone nodded approval. Bunghole even smiled slightly when he heard the bit about the cost.

"Good. Then that's settled. At this rate, we'll be done here in a flash."

Error. Ding-ding-ding.

"Let's pick a date then. President Sligh wants the affair to take place before the official end of the semester, which I interpret to mean before commencement. Let's see. Commencement is May 20, and we don't want to be too close to that, so how about some time around the first of May? How does that sound?"

Nods yes.

"Okay, let's look at some specific dates." I pulled out my smartphone and punched the calendar button. What about Monday, May 2? We'll have to clear it with the president, of course, but does anyone know of any other potential conflicts on that date?"

Nods again, mostly no. Then Brownnose began to mutter to himself.

"What is it, Dick?" I asked. "Is there a problem?"

"I'm afraid there is, Ty. There's a very important activity that day that might conflict with the reception. It's certainly something that I intend to participate in, and I suspect that there are lots of others here who will want to do so as well."

"What sort of activity, Dick?"

"Well, the SNAF-U Druids United against Defense Spending are having their annual rally, watermelon seed spitting contest, and square dance on May 2. I don't need to tell you how important defense spending is, and I for one intend to do all I can to support the DUDS. I know a lot of other people will be participating too."

"Okay, so May 2 is out. What about May 3?"

Again, nods. Again, mostly yes. But not Brownnose.

"What is it this time, Dick?"

"Sorry to be a bother, Ty, but Tuesday, May 3, is the date that has been set aside for our annual Buster Dukes appreciation dinner. I know the president wouldn't be willing to cancel that event, and I don't need to tell you how important it is that we honor Mr. Dukes each year."

I (barely) resisted the temptation to reply that he did, indeed, have to tell me how important it was and why. But that was a battle to join another day. Maybe.

"Okie dokie. May 3 won't do. What about May 4?"

No one responded. It looked like we had a date. Then Sparky snapped his fingers.

"No, Ty, that one won't work either. I just remembered, the president will be participating in a one-day retreat on May 4 at the local Rastafarian monastery. They do this every year, and this year, the theme of the retreat is "Surviving Puberty." President Sligh is really looking forward to it, and I'm sure he won't want to cancel."

"All right. Dare I suggest May 5, then? I presume the president will be back from the retreat by then.

Sparky nodded. No one else did, but no one indicated that May 5 would be a problem either.

"Okay, let's alert the press. We have a date. Thursday, May 5. Shall we say 6 PM? That way, we get things up, running, and over as quickly as possible. Is that time okay with everyone?"

"Well, Ty," Miranda offered, "I guess it only applies to me, but I usually devote the hour between five thirty and six thirty every day to transincidental meditation. So I couldn't get there before six thirty, but I guess you could start without me."

"Does anyone else have a conflict?"

"Now that you mention it, Ty, there is another problem with that time," Dick replied. "Mr. Dukes usually schedules his weekly appointment to have his nose hairs trimmed on Thursday afternoon. I'm not sure exactly what time it is, but I don't need to tell you that the president will certainly want him to attend Ima's reception… Oh, and one other thing. There are lots of students who have classes that don't end until right around six, so we need to choose a time that will make it possible for them to attend."

"Colleagues," I said with as much serenity as I could muster, "let me suggest that it will be almost impossible to find a time that will be convenient for everyone, and we all agree, I think, that we don't want to start too late. As I said, we want to get this affair up, running, and over with. So I for one think that six thirty is the absolute latest we can start. Shall we say six thirty then?"

"Yeah. Uh-huh. Okay. I guess so." Et cetera.

"Fine, then let's think about a menu for the affair. I would guess that the food service has a standard set of choices that they can provide for an event like this. Is there any reason not to use them?"

"Except for the fact that their food is frequently nasty, no, there isn't," said Lipless, a.k.a. Charity Butler. "But I must admit that they usually do a pretty good job with receptions. It is a good thing we decided not to do lunch or dinner."

"Hold on a second," said Bunghole. "How much is this going to cost? We do have to be conscious of budgetary considerations here."

"I don't know, Clark, but that's a question it should be pretty easy to answer. Why don't you have your secretary find out for us what the prices of the food service reception menus are? You can give me the information, and I'll pass it on to everyone else via phone, fax, or email. That way, we can probably make a decision about the menu without having to convene again. Does that sound reasonable?"

"That sounds fine, Ty. I'll do just that. As a matter of fact, I should be able to get back to you before the end of the day today."

"Okay, format, date, time, place, food, drink. Oh, drinks. Does anyone know if the food service schedules include beverages, and if so, whether alcoholic beverages are also included?"

"I'm pretty sure the answer is yes to both your questions," Sparky replied. "They'll provide wine, beer, even cocktails if we desire."

"Hold on a second," said Brownnose. "Who's going to check IDs to make sure that no underage students consume any alcohol? I don't need to tell you that we'd be in serious trouble if that happened."

"Dick, we haven't even decided that any students will be invited to this affair. So perhaps that's the next issue we need to consider, the guest list."

"Well," Sparky chimed in, "we'll need to invite all the executive officers of the U, of course, and board of trustees, and we should probably ask Ima if there are people she wants to invite and maybe some of her faculty colleagues from her teaching days."

"That sounds like a reasonable starting point, Tony. As I understand it, Tiffie Polk usually handles invitations to events like this, so why don't we leave it up to her to flesh out the guest list. Any objections to that suggestion?"

The Turkster raised her hand.

"Excuse me, Ty." She paused for a moment, then continued, "I apologize for saying this, but, oh, I feel I just have to. There's something inside of me that I just have to let out."

Uh-oh. Should I duck for cover? Was some creature about to pop out of her chest? Should I cover my face with a towel? Miranda stood and began walking around the table, pausing in turn to place her hands on our shoulders.

"My grandparents migrated here from Argentina because they believed that America was founded on the principles of equanimity and equilibrizing of opportunity, the land of the free and the home of the slave.

America! Oh, beautiful, for special skies, for ample wavy grain, for purple mounted magic trees, above the fruit airplane."

It took me several seconds to realize that Miranda had just recited what she thought were the words to "America the Beautiful."

Miranda continued, "And my parents worked hard to get their piece of the American dream and to provide a piece of that dream for their children. My father worked his fingers to the bone as an investment banker on Wall Street, and my mother worked her fingers to the bone as a certified public accountant, just to make life better for their children. And I know they would have worked even harder if I'd had any brothers and sisters. I can remember nights when I would hear them talking after they thought I'd fallen asleep. I can hear them now, talking about how hard it was to make ends meet on only $250,000 a year, and wondering what they were going to do so that I could have a better life than they had. I cried myself to sleep on those nights. But I never stopped believing in America and in the American dream. When I was old enough, I got a job so that I could help my parents, and I worked my little fingers to the bone, straightening up my father's desk in his office on Wall Street. It was hard, dirty work, but I did it gladly because I knew that we were all in this together. Not just me, not just my parents, but all Americans in all countries all over the globe. We were all in this together!"

Miranda's eyes were starting to puddle. Again. I wondered if maybe we'd all just entered the *Twilight Zone*.

"And we made it. My parents overcame their adversaries, and I overcame mine, and look where I am today. That's the kind of country we live in, a country that makes it possible for even working people like my parents to make something of themselves and to build something for the future. My parents paid income taxes too, you know. State and local taxes too. And they gave to charities too. They were good people. I wish you all could have known them."

"Excuse me, Miranda," I interrupted, trying my best not to sound completely insensitive, "but can you tell us please what this all has to do with the guest list for Ima's reception?"

"Oh, I'm sorry, Ty," Miranda responded, wiping the moisture from her eyes, "I thought I'd made myself clear. The point is simply that I'm terribly concerned that the kind of guest list that is usually put together for functionalities like this will fail to exclude many of the disenfranchised and disremembered members of our community. People like my parents and maybe even me. How can we be sure that there will adequate representation of blacks, native Americans, Pacific islanders, Macedonians, and Mollusks (Did she mean Moluccans?) at this affair? How can we ignore what's happening in other parts of the world, in Afghanistan, in Bosnia, in Kansas, as we activate this activity? Ima is vice president for External Affairs. Isn't it fitting that we externalize the departureship that we provide for her? That's what I meant to say."

Now the clever thing for me to say here was "Turkster, you're not in Kansas anymore." Thing was, I wished to hell she were.

"And what about the students?" Brownnose.

Yeah, and what about the Hutus and the Tutsis? I thought.

"Miranda, I think we need to think more locally about the event we're planning," I said, trying as best I could to remain calm. "While it's true that Ima is VP for External Affairs, we're only talking about a SNAF-U-specific farewell for her. My guess is that there will be other celebrations planned for her that may include a larger cross section of the community, but I think we have to confine our planning to a local context. Do the rest of you agree?"

Fortunately for me, they did.

"Oh, well, if you really think so," Miranda responded, obviously disappointed. She pushed out her lips in a very unattractive pout.

"With regard to the students, I trust the judgment of the committee. Does anyone besides Dick think students should be invited to the reception?"

No one did.

"Well," Dick sputtered, "I don't need to tell you that I don't like that decision. I don't like it at all. And I don't need to tell you that the students will be, excuse my language, really ticked off when they hear about this. But if that's the committee's decision, I'll abide by it, and that's what I'll tell the students when they ask me about it. But I don't need to tell you that I'll have to be honest and say that it wasn't a decision I agreed with. And, however, we may want to think about the *NONSENSE* rankings. I don't need to tell you that they may not be too happy to hear that we're excluding students from the celebration. I don't need to tell you."

Shit. He might have a point. I certainly didn't want to be party to anything that might jeopardize our reinstatement to the *NONSENSE* list.

"Tell you what, Dick. Why don't I ask President Sligh what he thinks about having students attend? Can we agree to abide by his decision? Good. The let's move on. What sort of gift should we give her?"

"How about a gold watch?" Brownnose, obviously demonstrating his remarkable recuperative powers.

"How much is that going to cost us?" Bunghole.

"How about a Caribbean cruise?" Lipless.

"How much is that going to cost?" Bunghole.

"If you don't mind, Ty," Miranda inserted, having apparently recovered from our response to her earlier suggestions, "I've thought about this matter, and I have several suggestions to make."

"Please do, Miranda."

Now what? I thought.

"Well, we might give her a pair of Rollerblades. You know Rollerblading has become quite popular lately. Or we could give her a gift certificate to go to a health farm. Muscle tone is important especially as we get older. Or maybe we could give her a riding lawn mower. You know how fast the grass grows around here in the spring. Or maybe a gift certificate for several visits to an aroma therapist, or maybe golf lessons or season tickets to the local Arena Football team. I saw an ad on TV to train people to treat hemorrhoids, maybe she'd like to take that up as a second career, and we could pay for the lessons."

I could see from their expressions that even Sparky and Charity were amazed at the Turkster's suggestions. Bunghole just asked his usual question.

"Those are all interesting suggestions, Miranda, but perhaps we ought to stick with something a little more traditional. I'm willing to be convinced otherwise, but I for one think that cash is always a good gift. That way, she can do what she wants with it. Of course, it probably shouldn't be the only thing we give her, and we would have to decide how much. An alternative would be a gift certificate. But maybe we ought to postpone making a decision about a gift. It might be useful for us to think a little bit more about that and maybe to get some additional information about her interests. I can also talk with President Sligh and get some suggestions from him. And," I added with a glance toward Bunghole, "I can get some sense of how much he wants us to spend. Does that sound reasonable?"

Nods yes except for Miranda, who was apparently pouting again.

"Okay, then," I continued before Miranda could come up with another brilliant suggestion, "according to my outline, there's only one item left to consider—the resolution. As I said, I got some background information from Tiffie and took a crack at drafting a resolution myself."

I passed out another set of photocopies.

"Since the president will presumably read it aloud at the reception, it might be a good idea for me to read it aloud now so that we can see how it sounds.

"Be it resolved:

For your thirty-plus years of yeoman service to SNAF-U;

For your faith in and dedication to the principles on which the institution was founded;

For your passionate efforts to preserve SNAF-U's traditions and for your conservative but sensitive approach in dealing with those inside and outside the university who might wish to modify or abolish those traditions;

For your many years of effort as a teacher of the history of democratic institutions;

For the convivial approach you always take in your interactions with colleagues and for the gaiety you have brought to SNAF-U's consideration of many a weighty matter;

For striving in your dealings with those outside the university to make the alien commonplace at SNAF-U;

The board of trustees and the executive officers of Small but National, Aspiring to be Famous University do hereby offer our thanks and appreciation to Dr. Imajean Plodter and declare this date, (fill in the blank), Imajean Plodter Day at SNAF-U.'"

Nobody said a word. Understand that I thought this was a pretty innocuous resolution, so I interpreted the silence to mean consent. Error. Ding-Ding-Ding.

"Well, what do you think?"

As I might have predicted, the Turkster was the first to speak.

"Well, Ty, it's okay in general, but there are some pacifics that need to be modificationed. At least we need to talk about them."

"What pacifics do you have in mind, Miranda?" I'm not a mean person. Really. But Miranda was such an easy and inviting target, and as I said, she was absolutely clueless.

"Well, for one thing, I don't think it's a good idea at all to mention how long Ima's been working here. That would make it way too easy for people to figure out her age. Then some people will surely think that her resignation was forcible, and we'd be accused of ageism. And in that same sentence, you use the word 'yeoman' (which Miranda pronounced *yo-MAN*). I don't think we want to use any rap music terms in the resolv... uh, resolution, do we? And anyway, I don't think we can use a word that has the word 'man' in it to refer to Ima. Then we'd be accused of sexism too."

I couldn't believe my ears, but she wasn't joking; she was dead serious. And two or three others around the table nodded their agreement. I could hear Brownnose mumbling to himself, "No rap music, no way."

"Well, I suppose we can modify that sentence if all of you think it's necessary," I conceded, "but maybe we should take a look at the whole thing before returning to it piece by piece. What other changes need to be made?"

"Well, Ty, I think we have to remove the word 'faith' from the second sentence." Brownnose. "I don't need to tell you that we don't want to give the impression that we're espousing any religious group, denomination, or belief system here, do we? And I think we should probably take out the word 'service.' It's a perfectly good word, I know, but I don't need to tell you that we don't want anybody to think that we just think of Ima as a servant. I don't need to tell you that *NONSENSE* certainly wouldn't like that. No, sir."

Miranda was nodding her agreement before Dick even finished his last sentence.

"And we can't use the word 'passionate' because, well, that's just too, uh, too, uh, dangerous," Miranda added. "And we can't use 'conservative' either. People might think that we're trying to politicalize the departureship."

"I'm afraid Miranda's right, Ty." Sparky. "And for the same reasons we can't use 'democratic' either. We don't want to appear to support one side of the political spectrum as opposed to another now, do we? And maybe we might need to omit the word 'history' too. There will be faculty from other departments there, and some of them might just be offended if we make reference to one department and not to any others. Better to be safe than worry, wot."

"Ty, I know you gave a lot of thought to your draft," Dick added, "and I hate to continue to suggest changes, but I think we have to drop the word 'gaiety' too. Otherwise, I think we run the serious risk of offending some of the gay, lesbian, and bisexual members of our family. I don't need to tell you that we don't want to do that, do I? And I, uh, I hesitate to say this, but I just think we have to drop 'abolish' too. There will be some African-Americans at the reception. You'll be there, and Clark will be there at the very least. And although we're all adults, since you decided not to invite any students, I just think we run the risk of offending someone. Abolish makes you think about abolition, which makes you think about slavery and, well, I don't need to tell you that we just don't want to run the risk of offending anyone. *NONSENSE* wouldn't like that. No, sir. I don't need to tell you."

"Dick's right, Ty," the Turkster added, "we have to be very careful about how this sounds to the farewellers. So I think we have to take out the word 'weighty' too. It might offend Ima, and it might offend the president, and it might offend, oh, I don't know who else."

"And, Ty," Dick continued, "if I'm not mistaken, the Immigration and Naturalization Service has recommended that the word 'alien' only be used when people are referring to people from other planets. So I think we have to take it out unless you think some people from other planets will be there."

I hoped this was Brownnose's attempt at a joke, but with him, it was impossible to know for sure.

"I don't need to tell you that I've already told you that we don't want to risk offending the black, Hispanic, and Asian members of our family."

I was stunned. But it wasn't the first time since my arrival at SNAF-U that such had been the case. What should I say next?

"Well, what's left then? Maybe someone should just suggest an amended resolution."

Sparky spoke up.

"How about this? We'll leave the 'be it resolved' in, of course, but given the concerns that we've all expressed about the draft, I move that we drop everything except the last paragraph."

"Second the motion." Brownnose.

You've probably noticed that we hadn't voted on anything else that we'd discussed in the meeting. I certainly did.

"Well, if that's what you all think is best." I wasn't about to join this battle either. "All in favor say aye."

A chorus of ayes.

"Opposed?"

"That's the resolution then. Is there anything else that anyone can think of that we need to consider?"

After this performance, I needed once again to go back to my office, lay my head on my desk, and listen for the sound of those electrons. There were no additional suggestions, at least not initially.

"Okay, I'll get back to you after I speak to the president."

"Oh, there is one more thing." Brownnose. "I know you'll have to handle this delicately because after all, he is the president, but you have to figure out some way to let him know." Dick hesitated. "That it's okay to shake hands with Ima, but he shouldn't try to hug her."

Where was Ty McTavish when the lights went out? Deaning at SNAF-U.

CHAPTER XI

W EBSTER DEFINES "TURPITUDE" AS "depravity" or "a base act." The American Association of University Professors is a bit more specific. To wit:

"The concept of 'moral turpitude' identifies the exceptional case in which the professor may be denied a year's teaching or pay in whole or in part. The statement applies to that kind of behavior which goes beyond simply warranting discharge and is so utterly blameworthy as to make it inappropriate to require the offering of a year's teaching or pay. The standard is not that the moral sensibilities of persons in the particular community have been affronted. The standard is behavior that would evoke condemnation by the academic community generally."

Okay, so moral turpitude can keep a perp out of the classroom or put him or her on the welfare rolls for a year. But more importantly, moral turpitude is one of the things that can get a faculty member kicked out of a university even if he or she is tenured. Now despite what the AAUP says, the operational definition of moral turpitude differs from institution to institution. But one thing most academics agree on is that it's not good to sleep with your students. And that applies to both males and females. Although it's not always the case, it *is* sometimes true that

---

sleeping with your students will get you kicked off the faculty. Moral turpitude. That's what happened to Titus. Remember him? He was the young hotshot who interviewed me at PERU. Turns out he was sleeping with a woman in one of his classes. If that wasn't bad enough, she was the dean's daughter. Last I heard, Titus was teaching general science at a junior college in Montana.

But sleeping with your students won't *necessarily* get you kicked out of the U, especially if you can dance around things like accusations, claims, complaints, and even evidence. In other words, moral turpitude may not present a serious problem if you're good at *moral terpsichore.*

So what does all this have to do with SNAF-U and particularly with the *NONSENSE* criteria? On the one hand, *NONSENSE* has no moral rectitude (pretty much the opposite of moral turpitude) criterion. And it's a good thing too. If they did, there probably wouldn't be anybody in their top twenty-five. On the other hand, even though there is no rectitude criterion, moral turpitude can hurt an institution if incidences of it come to the attention of the *NONSENSE* staff. And that's exactly what happened to SNAF-U. Somehow, Doug Little got wind of some hanky-panky involving one of the SNAF-U faculty. Doug communicated this information to Hermione Bull, who passed it on to the president, who passed it on to Olan Azkizur, who passed it on to—you guessed it—me.

The offending faculty member? One Jamais Dimanche. Yes, Jamais Dimanche, assistant professor of Romantic Interlocution and Poetic Evolution. She first came to my attention not as a result of direct contact, but by what might be referred to as reputation. I was soon to learn that Dr. Dimanche was well known by at least some of her students and by several nonstudents as well. It all began with a visit to my office by one of the undergraduates in the Literary College.

"Dean McTavish, Mr. Grabuttski is here."
"Thanks, Jarvis, send him in."

Sean Grabuttski had requested an appointment with me. I didn't attach any real significance to it because students came to see me for all sorts of reasons. Sean was a good student from all that I had heard and was also a star forward on the SNAF-U soccer team, a slim, good-looking lad with a winning smile.

"Come in, Sean, have a seat." I shook his hand and ushered him into my office.

"Thanks, Dean McTavish, and thanks very much for seeing me. Like, I know you're very busy, and well, I mean, I really appreciate you taking the time, y'know?"

"My pleasure, Sean. I don't have nearly as many opportunities to chat with students as I'd like, so I'm always pleased to have students come to visit me. What can I do for you?"

"Well, it's kind of awkward, Dean McTavish, y'know? I mean I don't feel very comfortable about it, y'know, but like, I had to talk to someone, and you seemed like the best place to start."

"Well, needless to say, Sean, I don't know what brought you to see me, but let me assure you that anything you tell me will be kept in the strictest confidence. You can be sure that nothing you say will leave this room."

"Thank you, sir, that makes me feel a little better about this. One other thing might help. Like, I feel a little awkward about that too, y'know? I mean, Sean is my given name, but, like, it's not what people usually call me. I might feel, like, more comfortable, and it might be easier for me to say what I have to say if you'd call me by, like, my nickname."

"And what's that?"

"Fuzzy."

"Okay, uh, Fuzzy. What exactly is on your mind?"

Fuzzy sighed, locked his fingers together and stared at his shoes.

"Well, lately, Dean McTavish, nothing seems to be going right. I mean, like until recently, I was doing pretty well in my classes. I'm a Computational Linguistics major and an Oriental Theater minor, and all of that was working okay. I'm on the soccer team, and although we haven't won many games, like, I was playing pretty well and having fun, y'know? There was even some talk that I might, like, make All-American. Life was, like, all right, Dean McTavish, and I was happy. But lately, all of that has changed. I mean, like, things just aren't going right. I mean, like, not at all. I'm not studying anymore. I go to classes, but like, I'm not paying much attention to what's going on. I'm still playing soccer, but like, I'm not enjoying it, and the coach has taken me off the starting team. I mean, like, things just aren't going right anymore, y'know?"

"Well, Sea… uh, Fuzzy, do you have any idea what might have happened to change things this way?"

"Yeah, I do, Dean McTavish. The problem is that I'm not gettin' any… uh, that I broke up with my, uh, girlfriend. And, like, I just haven't been able to get it all back together since that happened, y'know?"

Ah, the heart of the matter, both literally and figuratively. That didn't take long. Problem was that I didn't consider myself to have the least bit of talent as a purveyor of advice to the lovelorn.

"I'm not sure what to tell you, Fuzzy. These things happen. Have you talked with your former girlfriend? Are you sure the relationship is over?"

"I guess I am, Dean McTavish. I mean, like, the whole thing ended sort of all of a sudden and in sort of a strange fashion. We were together one night, and everything was, like, fine, y'know? At least I thought it was. Then the next afternoon, when I got back from classes, like, there was a message from her on my answering machine. She said the relationship had 'run its course.' That's what she said, and that she didn't want to see me anymore. Like, I was shocked. I mean, I thought things were going just fine, y'know? I mean, like, we had just been together the night before, and everything seemed okay then. And, like, she didn't even tell me face to face. She, like, left a message on my answering machine."

"Did you try to talk to her about the situation?"

"Yeah, I did. I mean, I called her on the phone several times and left messages on her answering machine, like, at her house and on her voice mail on her office phone, and I went by her office a bunch of times, and—"

"Whoa, hold on a minute, Fuzzy. You went by her *office?*"

"Yeah, I mean, oh, I guess I didn't tell you. My girlfriend is, uh, was... Dr. Dimanche, Jamais Dimanche, Department of Romantic Interlocution and Poetic Evolution, y'know? It's a long story, Dean McTavish, and I guess it was probably, like, wrong, but I was in one of her classes last term, and well, she seemed to, like, take an interest in me and helped me when I had some problems with one of my papers, and we started meeting after class so we could go over class materials. And the next thing I knew, like, she invited me to her apartment to help me prepare for an exam, and the next thing I knew, like, we were, we were, like, doing it. Y'know?"

Damn!

"And we saw each other off and on for the last several months, like mostly to, uh, do it, y'know? Then a couple weeks ago, I got the phone message, and well, my life has been pretty shitty, uh sorry... bad, since then. Like, I just don't know what to do, Dean McTavish."

Neither did I. But I took my best shot.

"Sean (Although Fuzzy might have been more appropriate here in one sense, it seemed totally inappropriate right then as a way to refer to this young man), I know it is hard for you to accept this right now, but it was unquestionably the best thing for you to get out of that relationship even if it's painful for you now. There's just no way, Sean, that the relationship could have worked out for you. And the longer it lasted, the harder it would have been for you when it finally ended. I know it's tough right now, but it was best for it to end. You're young, and you'll get over it. Think about it this way. It's extremely unlikely that your relationship with Dr. Dimanche had any long-term future. As long as you are at SNAF-U, you will be a student, and she will be a professor. Never the twain should meet, at least not romantically."

Did any of that make sense to him? Hell, it hardly made sense to me.

"I guess you're right, Dean McTavish. But, like, things were going so well, at least I thought they were. And now I just don't know what to do, y'know what I'm sayin'?"

"Yes, I do, Sean. And I'm glad you came to talk to me about it. What's more, I think you should probably talk to someone else about it, Sean, someone who has more experience in dealing with situations like this than I do. I think you should speak with someone at the counseling service."

Maybe I could foist him off on Jarvis's wife.

"That's why they're there. They'll handle your situation carefully and will keep anything you tell them in strictest confidence. If you like, I'll be happy to call the office myself and set up an appointment for you."

"Thanks, Dean McTavish. Like, maybe something like that would help. I feel pretty awkward about all this, y'know? I mean, nobody ever dumped me before."

"Happens to the best of us, Fuzzy."

"Well, thanks again, Dean McTavish. I do feel better now. Like, it was really nice of you to meet with me, and I mean, I will go to see someone at the counseling office, although I do feel a lot better just having talked to you, y'know?"

"I'm glad I could help, Fuzzy."

"Oh, one more thing, uh, I feel kind of awkward about all this, y'know? But I don't want you to think that I was, like, in love with Dr.

Dimanche or anything like that. I mean, I wasn't. I mean, we really didn't go out or anything except to a movie a couple of times, and then she insisted that we go to the cineplex, like, on the other side of town. So it wasn't like I was in love with her or anything. Mostly, we just, uh, did it, like I said. But that was great, Dean McTavish, I mean…"

"That's fine, Fuzzy. I understand what you're saying."

And I did I think, but in any case, I wasn't interested in hearing any more of the details.

"And one more thing, Dean McTavish. I'm not sure whether I should tell you this or not, but maybe I should, I mean, like, I went to the cineplex with some of my friends the other night, and Dr. Dimanche was there. And she was with a guy who was the Teaching Assistant in her class last term."

Like, thanks Fuzzy. As If I didn't have enough problems. I mean, like, y'know?

I said good-bye to Sean "Fuzzy" Grabuttski and returned to my desk. Apparently, there was a pattern here. At least one was developing. And what in hell was I going to do about it? Well, the short and immediate answer was nothing. I needed to think more about the situation and maybe talk to Leo before making a move. What I didn't know at the time was that Fuzzy Grabuttski was not the only one of Jamais Dimanche's paramours who hoped to benefit from my counsel. Not by a long shot.

It was about a week after my meeting with Fuzzy. Jarvis knocked on my door and stuck his head in. "Dean McTavish? I'm sorry to bother you, but there's a student here who would like to see you. He knows he doesn't have an appointment and seems quite willing to go away if I tell him to. His name is Dirk Wetrod (In keeping with my practice of providing a pronouncing gazetteer for your enlightenment, Dirk's surname was actually pronounced WE-trod)."

I had a few minutes between meetings and appointments, and I wasn't being disingenuous when I said to Fuzzy Grabuttski that I enjoyed meeting with students. I really didn't get as many chances to talk with students as I might have wished. So I decided to see Mr. Wetrod even though he wasn't on my official calendar. I went through the usual motions as he came into my office.

"Thanks for seeing me, Dean McTavish. I apologize for dropping in on you unannounced like this, but I have something on my mind, something that has been troubling me for some time now, and I need some advice. I've talked to some of my friends, and they've all told me that I should speak with someone in authority. You seemed like the logical choice."

"I'm happy to help in any way I can, Dirk. What exactly seems to be the problem?"

"Uh, well, maybe I should tell you a little about myself. I'm a second year graduate student in Romantic Interlocution and Poetic Evolution. I finished my comprehensive exams last semester and began looking around for a dissertation advisor. I talked to lots of faculty and finally settled on Professor Jamais Dimanche. Her work seemed most closely related to my interests."

Red flags and sirens.

"So I spoke with her, and she agreed to have me."

Yeah, I thought, *I'll bet she did.*

"Things went fine at first. I spent some time with her, usually in her office, talking about my dissertation prospectus and coming to some decisions about exactly the directions my research would take. Those office meetings gradually expanded to meetings at local restaurants and coffee shops, and then one day, she said that I should come over to her house that evening so that we could go over the outline for my prospectus in detail. I thought it was somewhat unusual for her to invite me to her house, but since she was my major professor, I agreed. Well, I got there, and things went fine at first. Actually, I guess that from one viewpoint, they went fine for the whole evening. Anyway, we talked about the project for a while, and I think I made some real progress in outlining my prospectus. We were sitting on her couch, side by side, looking over some of the material I had written up, and… and the next thing I knew, she put her hand on my knee, and then she put her arm around my shoulder, and I looked up at her. And right then, it seemed like the most natural thing in the world to do, so I kissed her or she kissed me… or we kissed each other. The next thing I knew, we were taking each other's clothes off, and the next thing I knew, it was the next morning, and I was waking up in the bed next to her. I was scared, Dean McTavish. It was great! But I was scared to death. I mean, she was my major professor."

A few seconds passed before I responded. Once again, I wasn't at all sure what to do about this situation.

"Let me see, Dirk, all this happened, what, a couple of weeks ago?"

"That's right, Dean McTavish."

Which meant that she had been sleeping with Fuzzy and Dirk at the same time, if you know what I mean.

"And what has happened since then?"

"Well, I spent one more night at her place about a week ago, and although she's asked me to come over a couple times since then, I've made excuses so that I didn't have to. Don't get me wrong, it's not like I didn't want to. I really did! I guess I shouldn't say that. But it was great! But I was scared shitless, I mean, I was scared to death, Dean McTavish. She's my major professor. If I say that I don't want to sleep with her, what will that do to my career here? If I do sleep with her, what will that do to my career? Will she continue to direct my thesis work just because I'm her lover? And what if she dumps me? What then?"

Dirk had clearly thought about all the possible consequences of his relationship, at least at some level. Too bad he didn't begin that analysis before he got into bed with her.

"Well, Dirk, I have to say right off that I'm no expert in situations like this." Although it appeared that I was destined to become one. "But I think you are right in refusing to sleep with Dr. Dimanche anymore. The situation can only become more complicated, and you are the one most likely to suffer the negative consequences of those complications. What you must do, I think, is to go to Dr. Dimanche and simply tell her, as difficult as it may be, that your relationship has to return to being strictly a professional one, if that's possible. See what she says. If she says, 'Fine, but I'm no longer willing to serve as your thesis advisor,' let me know, and I'll assist you in finding another one and will do everything I can to ensure that you're treated fairly by the department, and that no harm is done to your career by this indiscretion."

I hoped I wasn't copping out here. Maybe I should be the one to tell her that she had to stop screwing her students and to stop screwing *with* her students. But I wasn't ready to take that step just yet.

"If she agrees to continue as your advisor, you should still let me know. Given that your relationship hasn't been strictly professional up to now, it may be necessary for me to keep an eye on it once it returns to that status, just to be sure that Dimanche doesn't allow her response to this situation to influence her in her subsequent dealings with you. But you have to break the relationship off now. Understand?"

"Yes, Dean McTavish. I do understand. And I guess there's a part of me that was pretty sure that you'd respond this way. I pretty much knew that I should stop seeing her, at least the way I have been. But I felt that I needed to let you or someone in authority know what was going on so that I could be protected if things went wrong. And I did think I needed some advice."

"You made the right decision, Dirk. I'm glad you came to see me, and I think you'll set things right or at least take a big step in that direction by seizing the bull by the horns here and getting your ship back on course."

Do you think I threw enough clichés into that sentence?

"Thanks a lot, Dean McTavish, you've been a tremendous help. I was really nervous about coming to see you, but I know I made the right decision. I'm going to try to see Dr. Dimanche as soon as I leave here, while I have my courage up, and tell her that it's got to stop and that if that means that she doesn't want to direct my dissertation anymore, well, that's the way it will have to be."

Dirk rose and headed for the door.

"There's one thing, though, Dean McTavish. I'm going to do what you suggested. I know it's right. But I have to say, the sex was great! I mean the sex..."

Dirk left my office shaking his head.

It was reasonably clear that sooner or later, I would have to intervene in some substantive way in *l'affaire* Dimanche. I hadn't even heard her side of these stories yet. It was hard to believe, though, that two students, one of them a junior in the Literary College, would fabricate stories of this sort about a faculty member. Of course, stranger things had happened; and this was, after all, SNAF-U. So I decided to wait awhile before visiting with Dr. Dimanche and to mull things over a bit. I wondered how much *NONSENSE* really knew about all this.

A few days after my chat with Dirk Wetrod, I had an afternoon appointment with Anthony Atherton-Sparks to do some planning for a meeting in which he and I were scheduled to participate. I went over to his office and was shown in by his administrative assistant.

"Ty, old boy. Good to see you again."

Sparky shook my hand, put his arm around my shoulder, and ushered me to a seat in front of his desk."

"Would you like some coffee or a cup of tea?"

"A cup of tea would hit the spot, Tony."

Yes, Tony, as always. Never *ever* Sparky.

"Cream or sugar? And would you like a biscuit as well?"

Biscuit means Cookie, in case you didn't know.

"Sugar, two lumps please, if you have cubes. A couple of teaspoons otherwise. And I'll pass on the biscuits. Thanks."

"Well, let's get down to brass tacks, shall we? I think you've already been given the *scheduling* information. We'll be meeting with the Steering Committee of the Employees Association about setting up a continuing education and training program for SNAF-U employees. President Sligh wants my office to be involved because the employees association falls under my jurisdiction as VP for Internal Affairs. And of course, your office needs to be involved because setting up such a program is a curricular matter, and curricular affairs clearly fall within your bailiwick. So we need to put our heads together to see how best to handle the request and the implementation of a response to it."

"Exactly what does the employees association have in mind, Tony?"

"Well, I don't have a lot of detail. But the feeling seems to be that first, the continuing education programs we currently have in place aren't really suitable for many of our employees, that they seem to be tailored more for academics or for people with extensive academic training. Some of our employees would like, in fact, to be given the opportunity to get exactly that sort of training themselves. Many of the rest would like, as I understand it, to have the chance to enhance their job skills, develop some additional expertise, become competent in disciplines or areas that are related to their own, take courses that they think might just be fun, things like that. The Steering Committee has presented a comprehensive list of ideas to the president. One of the things we would hope to accomplish in the meeting is to gain a more thorough understanding..."

Tony was droning on, and I was tuning out. Our relationship with our employees, especially the nonacademic staff, was undeniably important. And it was commendable that they had taken the initiative to develop a proposal that would improve their lot. But that wasn't the relationship that was on my mind right now. I was still thinking about Jamais Dimanche, Fuzzy Grabuttski, and Dirk Wetrod. And goodness knew who else. If she was sleeping with two, there was a good chance that she was sleeping with three, maybe more. I still hadn't met with her yet but had pretty much concluded that it was time to do so. What I wasn't sure about was whether *I* needed to seek the counsel of a higher authority before talking with her. Thing was that I couldn't imagine that I would get any useful advice from Olan Azkizur, and it seemed even less likely to me that President Sligh would or could advise me in any meaningful way. Plus, bringing them into the loop might well put Dimanche, and possibly the students, in jeopardy, and since I hadn't spoken with her yet, I didn't think that was a chance I could afford to take. So I concluded I was pretty much on my own, and it was probably time to see Dimanche. I made a mental note to have Jarvis set up an appointment with her.

"And we can then see how they respond to that overture. What do you think about that approach, Ty? Ty?"

I was a million miles away. Or at least a million thoughts away.

"I'm sorry, Tony. I wasn't really listening. I am really sorry. It's just that I have this really tough situation to sort out. It's on my mind, and for the last few days, I haven't been able to think about much else because I'm afraid I'm going to pretty much have to tackle it on my own."

"No apologies necessary, old man. I know how this place can consume you if you let it. Is it anything I might help with?"

"I don't think so, Tony. It's a complex situation, at least it's becoming one. I probably shouldn't tell you the details, but on the other hand… perhaps the perspective of someone who is not directly involved might help me to sort it all out. Plus, it might be useful to get a different administrative viewpoint on this situation."

Despite what I considered to be his shortcomings, Tony seemed to be intelligent and level headed. I suspected he was able to keep counsel, and I was certainly in need of an additional perspective.

"Who knows, maybe it's a situation of a type you've dealt with before. I certainly know I can count on your discretion. In a nutshell, the situation is this. It seems that one of our faculty members is sleeping with her students. I suppose she's not the only one, but she's the only one I know about."

"Anyone we know?"

"Well, this is strictly confidential, Tony, and I probably shouldn't be telling you this, but it's one of the faculty in RIPE, Jamais Dimanche."

Anthony Atherton-Sparks sat completely motionless for a second or two as if frozen in place, and then he leapt out of his chair as if the seat had suddenly become red hot.

"What? Jamais? Jamais Dimanche? Sleeping with a student? Tell me you're not serious! You can't be serious! You're just doing this to upset me because you know about our relationship. That's it, isn't it? You bastard, I would never have thought you could stoop so low!"

And Tony started stomping around the room, kicking the desk, chairs, tables, whatever his foot could reach.

"Whoa, calm down, Tony," I said, hoping earnestly that he would calm down but not wanting to get too close to him if he didn't. I let him fume for a minute or so, then I finally convinced myself to get up and try to help him regain his composure. I put my arm around his shoulder and sat him down on his couch.

"I assure you that I had no intention of upsetting you, and I know absolutely nothing about your relationship with Dr. Dimanche. In fact, I didn't know there was one. And I'm certainly not making this up. But I've obviously struck a nerve here, Tony. Maybe you should tell me which one."

Tony was still fuming, but he seemed a bit calmer than he had a few moments earlier. He breathed a deep sigh and sat down again. He took a deep breath, trying quite obviously to compose himself.

"I'm sorry, Ty. I know you wouldn't do anything malicious. And when I think about it, I know that there's no way you could know about Jamais and me."

He paused and took a few more deep breaths. That seemed to help, and he appeared to have his emotions in control again.

"In a word, Ty, I've been seeing Jamais Dimanche myself for nearly a year. I had no reason to believe ours was anything but an exclusive relationship. She never ever gave me any reason to believe otherwise. And to find out now that she's been sleeping with someone else, and with a student at that, it's devastating. Just devastating. Devastating! Are you sure, Ty? Are you absolutely sure?"

"Well, Tony, for what it's worth, I have only these students' word that these relationships actually existed. I haven't spoken—"

"Wait a second! You said 'students' a few minutes ago, and you said 'these relationships.' Do you mean to tell me that there is more than one?"

I was reluctant to answer, but there seemed to be no obvious alternative.

"I'm afraid so, Tony. Two that I know about."

"Bitch! Bitch! Bitch! Bitch! Bitch!" And Sparky was up again, stalking around the office. "And to think I was planning to ask this woman to marry me. How could she? How could I? That bitch!"

"Take it easy, Tony. These things happen. As I said, I haven't talked to her yet, so I haven't heard her side of the story. In any case, if it is true, maybe it's just as well that you found out now rather than later."

Tony sighed.

"Yes, I suppose you are right. I just can't believe it, though. She just never gave me any indication that ours wasn't an exclusive relationship. None! I was this close to asking her to marry me."

He held up two fingers about an inch apart. That is close.

"Well, I do plan to speak to her soon. Perhaps she'll be inclined to talk to you once we've had that conversation. Because, Tony, as hard as getting this news has been on you, I hope you understand that what I said was said in confidence. I had no way of knowing that you were involved with Jamais Dimanche. If I had, I would have kept my mouth shut. I obviously should have done so anyway. So you have to give me your word as a gentleman and as an officer of this university that, as difficult as it may be for you, you won't say anything to her about this or to anyone else for that matter. I must have your word. I know it will be hard, but you absolutely have to do that. I mentioned this situation to you to get your advice as a colleague and as a member of the SNAF-U administration. And I promise that I will speak to her as soon as I possibly can. Will you give me your word?"

Tony was clearly insulted.

"Of course, you have my word, McTavish. I'm British, and I'll get over this! Now let's get back to business."

And we did. And as far as I know, although it really must have been hard for him, he never said word to Dimanche. But one thing he did say as I was leaving his office was that, you guessed it, as pissed as he was at her, he had to admit that the sex was great.

So that was it. It was time to have a long talk with Dr. Dimanche. I had put it off as long as I could, but I was resolved to finally do so. But fate once again intervened in my plans.

"Jarvis," I called to summon him into my office. "I need an appointment with Dr. Jamais Dimanche in the Department of Romantic Interlocution and Poetic Evolution. Please give her a call and have her come in to see me at her earliest convenience."

"Sure thing, Dean McTavish."

Jarvis made a note on his little pad and turned to leave the office, then turned again toward me.

"Dean McTavish, if you have just a moment. There is something I'd like to talk to you about."

Oh no, I thought. Don't tell me that Dimanche has been sleeping with Jarvis too. He closed the door and sat down beside my desk.

"I hate to bother you with this, Dean McTavish, especially because I know you have a lot on your plate right now. But I respect your opinions, and in the short time I've known you, I've come to trust you and to admire the way you deal with things here. So here's the story. I have a friend who's a secretary in RIPE. We have lunch together sometimes, and we've gotten to know each other pretty well. She's a nice person, and I like her a lot, and so does my wife, and we've noticed recently that she seems kind of down in the dumps. I haven't been able to get her to tell me exactly why, but I know it has something to do with her job. I thought that maybe you could talk to her and that if it is job-related, there might be some way you could help. I know that stuff like this isn't a part of your job description, but she is a nice person and... well... I'd like to help her if I can."

"Sure, Jarvis. Make an appointment for her. If she's willing to talk to me, I'll be happy to talk to her. Make it clear, though, that I can't promise anything."

"Good enough. I'll get right on it, and I'll get an appointment for Dimanche too.

Turns out that the two appointments were scheduled for the same day, the RIPE secretary in the morning and Dimanche in the afternoon. Jarvis escorted Samantha Diddle into my office.

"Dean McTavish, this is my friend Samantha, Samantha Diddle."

"Pleased to meet you, Ms. Diddle. Jarvis has told me a little bit about you, and I'm delighted that you were willing to come see me. Please sit down. Thanks, Jarvis."

"Thank you, Dean McTavish... thank you for seeing me," she said, somewhat tentatively. "I didn't really want to come, but Jarvis sort of insisted. He said he thought you could help."

"Well, I'm not sure, Ms. Diddle, but I'll help in any way I can. Perhaps you should tell me exactly what the problem is."

"Uhhmm, I… I'm worried about my job, Dean McTavish. I'm a secretary in RIPE, and I think I'm good at my job. I work hard, and I stay out of trouble, at least I've stayed out of trouble up to now. But now I'm afraid that I might lose my job, and I just can't afford to have that happen."

"What have you done that might cost you your job, Ms. Diddle?"

"Well, I'm not sure that I've done anything yet. It's what I think I should do, what I think I have to do that may cause me to lose my job."

"And what is that?"

"Well, maybe I should… Do you think you can help me, Dean McTavish? Because I don't think I want to tell you all this if you can't. It's so embarrassing as it is, so if you don't think you can help me, you should tell me now, and I'll just leave."

"I don't know, Ms. Diddle. And I can't know until I have some idea of the nature of your problem. Please understand that you don't have to tell me if you don't want to, and I'm not going to try to force you to say anything you don't want to say. If you leave now, it will be as if this meeting never happened. But I certainly can't help if I don't know what the problem is."

"Yes, I can see that."

"One thing I can tell you is that anything you say to me will stay right here. You don't have to worry about that."

"Okay, here goes. I'm a secretary in RIPE. Did I say that? Anyway, in my job I have to deal with all of the faculty in the department, and sometimes I'm asked to help them out in particular ways, not anything that's not appropriate, but I help them prepare manuscripts and materials for classes and things like that. Well, a few weeks ago, one of the faculty members asked for my help with a manuscript. I was glad to help, so we began getting together in the office when I was free to help organize the notes so that I could begin typing them up. Then one day, this faculty member suggested that we get together for lunch so that we could go over some changes. I didn't think anything about it, and since I would get a free lunch out of it, it didn't seem to be a problem. There were a couple of additional lunches, and then one day, this faculty member invited me to her house for dinner so we could continue our work. I still didn't see anything wrong, it still seemed pretty much in line with my responsibilities, and I was going to get paid extra for working outside of my regular hours. So I went.

"We had dinner, and things were going along just fine. We had some wine, and then we were sitting side by side on the couch, looking over her manuscript, and the next thing I knew, we were kissing. Then we were taking each other's clothes off, and before I knew it, it was morning."

"Do you want to tell me who this faculty member is, Ms. Diddle."

As if I didn't already know.

"Do I really have to?"

"No, you don't, of course. But if I'm going to do anything about the situation, I think I need to know who else is involved in it."

"Well, yes, I guess I should tell you. It was Professor Dimanche. Jamais Dimanche."

Busy girl.

"I know I shouldn't have done it, Dean McTavish. I mean I don't even think I'm gay or bisexual or whatever. I mean I have a boyfriend, and I really care about him, and I don't want this to mess up our relationship. I mean the thing with Dr. Dimanche, it just happened, and now I'm scared stiff."

"Well, I think I can understand that, and I can understand why. You don't want to continue the relationship, but you think that if you break it off, it will put your job in jeopardy because Professor Dimanche may not react positively, let's say, to your decision. Is that close?"

"Yes, sir."

"Well, I suspect you know, Ms. Diddle, that you should probably have used better judgment here, but I guess you had no way of knowing what Professor Dimanche had in mind. And in any case, it's not my place to pass judgment on you. Jarvis may have told you, I have an appointment to speak with Professor Dimanche this afternoon. I won't mention you specifically if you don't want me to, but I'll try to make it clear to her that in her position, she shouldn't even give the appearance of taking advantage of people who report to her."

"Thank you, Dean McTavish. I would appreciate it if you wouldn't mention my name."

"Fine. I think I can do that, at least I'll try. Thank you for coming to see me, Ms. Diddle."

And with that, Samantha left. No, she didn't leave me with a parting comment about the quality of the sex, but I could tell by the look on her face as she described the episode, as brief as that description was, that even if she wasn't gay or bisexual or whatever, she had *really* enjoyed it.

I wondered again, how much did *NONSENSE* know about all this?

It was clearly time for me to meet Jamais Dimanche, but I still wasn't quite ready yet. There was one more stop to make before I arrived at that final destination. I needed a bit more background if I could get it, so it was time to put in a call to Leo Da Vinci.

"Leo? This is Ty. How's tricks?"

"Can't complain, dude. What's on your mind? Make it quick because I have an… uh, appointment in a few minutes."

"This shouldn't take too long. I need to pick your brain once again about one of our faculty colleagues, one we haven't talked about before. What can you tell me about Jamais Dimanche?"

No response.

"Leo, you still there?"

"Yeah, I'm still here. Listen. If you want to talk to me about Jamais Dimanche, you're going to have to treat me to lunch. I get to pick the place, and you have to come pick me up in your chauffeured limousine."

"Leo, I don't have a limousine or a chauffeur. I drive a five-year-old Jeep, but I'll be happy to take you to lunch. I will come pick you up, and you can pick the place."

"Great! See you in about twenty minutes."

I told Jarvis to cancel my next appointment and headed to the parking structure to collect my car and Leo. Why did Leo want me to take him to lunch? And why did he hesitate when I asked him about Dimanche? Had Leo been sleeping with her too? Naw. That couldn't be, could it? I didn't even want to think about that possibility and the additional complications it would create, so I tried to imagine what sort of place Leo might pick for lunch. Despite his eccentricities, there was always the possibility that his favorite place might be the most expensive restaurant in town. I hoped not. Traffic was light, so I got to the NUThouse in about fifteen minutes, and to my pleasant surprise, Leo was at the curb, waiting for me.

"Hey, dude. Where's the chauffeur? Okay, we're going to the Burgermeister, best burgs and brews in town. Turn right at the next corner."

He got in, and we headed off. I had just turned the corner when he told me to stop. And just ahead of us, not even a block away from where I'd picked him up, was the Burgermeister.

"Leo, you could have walked here from your office, and I could have met you here."

"Yeah, but then I wouldn't have been able to ride in the chauffeur driven limo. You know that the guy who was in this job before you did have a limo, don't you? Maybe you didn't get one because you're not the right ethnic persuasion. Maybe you should ask Sligh and Asskisser about that."

Maybe I should. I parked the car a half a block down from the restaurant, and we went in. It was still a few minutes before noon, but the place was already bustling. We got a table near the front window and sat down. A middle-aged waitron, who looked like she'd been working there forever, came to take our order.

"Hey, Judy," Leo said brightly. He was obviously a regular here.

"How ya' doin', Dr. Da Vinci?" she answered. "Shall I bring you your usual?"

"Abso-damn-lutely! Cholesterol Bullet, large fries, and a pint of Guinness."

"And you, sir? I don't think I've seen you here before."

Leo introduced me. "This is the new dean, Ty McTavish. Ty, this is Judy, best damn waitress in the business."

"A pleasure to meet you, Judy. Well, let me see. Leo obviously knows what he wants, but I need another second to look over the menu. Do you have any specials?"

"Why yes, we do, we have—"

"Hell, he doesn't want any specials," Leo interrupted. "He'll have a Cholesterol Bullet, fries, and a beer same as me. What kind of beer do you want?"

Since I needed to stay in Leo's good graces at least for the next hour, I demurred. "I'll have a Honey Brown."

Judy left to place our orders, and I decided to get down to cases with Leo.

"So, Leo, my friend, let's get back to the question I asked you earlier. What can you tell me about Jamais Dimanche?"

The biggest smile I'd ever seen from him lit Leo's face. He was quite obviously going to enjoy talking about Dr. Dimanche.

"Well, I can tell you that she's one hell of a beautiful woman. What a built! Man! Have you ever seen her in a miniskirt with one of those tight blouses that she wears? Man! A look at that woman would give sight to the blind. I've asked her out about twenty different times, and she always says no. Shows that she's an intelligent woman, and that makes me want her even more. I even asked her to marry me once, but she said no to that proposal too. When I think about it, I can't say that I blame her. I'm sort of like Groucho Marx when it comes to stuff like that. I'd be afraid to marry any woman who would have me. Still, I probably would have taken a shot at it if she'd said yes. Scuttlebutt, though, is that she sleeps around a lot but unfortunately not with me."

I breathed a sigh of relief.

"Why do you want to know?'

I'd already shot my mouth off once too often. Even though I trusted Leo, I wasn't about to do it again.

"What else can you tell me about her?

"All I have is rumor and innuendo, Ty, but as you know well, rumor and innuendo is frequently based on fact, especially around this place. For one thing, I've been told that Dimanche was married at one point, about ten years ago, before she came to SNAF-U. Guy was younger than she was by several years and had been a professional athlete of some sort. Rumor is that he died of a heart attack in bed, a year or so after they were married. They say that when the paramedics wheeled him out of the house, he had a big smile on his face. No one knows for sure, of course, but you can guess what they say caused the heart attack. What the hell, the whole story may be apocryphal. But it's a hell of a good story isn't it."

"Yeah, it certainly is that. Listen, Leo, I can't go into any detail about Dimanche, but I can tell you that it involves her alleged sexual prowess. So anything else you can tell me that might be helpful will be appreciated."

"So she's been sleeping with her students, has she?"

I didn't answer, but I didn't need to. Leo was perceptive enough to know that if a faculty member's sexual activities ever required the intervention of a dean, those activities almost always involved a student.

"Well, there's not a lot more that I know, Ty. I know she's currently involved with Atherton-Sparks (as always, Leo knew a lot more about what was happening at SNAF-U than I did), but that apparently hasn't stopped her from exploring other opportunities, if you get my drift, and I've heard that she made a play at one point for the chair of the French Department, Laforge. Problem was, she found out that he's gay. If you have to do something to curtail her sexual activities, all I can say is good luck. I certainly don't envy you that responsibility. I sure as hell wouldn't know how to do it. Maybe you could threaten to make her get a clitorectomy or whatever they call it if she doesn't shape up. Or better maybe you can threaten that if she doesn't shape up, you'll make her sleep with me. That might slow her down. Whatever you decide, lots o' luck."

"Well, thanks for trying, Leo." I sighed. "At least I know a little bit more about her now than I did. I do have one more question for you, and I admit up front that I may be risking our friendship by asking it."

"Well, you know what they say. Friendships come and go, but a good bacon cheeseburger is forever."

"I'll assume that means that I can ask my question. Anyway, somehow, Leo, the big wigs at *NONSENSE* found out about Dimanche's doings, no pun intended, and they contacted Charity Butler, who contacted the president, who contacted the provost, etc. You weren't the source of that information, were you?"

"No, I wasn't, Ty, although it sure as hell sounds like something I would do, doesn't it? Damn! I wish I had thought of it, but… naw, it wasn't me."

"Okay, thanks, Leo. And thanks for not being offended."

"My pleasure. I do have one piece of advice for you though, Ty. If everything I hear about this woman is true, and I bet I haven't heard the half of it, I would strongly suggest that you try to find a good strong chastity belt and lock it securely… on yourself. And give *me* the keys."

Judy arrived with our Cholesterol Bullets, and I came quickly to understand what Leo meant about a good bacon cheeseburger. The Bullet was, without question, the best bacon cheeseburger that I'd ever tasted—thick, juicy, with a nice peppery flavor and mounds of crisp bacon and pepper jack cheese. I was sure that I could feel my cholesterol level rising with every bite. But, man, was it worth it.

So it was finally time for Jamais Dimanche. Jarvis had made the afternoon appointment for her, and she arrived promptly. I thought it prudent to collect her from the outer lobby myself. It would give me at least a few moments to size her up before I had to get down to cases. Leo's brief description of her did her little justice. She was indeed *stunningly* attractive. I could see why all these guys (and girls) were seduced (in all the senses of that word) by her. She was drop-dead gorgeous! A tall (almost six feet), willowy brunette with everything in exactly the right place. Hers was a classic beauty in the Greta Garbo mold—skin like ivory, long, slender fingers, a smile that lit up the room as if someone had turned on the sun. I had wondered how she would be dressed, imagining almost every possibility, including completely nude. As it turned out, she was dressed quite conservatively, in a dark green, ankle-length skirt and a yellow blouse. Her blouse was unbuttoned at the top presumably, or perhaps obviously, to accentuate her charms. It did exactly that as did the rest of her outfit. Conservative it may have been, but a suit of chain mail would not have been able to disguise the fact that Jamais Dimanche was one incredibly beautiful woman. Although she was clearly from some Francophone country, the pleasantries we exchanged as we walked into the office didn't reveal much of an accent.

"Thank you for coming to see me, Dr. Dimanche. Please make yourself comfortable."

She took the chair in front of my desk, folded her hands in her lap, and leaned forward to face me. As she did, a lock of her hair slipped onto her forehead. She brushed it back into place with a graceful, practiced motion that gave me an even closer look at one of those exquisite hands. The position she assumed also brought her close enough for me to catch the scent of her perfume—subtle but enticing, neither too sweet nor too flowery. I'm certainly no expert on perfumes, and many of the newer scents actually make me nauseous, but hers was quite appealing as was just about everything else about her. This might be pleasant, but it wouldn't be easy. And it might be quite dangerous.

"Thank you for the invitation, Dean McTavish. I have so wanted to meet you. I've heard so many wonderful things about you. And please, please call me Jamais."

I decided not to go through my and-you-can-call-me-Ty routine since I was pretty sure that she had already made the decision to do just that.

"Fine. Let's get down to business, shall we?"

"Ah, yes. I think you have already gotten down to my business, have you not, Ty?"

Shit. Someone had talked. But since I had, in fact, told at least some of them to do so, I should be pleased that they did.

"I'm not sure I take your meaning, Jamais."

"Dirk Wetrod did come to see me a few days ago. He told me that he was following your advice and that he did not plan to sleep with me again. He said that he hoped that would not jeopardize our professional relationship, but that you had promised to assist him in case it did. I presume he was representing the situation correctly?"

The fact that I was unprepared for this turn of events was quite clearly irrelevant. I had to deal with it.

"Yes, Jamais, that was precisely my advice to Mr. Wetrod. And I do hope that his decision will have no adverse effect on his relationship with you or on his career in RIPE. He's a bright young man, and he has a good record here at SNAF-U. I don't want to see his career go down the drain because of this indiscretion."

"Nor do I, Dean McTavish. You see I *am* a professional, and I am well capable of separating considerations that relate to my personal life from those that relate to my professional life. As Dirk Wetrod's scholarly interests are most closely allied to my own among the faculty in RIPE, it seems appropriate for him to continue to work with me. Dirk is a very bright young man, as you say, and I think he has an excellent future in RIPE. And to assure that his situation is handled objectively, I have asked one of my colleagues to serve as codirector of his dissertation. I hope that meets with your satisfaction."

"That's fine, Jamais, and seems an appropriate expedient in this situation. I do hope you understand that I intend to keep an eye on his progress."

"As you wish. And what would you like me to do about Samantha Diddle?"

Damn. This woman was good.

"To what exactly are you referring, Professor Dimanche?"

"Come on, Ty. If you've spoken to Dirk, you've almost certainly also spoken to Sean, and if you've spoken to the two of them, the odds are that you've talked to Samantha too. Don't toy with me."

"All right. I have spoken to Samantha. And formally, I consider her situation to be the same as Dirk's. She is someone who effectively reports to you, and that requires, in my opinion, that your relationship again be a strictly professional one. I would think that you would agree with that. You say that you are a professional. I'm sure that you feel that you are, so I am appalled that, as a professional, you would put those who report to you in compromising situations."

"I am a professional, Ty, but I am also a woman. And I can tell from your response to me, as hard as you're obviously working to disguise it, that even you find me to be an attractive one. I am not ashamed of my sexuality. I am attracted to men and sometimes to women. They are attracted to me. Things happen. I did not plan any of this, but I don't apologize for it either. I can assure you that all of those relationships have ended. In the case of that charming young man, Mr. Grabuttski, I assure you again that his grade in my course was based entirely on his performance on the relevant assignments, not on his performance, uh… elsewhere. Moreover, I did not provide Mr. Grabuttski with any assistance with the class that wasn't also available to my other students. I did, in fact, invite other students, male and female, to my home to help them with their coursework."

Commendable, I thought. *I hope you didn't sleep with all of them.*

"No, I didn't."

Damn! I hadn't said a word. Does she read minds too? I ignored her statement. I was about to lose (had already lost?) control of this situation, and I had to keep that from happening.

"And can you also assure me that you will avoid establishing, no, let's call a spade a spade. I want your word, Professor Dimanche, that you will not establish any further sexual relationships with students, graduate or undergraduate, or with others here at SNAF-U whose professional situations might be compromised by those relationships. Will you give me your word on that?"

Dimanche hesitated. She got up from her chair and walked over to the window. She stood looking out at the quadrangle, running her fingers through her hair, for several moments before returning to her chair.

"All right. Yes. I will give you my word. But what do I get in return?

What I really wanted to say here was "You get to keep your job," but I decided to be a bit more statesmanlike.

"In return, Dr. Dimanche, I will chalk the previous episodes up to your, let's say, exuberance for your students and coworkers. I will not report the details of the incidents to the provost or the president. Although they know that there is a problem that involves a faculty member and that person's students, they don't know that you are that faculty member. I'll simply report to them that I have resolved the situation, and I will make every effort to see that the details reach no other ears. But if I hear of any further incident that represents an abrogation of your commitment, I'll do everything I can to have you dismissed from this university. Are we clear on this?"

She nodded assent.

"One thing more, Professor Dimanche. I'm sure you are aware that SNAF-U is working diligently to return to the *NONSENSE* top twenty-five listing of American universities. We have been told that someone at the magazine has gotten wind of the… uh, exploits, for lack of a better term, of one of our faculty members. As far as I know, they have no details, and I obviously intend to do all I can to see that things stay that way. So I hope you understand that any consequences of your actions that might accrue in a negative fashion to our attempts to get back into the *NONSENSE* top twenty-five will have serious consequences for you. Is *that* clear?"

"As clear as glass, Dean McTavish. Is there anything more?"

There was no reason for me to say anything about Sparky nor any for her to mention her relationship with him. But I did wonder if she knew that I knew.

"Nothing that comes to mind."

"Then I'll be off. Thank you again for seeing me. It's been... interesting."

She rose and walked toward the door, pausing before opening it to leave. I wondered if she was going to tell me how great everyone thought the sex had been. I was close. She extended her hand to shake mine, and she held my hand for a long moment after the formal handshake was done.

"Ty," she said, smiling, "we've obviously gotten off to a rather bad start, and I'm unhappy about that. Perhaps we might get to know each other better over dinner some evening."

Moral terpsichore. But then few of us are saints.

CHAPTER XII

To MY RELIEF, AND I must say somewhat to my surprise, things quieted down quite a lot after *l'affaire* Dimanche. As far as I could tell, she kept her word, at least through the end of the spring term. For me, the end of the academic year brought the prospect that I'd finally be able to spend some quality time in the lab. Working on my research had pretty much been hit or miss up to that point. I had hired a technician and, more recently, a postdoctoral fellow and the graduate student I'd brought with me from HUT was still plugging along. All things considered, my research was actually going pretty well, even though I wasn't able to spend much time at the lab bench myself. The grant I brought with me to SNAF-U had run out, so I no longer had any external research support, but the funding I got from SNAF-U as a part of my agreement to become dean would keep me going for at least a couple of years. I did hope to spend some time during the summer months, writing grant proposals. My experience had been that universities slowed down considerably during the summer months, even for an administrator. And for some weeks after commencement, that was exactly the case. There were no fires to fight, far fewer meetings to attend, and much more time to spend at the lab bench, something

I still really enjoyed. I should have known it was too good to last. One morning in mid-June, Jarvis announced that the president and the provost were coming down to see me. I cringed. I knew it couldn't be with good news.

Sligh and Asskisser came into my office. Sligh closed the door behind him.

"Good morning, Ty." I stepped from behind my desk and accepted Sligh's handshake. Olan and I shook hands as well. "I hope you've been enjoying your summer break. Olan tells me that you've been working in your lab. I hope that's going well."

"Thanks for asking, President Sligh. Yes, the work is going quite well. I have a couple of people working in the lab, and since things have quieted down, I've been able to do some experiments myself. I still enjoy research, and apparently, I haven't completely lost my experimental touch. And I'm planning to write some grant proposals this summer so that I won't have to depend entirely on my start-up funding to support my lab."

"Glad to hear it," Sligh replied, though in a tone that suggested that he really didn't care that much about what was going on in my lab. I thought at the very least he'd be happy to know that I was hoping to let the U off the hook for my research support.

"Please," I offered, directing Sligh and Olan to the sofa across from my desk.

"No, thanks, Ty, I think we'll stand. This shouldn't take long, so let me get right to the point. We haven't talked much recently about the *NONSENSE* top twenty-five, but as I'm sure you know, every day brings us closer to the announcement of the rankings for this year. We've kept in close contact with Doug Little, and I regret, I very much regret to say that the news he has given us isn't good. Of course, he can't divulge the rankings ahead of the formal announcement, but based on what he has been able to tell us, it doesn't look like we're going to make this year's top twenty-five."

I sighed. So did Asskisser. In my case, though, it wasn't only because I felt badly for the university but also because I didn't want to go through another year of hand-wringing and general anguish about that stupid ranking.

"I'm really sorry to hear that, President Sligh." I know how hard you and all of us have worked to get us back into the top twenty-five."

And I had worked hard at it. There was Ima's reception, the business with Jamais Dimanche, and all those interminable executive staff meetings.

"Despite the fact that I don't think those rankings serve any useful purpose," I continued, "I know that it's better to be in the top twenty-five than out of it. Is there anything at all that we can do at this point?"

The question was a sincere one, but I still hoped the answer was no.

"I'm glad you asked that question," Sligh replied, "because I do have a specific idea. Olan and I have discussed the matter, and he agrees with me. What we think we need is a new approach, some fresh ideas, new energy, a different strategy. We've done everything we can think of to meet the *NONSENSE* criteria. What we feel we need is some fresh thinking, and as the new kid on the block, we think you're the person to give us that fresh perspective. You've shown yourself to be capable and creative in your first year here, Ty. You did a great job in chairing the committee to plan Ima's retirement celebration, and Olan and I think you're just the man for the *NONSENSE* job. So, Ty, I would like for you to take on the responsibility of getting SNAF-U back into the *NONSENSE* top twenty-five. Put us over the top!"

I was dumbfounded. "You mean for… for… for next year, right?" I stuttered, hoping at least to have a year to put something together.

"No, no, Ty, I mean for this round, for the rankings that will come out in the fall."

"But that's impossible!" I protested. "That only leaves me a couple of months, and you just admitted that everyone else at SNAF-U has done everything they can think of to do."

"And that's exactly why we're giving the job to you," said Olan. "Bob and I feel that you're the man to make this work. And I have to be candid, Ty, and point out that you haven't been as much help as you might have been in dealing with the problem up to now. You didn't give any input when we prepared our responses for the various NONSENSE categories, and you haven't really been very supportive of our other efforts to get back in the rankings. Apart from dealing with that case of moral turpitude, you haven't been of much help at all. Bob and I feel that this is a chance for you to show that you're a team player, that SNAF-U means something to you, and that you're one of us."

I was tempted to point out, in the strongest possible terms, that no way was I one of them, but the reality was that I was. I was now a member of the SNAF-U team, and although I had done much, much more than Sligh and Asskisser knew to help get us back into the top twenty-five, there didn't seem to be much point in saying so. In fact, I concluded that I was quite neatly painted into the proverbial corner, in part by I brush that I myself had wielded. There seemed to be little choice but to accept the challenge, although I didn't have a clue how I would meet it.

"I'll do my best," I said weakly. "I'll give it my best shot."

"Good!" Sligh said, smiling. He put his arm around my shoulder. "I knew we could count on you. When do you think you'll have something for us?"

"Give me a few days, President Sligh, and I'll get back to you."

"Great. Olan and I will look forward to hearing from you. I know you're the right man for the job. Remember, SNAF-U will be counting on you."

We all shook hands again; Sligh patted me on the back, and they left. I slumped back in my chair. What had I gotten myself into? I had no clue about what I was going to do. I certainly didn't intend to play the silly game of looking for loopholes in the ranking categories. Besides, there didn't appear much else that could be done about that. What the hell was I going to do? Maybe a good start would be to hear myself think out loud a bit. I called Leo.

"Leo, it's Ty."

"What's up, guy? Haven't heard from you in a while."

"I was hoping that you and I could get together for lunch. I haven't had a Bullet in a while, and I could use one."

"Okay… what do you want?" he asked in a tone dripping with cynicism.

"Really, Leo, I don't want you to do anything. I just need to talk, I would really like to have a Bullet and a beer, and it has been a while since we got together."

"Well, I'm still suspicious, but if you're buying, I'll go along. Pick me up around one. Things will have quieted down some at the Meister by then. See you then."

I picked Leo up in front of the NUThouse and repeated the usual pattern of driving a block and parking at the restaurant. We sat at our favorite table by the window, and Judy took our orders, which by now she knew by heart for both of us.

"Well, if I may say so, Dean McTavish," Leo began, "you look like shit. It's a beautiful summer's day. We're at the home of the world's best bacon cheeseburger, and all should be right with the world. I certainly can't complain. So what the hell is wrong with you?"

"It's *NONSENSE*, Leo."

"You mean my statement, or the magazine?"

"The magazine. I got a visit from the president and the provost this morning. They have heard from one of the *NONSENSE* guys that our chances of getting back into the top twenty-five this year aren't too good. That in itself would be bad enough, but they've decided to make a last minute push to get us there. And guess who they've elected to lead that push? *Me!* I didn't see how I could say no, but I don't have any clue about what to do. I don't know any of the people at *NONSENSE*, I don't know anything about how they do their actual rankings, and in any case, there's not much time left before they make their final decisions. I don't have any reason to think that what I do or don't do will jeopardize my job, but I can't imagine that it will endear me to anyone here if we don't make the top twenty-five and if people learn that I had a chance to do something about it and didn't. And I am 100 percent dead-certain positive that Sligh and Asskisser will blame me, and publicly at that, if we don't make the list, even though they're absolutely clueless themselves about what to do. As a matter of fact, there's a part of me that thinks that they know we won't get into the top twenty-five, and they're just looking for a scapegoat to blame when we don't. And they've decide that it should be me."

Leo sat quietly for a few seconds.

"Don't say anything for a few minutes. Give me a moment to think." He rubbed his chin and looked out the window. Judy came over to the table, and he waved her away. He sat like that for some time, almost five minutes. Then he turned back to face me.

"I think I can help you out, Ty. I can't guarantee anything, but I have an idea. The kicker is that you'll have to give me complete freedom to do what needs to be done. Are you willing to do that?"

"Well, within reason, Leo. I'm not going to condone assassinations or bombings or anything like that."

I was only half joking. I had no idea what sort of scheme Leo might come up with.

"It won't be anything that extreme, Ty, but it will be tricky."

"Okay," I responded, "I'm willing to give it a go because I certainly don't have any viable ideas at this point. What do you have in mind?"

"I don't want to answer that question right now, Ty. I need some additional time to think things through. But as I said, it will be tricky."

"Okay, then, tell me this. Why are you volunteering to help me with this?"

"For several reasons, Ty. First, as I think I said to you when we first met, my relationship with SNAF-U is something like the relationship between a virus and its host, and what's good for the host is good for the virus. And of course, I'm the virus. At least people think I am. Anyway, if SNAF-U is in the top twenty-five, everyone will be happy, the university will prosper, and that will be good for me. Plus, people will be inclined to leave me alone, and as you know very well, that's exactly the way I like it. Second, if what I have in mind works, we'll stick it to the magazine. I think this ranking shit sucks. I know you do too, and if we can stick it to them, we should. Last but not least, and if I was a sensitive guy, which, of course I'm not, but if I was, I would be offended that you didn't come up with this reason yourself. I'm willing to help you because you're my friend."

He meant that, and I was touched. "Thanks, Leo, and I mean it when I say that I'm glad you are my friend."

Judy brought the Bullets and the beer, and they were both as good as always. I was actually starting to feel a bit better about all of this even though I had no idea what Leo was going to do. And that scared me a little bit. He had said that it wouldn't be as extreme as bombings or assassinations, but that didn't mean that it still wouldn't be extreme. We finished our meals, and I dropped Leo off in front of the NUThouse.

"I suspect you're wondering what the next step will be," he said as he opened the car door. "Come to my apartment at eight o'clock on this

Saturday evening. That should give me more than enough time to think this all through. I'll email you my address."

"Okay, I'll see you then."

The rest of the week was uneventful, but I must admit that I was anxious about the meeting with Leo. What in hell did he plan to do? I was convinced that it would be something extreme. The question was, how extreme? I arrived at Leo's place a few minutes before eight on Saturday evening. He opened the door. He was dressed in shorts and a T-shirt. It was summer after all. I walked into his apartment, surveyed the surroundings, and stood there with my mouth open. I expected a pig sty or the cave of the Abominable Snowman. Leo's apartment was immaculate. It was a large loft with lots of wood paneling and a collection of artwork that was enviable. There were Asian and African sculptures, some gorgeous Indian batiks, and a number of impressionist paintings that I assumed were originals. Leo noticed my astonishment.

"Not what you expected, eh, Ty?"

"No, Leo. I'm not sure exactly what I expected, but it certainly wasn't this."

"Well, I admit that I'm eccentric. I even flaunt that fact, but I'm not a philistine. I told you once that I like nice things. My situation allows me to have them, and I do. Want a beer?"

"Please. What have you got?"

"Well, since I knew you'd be coming, I stocked some Honey Brown." He went to the fridge, got a bottle, and filled a mug.

"So," I offered, "are you ready to tell me what you have in mind?"

"Not quite, yet, Ty. There are some other people coming."

"Who?"

"You'll see, and you shouldn't have to wait long."

I didn't. The doorbell rang, and Leo went to answer it. Stoy Urgek and Michael Baccaliprati walked in. Urgek was disheveled, as usual, and was obviously continuing his practice of not using deodorant. I tried to stand upwind of him.

"I do not know why you invite me here, Da Vinci," Urgek said, "but curiosity made me come."

"Well, for my part, I was delighted to get your invitation," Baccaliprati said effusively. "I've never ever been invited to the home of a fellow faculty member before. Wow, Leo, you have a terrific place. I wish I had a place like this. Where'd you get all this great art stuff? How much—"

Leo didn't let him finish. "Come on in, guys. Can I get you something, beer, wine, something stronger?"

"I'll take a vodka, neat, if you have," said Urgek.

"Beer will be fine for me," added Baccaliprati.

"Is this the crew?" I asked.

"Not quite," Leo replied. "There are still two more to come."

The bell rang again. I had been surprised that the first two arrivals were Urgek and Baccaliprati. I was astounded by the identities of the other two. It was Ola Ebola Shalaka and… Jamais Dimanche. Leo welcomed them and offered them drinks, white wine for Dimanche, nothing for Ola; and we all sat down in Leo's conversation pit, which was comprised of plush leather chairs and a sofa around a glass top coffee table.

"You're probably all wondering why I asked you here," Leo began. Heads nodded. "Well, let's get right to the point. Ty and I need your help." Looks of surprise. "Ty, why don't you explain your, uh, our dilemma to our friends."

I cleared my throat in the typical faculty manner. I had hoped Leo would run with the ball here.

"Well, in a nutshell, the situation is this. As you are all no doubt aware, SNAF-U fell out of the *NONSENSE* top twenty-five rankings last year. That caused no end of embarrassment, consternation, and concern, and the administration has worked hard to get us back into the next rankings. Now I suspect that all of you are like me and that you think that the *NONSENSE* rankings are just that, nonsense. But the folks on the top floor of the administration building feel very differently, and if I'm honest, I have to admit that it's better to be on the list than off it. Unfortunately, the word we get from those in the know at the magazine suggests that we're not going to make it back into the top twenty-five, at least not this year. The president and the provost, in their infinite wisdom, have given me the responsibility of doing something about that. I asked Leo for help, and he came up with a plan, which he's going to reveal to us tonight. Leo?"

"Yeah, I do have a plan, so let me cut right to the chase. We can't do anything about the categories. We can't make ourselves any better than we actually are. What we can do is make ourselves *look* better than we actually are, at least to *NONSENSE*. The question is how do we do that in the amount of time between now and when the rankings are released? I can think of only one sure way to get the job done. We're going to hack into the *NONSENSE* computers and change our scores."

My jaw dropped again. I sputtered for a moment before I could even get out a response. "Leo, we can't do that! It's illegal not to mention unethical. And it's certainly not something that I can be a party to."

"I was sure you'd say that, Ty, and I can't say I blame you. But first of all, I'm not sure that it is illegal. The case law on computer hacking is still pretty murky. Second, I think we could have a very productive debate about the ethics of these ranking systems in the first place. You and I both know that *NONSENSE* doesn't give a damn which school is number one, number twenty-five, or number 1056. They rank schools for one purpose and one purpose only—to sell magazines. That's why they change the system every year or two. No one would buy the magazines if the same schools were given the same rankings year after year after year. So they manipulate the rules so that schools change places and so that some schools drop out altogether. That's not ethical. So I look at what I have in mind as simply beating them at their own game, sticking it to the man, you know. They change the rules, so can we. Plus, as I know you know, all these schools cheat. We're just going to be a bit more creative than the rest of them."

"Well, when you put it that way, Leo, it almost makes sense. But for a dean to be involved in something like this, it just doesn't seem right."

The term "moral terpsichore" was beginning to take on new meaning, at least for me.

"Ty, I guarantee you that deans at every school in the top twenty-five are involved up to their ears in what their universities are doing to stay there. But my plan doesn't involve your being anything but an observer, except for one thing. And I'll get to that," he said, anticipating my next question. "Other than that, your hands will be clean."

"So here's the plan. We'll use Urgek's and Michael's computer skills to hack into the *NONSENSE* computers, and once we get in, we'll adjust our numbers so that we make the top twenty-five. Now getting into the computers won't be easy. The files will be protected, and while I know that Urgek and Michael could figure out the access codes in time or a way to get around them, we don't have a lot of time as you know. So we need to get the access codes from a *NONSENSE* operative and as quickly as possible at that. That's where you come in, Jamais. I think the likely target for that part of the operation is Doug Little, the *NONSENSE* guy who is responsible for the rankings."

"Wait, a second, Leo," I interrupted. "Just how do you propose that she get the access codes?"

"What the hell kind of question is that? It should be obvious, why, with her charms, dude! Her very obvious charms! What else? She's going to charm the codes out of him. Just look at her! She could charm the sun from the sky! She could charm white off rice, she could charm milk out of cheese, she could charm stink off shit, she could—"

"We get the point, Leo!" All four of us certainly did.

Leo had been sitting in the chair next to Jamais. He slid off his seat, got down on his knees, and took her hand in his.

"Will you marry me?" he asked, a huge grin on his face.

Jamais blushed ever so slightly but composed herself quickly. For once it appeared that she was the one who'd been caught off guard.

"No, Leo, I won't." She took her hand away.

Leo got up and went on as if nothing at all had happened.

"Anyway, Ty, the one thing you'll need to do is to set up an opportunity for her to meet with Little, and, Jamais, you'll take it from there. Are we all in?"

"Well, I will do it," said Urgek. "It will give me chance to use my not inconsiderable skills and intellect, as you say, Leo. It is about time someone recognize that I have abilities far beyond those of average faculty, here or at any other university. This will be opportunity for me to show to SNAF-U and the world that Urgek is brilliant, that Urgek is—"

"Shut up, Urgek!" Leo snapped. "What about you, Michael, are you with us?"

I looked at Baccaliprati, and a small tear was forming at the corner of his eye.

"Oh, yes," he said gratefully. "I'm just so happy that you've included me in your plans! I can't tell you how happy it makes me that you think enough of me to want me to help you. It gives me such a feeling of camaraderie, and I don't think I've had that feeling in all my time here at SNAF-U, and I've been here for fifteen years. Thank you so much, Leo, for including me. It just means so much, I—"

"Shut up, Michael! Ola?"

"Well, to be honest, Da Vinci, I don't know why you asked me here in the first place. I don't know anything about computers, and I'm certainly not going to seduce anyone."

Leo scowled. So did I. So did Jamais.

"First of all, Ola," Leo said, "I'm not asking anybody to seduce anybody. Second, this is a NUThouse project, and like it or not, you are member of this department. There will be something important for you to do."

She perked up a bit at that last statement. "Well, if you put it that way, you can count me in. I certainly don't approve of those magazine rankings."

"Fine," Leo said and then turned to Jamais, "What about you, sweetheart?"

"I must admit, it does sound interesting, but I must ask the pertinent question… What's in it for me?"

Leo turned to me. "Ty?"

I had no ready response and so came back with the best one I could muster. "What do you want?"

She rested her chin on her folded hands and looked seductively at me. Maybe Leo *was* asking her to seduce someone. Me.

"I'll think of something, Ty. For now I admit that I am intrigued by the plan. It should be fun, and like the rest of you, I find these rankings totally useless. In fact, they probably do more harm than good." She leaned closer. "Besides, Ty, it might be useful to have you in my debt."

I was sure that I didn't like the sound of that, but there wasn't much I could do.

"Then it's settled," said Leo. "The first step will be to hook Jamais up with Doug Little, and, Ty, that's where you come in. That's the one point where you'll need to do something other than observe. You'll need to arrange for a meeting for the two of them."

"Okay," I said reluctantly, "I still don't like this, Leo. I don't like it at all, but I have to be honest and admit that I don't have a better idea. In fact, I don't have any other ideas, better or worse. So I guess we're all in, including me."

"Good. Once Ty arranges the meeting and Jamais gets the access codes, we'll meet here again to make our move."

We all left together. I gave one glance back at Leo as I walked out of his apartment. He smiled, and I somehow had the sense that although he was enjoying this and didn't much care what happened to him, he *was* my friend and would try to keep anything untoward from happening to me. That meant a lot.

CHAPTER XIII

A S LUCK WOULD HAVE it, when I got back to the office the following Monday and made some inquiries, I learned that Doug Little was scheduled to visit with Charity Butler later that same week. I had Jarvis schedule an appointment with him and arranged for Jamais to come to my office around the same time. Doug showed up promptly on the scheduled date, and Jarvis showed him into my office. We exchanged the usual handshake and took seats across from one another.

"I'm pleased to get the chance to meet you, Mr. Little. I know you have a busy schedule, so I appreciate your taking the time to meet with me."

"No, problem, Dean McTavish. I always appreciate the chance to meet my constituents, as it were. And I wanted to thank you too for helping my niece, Muffy. I've spoken with her, and she said that you were very sympathetic and helpful. Thanks so much."

"I was happy to do it, Mr. Little. Our students are our greatest asset, and I was happy to help Muffy with her dissertation committee. I haven't heard from her recently, so I certainly hope her writing is proceeding smoothly at this point."

Little leaned forward in his chair and folded his hands.

"I spoke with her a few days ago, and things seem to be fine. So thanks again. Now what did you want to see me about?"

"Well, my question is simple, Mr. Little. You know quite well that all of us are hoping that SNAF-U will move back into the *NONSENSE* top twenty-five, and I simply want to know whether there is anything I can do as dean to facilitate that."

Little scratched his chin.

"Unfortunately, Dean McTavish, I'm afraid the short answer is no. You understand how the system works, I'm sure. We have the data, it's being massaged even as we speak, and we'll see how the numbers fall out."

"So there's nothing additional that I can provide for you that might help our case?"

"No, I'm afraid there isn't. I should say, though, that SNAF-U's case is strong, and the fact that you've been in the top twenty-five before makes for a reasonable probability that you'll get in again. Of course, there are no guarantees."

Little was obviously being coy, but I guess he had to be. We already knew that we weren't likely to make the coming year's top twenty-five.

"Do you think the magazine has all the data it needs? My office is a repository for statistical information on graduate and undergraduate students and faculty, and we would, of course, be more than happy to provide any additional information you might need and which might help our case."

"Thanks for the offer, Dean McTavish, but I honestly don't think there's anything else that you can do. Your administrative offices have provided the data we requested, and as I said, we're compiling that information now. I know my assistants are working on the rankings at this very moment."

The phone rang. I excused myself and answered. Jarvis informed me that Jamais was outside. I stood up, offered my hand, and escorted Little to the door.

"Well, thank you for taking the time to meet with me, Mr. Little. I do hope this wasn't a waste of your time, but I wanted to be sure that you and the magazine have everything you need. And if there *is* anything else I can do, please let me know."

"I'll do that, Dean McTavish, it was a pleasure to meet you. Good luck."

I opened the door, and Jamais was standing a few feet away, directly in Little's path. He stopped and stared at her. Ten or fifteen seconds passed before I said anything. I figured that was enough time to get him on the hook, so I intervened.

"Oh, Mr. Little, this is Dr. Jamais Dimanache. She's a faculty member in the department of Romantic Interlocution and Poetic Evolution. Dr. Dimanche, Doug Little from *NONSENSE*."

She shook his hand and held it. She was good at that.

"It's a pleasure, Mr. Little. I do hope Ty has convinced you that SNAF-U belongs in the top twenty-five this year."

"Well, he did his best, Dr. Dimanche, and let me say that the pleasure is all mine."

"Well, thanks again for coming by, Mr. Little." Then, to Jamais. "Come on in, Jamais, and tell me what's on your mind."

She released his hand. Little walked to the door of the office but turned again to look at Dimanche before he left.

"I think we have him," I said, smiling.

"I know *I* have him," she replied. "Who should make the next move?"

"Let's give him a chance. I'll call you one way or another."

"I'll look forward to it," she said, smiling. This woman never let up. Maybe she couldn't, and perhaps that was just as well.

Jamais stayed for another five minutes or so, then left. It didn't take long for Little to bite. About an hour later, Jarvis directed his phone call to me.

"Dean McTavish, it's Doug Little. Sorry to bother you again, but I wonder if you can help me?"

"Happy to be of service, Mr. Little, what can I do for you? Did you think of something more you need to evaluate our ranking?"

I knew this was an unnecessary artifice, but I couldn't resist.

"Well, I feel a little awkward. I'm not actually calling about SNAF-U or *NONSENSE*. It's about the woman I met in your office, Dr. Dimanche. I just can't get her out of my mind. I'm hoping that I might be able to see her again. I'm not a married man, and well, I guess… well, I guess my first question should be… is she married?"

We have him by the short hairs, I thought. *Let's just hope we can hold on to him.*

"No, as far as I know, Mr. Little, she is not. My understanding is that she is engaged to Tony Atherton-Sparks, but I could be wrong about that. I suspect you've met him."

"Yeah, I have. But I guess I shouldn't feel that I have to let a fiancé stand in my way. Do you think she would go out with me? I know that's a strange question, but I'm not here for very long this week, and you do seem to know something about her, so…"

"Well," I said slowly, getting my lie together, "she did seem to be somewhat taken with you after your meeting this morning. She asked me about you in our meeting, and I told her about your connection to *NONSENSE*. Needless to say, there wasn't much else I could tell her. As far as going out with you is concerned, I don't know, but it certainly wouldn't hurt for you to ask. I think she was planning to go back to her office in RIPE after she left here. You should be able to reach her there."

"Thanks so much, Dean McTavish. I owe you one."

And I certainly intend to collect. I quickly called Jamais.

"The game's afoot. He's going to call you." I added without thinking about it but sincerely nevertheless, "Be careful."

"Thanks, Ty. I will."

She called me about a week later.

"Ty, I think it's time to get the conspirators together again."

"You have what we need?"

"It appears that I do."

"Okay, I'll get in touch with Leo. Unless you hear from me otherwise, let's plan to meet at his place at eight o'clock on Saturday evening."

I got there at eight, and everyone else, except for Jamais, was already there. She arrived a few minutes later. She was smiling as she came in, and she pulled a piece of paper from her purse and waved it around in front of us, turning and posing as she did so. She was obviously quite proud of herself. I didn't want to be the one to ask the obvious question, but as no one else seemed inclined to do so, I did.

"Okay, Dr. Dimanche. While I'm not really sure that I want to know the answer to this question, I have to ask it. I presume that those are the *NONSENSE* codes and passwords. How exactly did you get them?"

"Well, I didn't sleep with him, Ty, if that's what you're afraid of."

She seemed to be genuinely offended by my question.

"Although I wouldn't be surprised if he thinks I did."

I breathed a sigh of genuine relief. I felt bad enough about what we were doing already. I didn't want to feel like a pimp too.

"In fact," she continued, "I had absolutely no desire to do so. As you all know, he called and he asked me out to dinner. I agreed, of course, and we went to a little French restaurant that I know. I enjoyed the meal but not much else. I didn't find him attractive at all. He isn't very smart, and he was definitely conversationally challenged. All he could talk about was himself and *NONSENSE*. After dinner, I invited him back to my apartment. I'm sure he thought that he was going to get into my pants, but I assure you that was *never* in my plans. When we got to my place, I offered him a drink, and that's when things started to get interesting. In fact, it turned out to be pretty easy to keep him talking, to get the information I wanted from him, and to keep him out of my bedroom. And it was even easier after he'd had a few glasses of Chartreuse Surprise."

"What the hell is Chartreuse Surprise?" asked Leo.

"You can thank Ola for that. Normally, it's a mixture of Lime Kool-Aid and vodka, but instead, I used lab alcohol that Michael supplied. It made for a much more potent concoction, I think."

Ola smiled, obviously pleased to have been able to contribute to the conspiracy. Michael started to cry.

"So after a couple of drinks, I asked him to tell me more about his work at *NONSENSE*. He was a little reluctant at first to give me the information I wanted, but I kept pouring Surprises, and he kept drinking them. And as more Surprises went in, more information came out. It took a while, but I got everything I thought we needed. By that time, he had passed out. I put him in a cab and had them take him to his hotel."

"Brilliant." Leo beamed. "Absolutely brilliant!"

Jamais handed the paper to Leo. It had the web address for the *NONSENSE* files, two access codes, a user name, and a password. I hoped it would be all we'd need.

"So what's the next step?" Leo asked. "Do we need any special computing facilities to hack in?"

"Do you have internet connection here?" asked Urgek. "If yes, that should be all we need. We can do everything we need to do from your computer. Only problem, if caught, they will be able to trace to here. Is that problem for you?"

"Of course not," Leo replied. "If that were a problem, we wouldn't be here at all. Let's get on with it."

Leo went to his computer and logged on to the internet. Jamais gave Urgek the paper with the access information, and he typed in the address for the *NONSENSE* file server. We all breathed a sigh of relief when, after a few seconds, a dialog box opened, asking for the access codes. Urgek typed those in, and after a few seconds more, another dialog box appeared that asked for Little's user name. He glanced at the paper Jamais had provided and typed in DLDALAP, and the password dialog box popped up.

"In case you're interested, after about the third Surprise, Dougie told me what DLDALAP stands for.

"And what was that?" Leo asked obligingly.

"Doug Little Does As Little As Possible."

Urgek turned to Jamais and pointed at the paper.

"Sorry, Dr. Dimanche. I cannot read writing here. What is word here for password?"

"Pis…" Jamais hesitated and started to giggle. "I'm sorry," she said, "but I have to laugh every time I read his password… It's… *pistonpants*." And she burst out laughing.

"What?" asked Leo with a big grin on his face.

"Pistonpants!"

Leo burst out laughing as well and after a few seconds, so did I.

Even Urgek got it. He smiled and typed in the password. In a few seconds, we were in. I don't know that any of us thought this was really going to work, but there before us were the numbers in each category, assigned to every school in the rankings. The totals were there and the rank order for all the schools. The rumors had been right. SNAF-U was number 31.

"What we do now?" asked Urgek.

"Ty," said Leo, "I think this has to be your baby from here on."

"Yeah, I guess you're right. Okay, here's what we need to do. First, Stoy, what are the total numbers for the schools in the top twenty-five? What are the ranking scores for number one and number twenty-five?"

Urgek scrolled through the file.

"You not believe this. The score for number one school is 97.671. The score for number twenty-five school is 97.641. There is only 0.03 point difference between number one and number twenty-five."

"Wow!" Michael exclaimed. "Those top twenty-five schools must really be good! No wonder we can't get in."

"They're not that good." I responded. "I think the chances are high, very high in fact, that they got those scores by cheating, just like we intend to do. Let's just hope that nobody else has thought of hacking into the files. Let's get on with it. Urgek, where would a score of say, 97.651 put us in the rankings?"

"Give me second." He scrolled through the file again and wrote some numbers down on a pad next to the computer. "That score make us number twenty-two. That good enough?"

"I think that's more than good enough. We don't want to make too big a jump. That would attract too much attention. Besides, we were number twenty-two once before, so it won't seem too strange for us to have that same rank again. You'll need to change the numbers in two or three categories so that our total comes out right. Let me take a quick look to see which ones we should choose. Let's choose Tuitional Aggrandizement Originality. We can always say that we raised our tuition a few thousand dollars more. And... Cosmic Placement Perception. That one is about a subjective a measure as you can get. And... Quadrennial Baccalaureal Efficiency, whatever the hell that is. Will changing the numbers in those three categories do the job, Stoy?"

"Let me see... if I change this to... and change this to... Yes... and finally, this one to... Yes! That does it, 97.651... number twenty-two."

"Okay, do it, I presume you'll need to save the file, and then let's get out of there."

Urgek completed the process and turned off the computer. Leo brought out glasses and a bottle of an excellent single-malt Scotch. He did like nice things. We all had a drink, even Ola, and congratulated ourselves on a job well done. I thanked everyone as they left, but I stayed for a bit to talk to Leo.

"Leo," I began, "I'm not at all sure we did the right thing here, but I'm no longer sure that what we did was wrong either. We did hurt someone by what we did. The school that was number twenty-five is now number twenty-six, and I wouldn't wish the agonies associated with falling out of the rankings on anybody. Still, and I hate myself for feeling this way, better them than us."

"Maybe, there's hope for you yet, Ty. As I said, when I met you, you're not as dumb as you look."

"Thanks, Leo." We had another Scotch and called it an evening.

Things went fairly smoothly through the rest of the summer. As I expected, Sligh and Asskisser phoned or emailed me at least once a week to ask how things were going. I always responded with "I'm working on it," and somewhat to my surprise, that response managed to keep them off my back for the rest of the summer. I went back to part-time deaning and working in my lab, and I kept my fingers crossed that nobody at NONSENSE would discover what we had done. I told myself that even if Doug Little had figured out what had happened, the fact that he had given up the access information might induce him to keep his mouth shut, assuming that he actually knew he had given it up. Of course, if push came to shove, we could prove that he did. I dearly hoped it would never come to that. And as the beginning of the new term came and went without any accusations from NONSENSE, it looked like we'd gotten away with it. But we still hadn't seen the rankings yet.

The big day finally arrived. It happened to coincide with the date for an executive staff meeting, one that once again, I'd been invited to attend. There was a full agenda. Even with the *NONSENSE* nonsense, the university had to keep going. Sligh tried to get us on point, but everyone, including me, was so nervous about the *NONSENSE* rankings that we couldn't get anything done. The letter announcing the new rankings was supposed to arrive by courier at around ten that morning. The meeting had begun at nine, and for most of the hour, we sat there, squirming, sweating, drumming our fingers on the table. Finally, at about a quarter to ten, Charity left the room to wait for the messenger. The next fifteen minutes seemed to last forever, but she returned with the envelope in her hand. She gave it to the president. He opened it, slowly removed a second envelope from inside the larger one, and extracted the long-awaited letter. He opened it and began to read to himself. Without warning, he began to smile broadly. He stood up from his chair and actually began to dance a little jig. He then turned to us and read.

"Dear President Sligh. I am pleased to announce that in the *NONSENSE* rankings of American universities, Small but National, Aspiring to be Famous University is ranked… number twenty-two!"

A collective cheer went up that surely could have been heard throughout the administration building and maybe all across the campus. I had to cheer myself because until that moment, I had no way of knowing whether our conspiracy had succeeded. But apparently, it had. There were tears, more dancing, lots of backslapping, handshakes, etc. Sligh came around the table and took my hand.

"Ty," he said, "I don't know what you did, but whatever it was, thank you so much. SNAF-U owes you a debt we can probably never repay."

What I wanted to say was "You got that right! You have no idea what I and several other loyal SNAF-Ugees had to go through to get us back on that list." But what I said was "Oh, I didn't do much." I obviously wasn't going to tell him what I'd actually done.

"I'm sure that in the end, it was your work, the work of the others around this table, and the university's own merits that got us back in the top twenty-five. Whatever it was, it worked, and I'm glad it did."

Sligh went back to the head of the table. "This calls for a celebration. Charity, announce throughout the university that classes will be canceled at noon today. Let everyone know that there will be a celebration on the quad, let's say around three in the afternoon. Get in touch with catering and tell them to get food and drinks prepared for the crowd. I know it's short notice, but we have good cause to celebrate, hell, great cause to celebrate and by gosh we're going to. So tell everybody, students, faculty, staff, everybody, to be on the quad at three. I'll get in touch with the board chair, but, Charity, you should contact the other board members and tell them to be there. This is one of the greatest days in the history of the university, maybe *the* greatest day, and I'm not going to let it pass without celebrating it."

Then, as if on cue, "*Who's the boss?*"

"*You's the boss!*"

"*Who's the boss?*"

"*You's the boss!*"

"*Who's the boss?*"

"*You's the boss!*"

And once again, this time, in genuine triumph, Sligh strode from the room.

The celebration was a splendid affair! There were lots of students, faculty, and staff there. To my great surprise, even Leo showed up and really seemed to enjoy himself. No alcoholic beverages were served with students in the mix, and after all, there was still next year's ranking to think about. Still, Leo was obviously getting progressively sloshed as the afternoon progressed. He'd obviously brought his own libations. As the celebration was winding down, Sligh took a microphone to speak to the citizenry.

"Calm down everyone, just for a minute. I'd like to take this opportunity to thank all of you for everything you've done to make this day possible. This time a year ago, we were at the beginning of one of the darkest periods in SNAF-U history. Now we're at the beginning of one of the brightest. Thanks so much to all of you. Charity, Clark, Sparky, Ty, all of you from the executive staff, come up here with me. First of all, I want everybody to know that these are the people you have to thank for the fact that we're back in the top twenty-five. Let's give them all a hand."

And there was a rousing round of applause.

"Now before we go, I want all of you to join me in a cheer, a cheer for SNAF-U."

Surely not "*Who's the boss?*"

"Come on, Charity, Clark, Sparky, join in with me here." And Sligh started to chant, "*We're number twenty-two! We're number twenty-two! We're number twenty-two!*"

And soon, the entire crowd joined in, including yours truly.

Given everything we'd been through, for SNAF-U, being number twenty-two was probably just as good as being number one.

EPILOGUE

S O IT WENT. AND just as I said and as now you know, the way these institutions get us to think they're great is... they cheat. Maybe not in the same way that SNAF-U cheated, but they cheat all the same. And given that there are lots and lots of universities in the United States with cultures that are every bit as bizarre as SNAF-U's, it's perhaps understandable that they have to cheat.

It goes without saying then that my first eighteen months at SNAF-U were interesting ones, and I'm now well into my fourth academic term here. There is a lot more that I could tell you about SNAF-U and the SNAF-Ugees. But I don't think I will. That will have to wait for my second book, and if this one gets published, I guarantee that there'll be a second. But for now, let me bring you up to date on some of the stories I've already told you. You're probably wondering what happened to various and sundry, so here's the scoop.

For reasons that weren't entirely related to the help they provided with the *NONSENSE* nonsense, I tried to be as supportive as possible of the residents of the NUThouse. Stoy Urgek is still there, still as insolent and content as ever. Michael Baccaliprati has been given a small lab in the new Physics Building but with significant constraints on his research. He can't work with anything even remotely explosive or with anything alive. But he's happy as a clam just to be able to do research and use laboratory wipes again. Problem is, now he thinks he should be released from the NUThouse. Not a chance, though, at least not yet.

Despite my best efforts to convince her otherwise and my commitment to provide her with as much assistance and support as I could, Ebola-Shalaka did file suit against the university. When her case went to court, she insisted on a jury trial. She might have won if she hadn't also insisted on making a closing statement to the jury herself. She thanked them for their patience in hearing her case, then told them that to be sure that their deliberations went smoothly and fairly, she needed to sit with them and watch them deliberate. She promised them all peanut butter sandwiches and lime Kool-Aid if they'd agree. They didn't, and they found for SNAF-U. Hyphen-Shalaka is planning to leave the university and, simultaneously therefore, the NUThouse at the end of this academic year. I admit that in some ways, I'll be sorry to see her go. I suspect that someone will surface to take her place. Goodness knows that there are plenty of candidates around here.

Muffy Torkelson-Little did finally figure out how many pages a hundred grams worked out to be and turned in her thesis at the end of last year. I tried to read it, but couldn't. It was completely unintelligible. I hate to admit this, but I have no idea whether she deserved a PhD or not. But she has one.

Miranda Turquette. She must have copies of the squirrel pictures. As I understand it, at a recent executive staff meeting, one that I missed, Sligh raised the possibility of starting a school of architecture. In the same vein, you'd be interested in knowing that Buster, Duke of SLOPP, is currently touring the former Soviet Union with the president, probably the first time in history that the head of the facilities operation has gone on a fund-raising tour with a university president. I *have* to see those pictures.

Remember Professor Titus, exiled to a community college in Montana for screwing the dean's daughter? Well, strange as it may seem, Mo Tormouth ended up at the same community college. If this keeps up, Montana CC may end up having one of the country's most prestigious science faculty. Then again, maybe they won't.

What about Bucky Bier? Well, you'll be pleased to know that he didn't end up as a driver's ed instructor. He did stay in school, and he did get an A- in another course. And I got another round of phone calls from Sligh, Azkizur, and Brohwknoz… and from Bucky's parents. But I refused to see them, and I made it clear that I did not intend to become involved in the matter in any way. Burleigh Bier swore at me when I told him that, called me a dirty name, and slammed down the phone. Pretty much as I expected. But… Bucky did graduate with a 3.95 GPA and did get into med school. Not one in Ghana, Uzbekistan, or England, but one at a PNEU. Both he and his parents were ecstatic, as you might imagine. Shortly after graduation that year, I got a call from an apparently very contrite Burleigh Bier. I say apparently because Jarvis spoke with him. I refused to do so. Anyway, Bucky is in med school as I write this account. Remind me never to have any problems that require an acoustical pyrophysician, at least not one under forty.

You're probably also wondering how Ima Plodter's reception turned out. It was actually pretty nice. We had it on May 5. It was well attended; and a good time was apparently had by all, faculty, staff, *and* students. We did give her a cruise as a parting gift, but a Mediterranean rather than a Caribbean one. The resolution? Well, the president, to his credit, was as astounded as I was at the way the committee chewed up my draft. So the final resolution that he read that evening went something like this:

"Be it resolved:

For thirty-plus years of yeoman service to SNAF-U;

For faith in and dedication to the principles on which the institution was founded;

For your passionate efforts to preserve SNAF-U's traditions and for your conservative yet sensitive approach in dealing with those inside and outside the university who might wish to modify or abolish those traditions;

For your many years of effort as a teacher of the history of democratic institutions;

For the convivial approach you always take in your interactions with colleagues and for the gaiety you have brought to SNAF-U's consideration of many a weighty matter;

For striving in your dealings with those outside the university, to make the alien commonplace at SNAF-U;

The board of trustees and the executive officers of Small but National, Aspiring to be Famous University do hereby offer our thanks and appreciation to Dr. Ima Plodter and declare this date, May 5, Ima Plodter Day at SNAF-U."

Sound familiar? It should. It's the exact text that I suggested originally. And by the way, the president did, indeed, give Ima a hug. At least he tried to. Remember that Ima is a *big* woman. The best the president could do was to lean forward and sort of pat her on the sides. No way could he have gotten his arms around her. I bet Wilt Chamberlain would have needed at least six more inches on each arm to get around that waist, or whatever you call it in her case.

Jamais Dimanche. My relationship with Jamais stabilized, and for a while, I thought that our roles as coconspirators and the friendship that developed as a result might make for smooth sailing with her for the foreseeable future. But no such luck. In the end, Jamais did not keep her promise to me. She continued to sleep with her students, both male and female, graduate and undergraduate, with male and female faculty members and staff, and with just about anybody, as it turns out, that she could lay her hands (and body) on. Except for Leo, of course, and as far as I know, Doug Little. And despite the fact that her help with the *NONSENSE* business had been invaluable, I had other issues to consider. So we/I finally had to dismiss her from the university. I was able to allow her to resign rather than be fired. I think she appreciated that. After she resigned, she did marry Sparky Atherton-Sparks. I wonder if she kept her "promise" to him. I seriously doubt it. Either way, it was probably a good thing that Sparky was physically fit. Although based on what happened to her first husband, that wasn't guaranteed to ensure his survival. By the way, even though I felt that we had developed a good and positive relationship, at least at one point, I never took Dimanche up on her dinner invitation. It wouldn't have been politic or prudent for me to become any more involved with her than I had in the context of the *NONSENSE* business. But that wasn't the only reason. I know my limitations, and Jamais Dimanche very clearly exceeded them.

One more note about Atherton-Sparks. President Sligh decided to implement his parking plan, which he referred to as Sparky's Parky, a name which was just as goofy as the plan itself. Here's what happened. The first day of the implementation was a Monday. By nine o'clock that morning, there were lines of cars a mile long outside every parking deck at SNAF-U. On Tuesday, the decks were almost empty. On Wednesday, the lines were back again, Thursday, the decks were empty, and so on and so forth. This went on for two weeks when someone, probably Bunghole, figured out that this wasn't working and wasn't going to work. So they decided to go back to the old system, with one modification. They raised the annual parking fee to $5,000. As you can easily imagine, a lot of people, including me, started taking public transportation. In my case, that turned out to be a marked improvement over driving to work. Wish I'd thought of it sooner.

Leo Da Vinci is still the head nut in the house of NUTS, and he continues to be an invaluable resource for me, and a great friend. We go out for a Bullet and a brew at least once a month, and he's introduced me to some of his other favorite haunts in SNAF-Uville, all of which are excellent. Leo is quite obviously a major reason for my having successfully survived for nearly two years at SNAF-U—not an easy place to be an administrator—and I doubt if I would have made it this far without his help. Oh, by the way, I did find out the source of at least some of Leo's wealth of information. Turns out that he was very well acquainted with Charity Butler, Hermione Bull, *and* Cloris Stargell (Program in Literary Psychotherapy). *Very* well acquainted, if you get my drift. And you thought Jamais Dimanche was good. One more thing about Leo. Neither Jamais Dimanche nor any of the others ever raised the issue of our relationship as coconspirators in the *NONSENSE* business. I was never sure whether that was because of their integrity or because of what Leo may have threatened to do to them if they did, but I'm inclined to believe it was mostly the latter.

We're still in the *NONSENSE* hunt, as you might well imagine, and Hermione has learned that next year, one of the new criteria will be average age at graduation, a.k.a. the Baccalaureal Lifespan Index. As you might imagine, the idea is that the better the university, the younger its students will be when they graduate. When they got this news, Sligh and Co. apparently considered, seriously, admitting students to SNAF-U when they finished eighth grade. As far as I know, although they did give the idea serious consideration (two executive staff meetings worth), they ultimately rejected it. As far as I know. One thing I'm sure about, I have done my last bit to keep SNAF-U in the top twenty-five. At least I hope I have.

And finally, I know you've all been wondering about my name, so let me clear that up for you right now. My great-grandmother was a slave in Virginia, owned by one Angus McTavish. They fell in love, married, and moved to Massachusetts, where my grandfather, Attila McTavish, was born. My grandfather married and moved to Connecticut, where my father, Cleophus McTavish, was born. And so on and so forth. Simple, no?

So life has been good for Tyrone, i.e., me, at SNAF-U. Strange but good. You may wonder then why I decided to write this book. The answer is simple. It's because life at SNAF-U is so damned funny! Leo was absolutely right. Most faculty, and administrators I might add, at SNAF-U and at all of our colleges and universities, for that matter, are smart, committed, hardworking (frequently overworked), skilled, talented, concerned, caring, et cetera, et cetera, et cetera. (And most of them are scrupulously honest. It's the *NONSENSE*s of the world that make us do bad things.) They are good, frequently great, teachers and exceptional scholars. They are, indeed, what makes American education what it is. And what it is, is by and large outstanding and something of which the country can be proud. But the rest. Ahhh, the rest. Those folks. Well, draw your own conclusions.

In any case, I *am* going to try to have this book published. And unless I'm able to keep my identity a secret—which, of course, I won't if the book is a success—and I do TV interviews and get my picture in the *Times Book Review* or maybe even the *NONSENSE Book Review*, it means that all the SNAF-Ugees will know who I am, and my administrative position here will be in jeopardy, to say the least. I just hope I don't get arrested. But if you are in fact reading this book, it means that it has been published, and if I'm lucky, it has sold lots of copies. So one thing is for damned sure: one way or another, and even though I'm pretty happy here right now, once this tome hits the streets, I'm likely to be released from SNAF-Ugee camp.

CPSIA information can be obtained at www.ICGtesting.com
Printed in the USA
BVOW08s1908021213

337929BV00006B/361/P